P9-BYQ-512

HEART
AND
SOUL

DATE DUE

OCT 10 1997	
NOV 12 1997	
NOV 24 1997	
DEC 12 1997	
JAN 13 1998	
JUN 12 1998	
JUN 26 2001	
JUL 11 2011	
MAR 12 '03	
AUG 9 '03	
SEP 11 '08	
AUG 16 2012	
OCT 17 2012	

BRODART   Cat. No. 23-221

THE INNOCENT YEARS
★ ★ ★

Love and Glory
These Golden Days
Heart and Soul

Geneva Public Library
1043 G. Street
Geneva, NE 68361

HEART
AND
SOUL

ROBERT
FUNDERBURK

BETHANY HOUSE PUBLISHERS
MINNEAPOLIS, MINNESOTA 55438

Cover illustration by Joe Nordstrom

Copyright © 1995
Robert W. Funderburk

All rights reserved. No part of this publication may be reproduced, stored in a retrieval system, or transmitted in any form or by any means electronic, mechanical, photocopying, recording, or otherwise without the prior written permission of the publisher and copyright owners.

Published by Bethany House Publishers
A Ministry of Bethany Fellowship, Inc.
11300 Hampshire Avenue South
Minneapolis, Minnesota 55438

Printed in the United States of America

Library of Congress Cataloging-in-Publication Data

Funderburk, Robert, 1942–
    Heart and Soul / Robert Funderburk.
      p. cm. — (The Innocent years ; bk. 3)

    1. Korean War, 1950–1953—Veterans—Louisiana—Fiction.
2. Legislators—Louisiana—Election—Fiction. I. Title.
II. Series: Funderburk, Robert, 1942–   Innocent years ; bk.
3.
PS3556.U59H43   1995
813'.54—dc20   95–22383
ISBN 1–55661–462–4   CIP

899

Renew

To my dad, Ezra B. Funderburk,
1920–1986

Strange that my memories of you are most often:

Of us staking out a foundation
Beneath a blistering July sun
With a sixteen-pound mall
that you named "John Henry,"

Or sheeting a roof side-by-side
In a cold December wind,
Or sitting together
On the tailgate of a pickup
After a long day.

When I get to Heaven,
you're the second carpenter
I'll look for.

See you then,

Bobby

9-5-97

34475

ROBERT FUNDERBURK is the coauthor of six books with his friend Gilbert Morris. Much of the research for this series was gained through growing up in Baton Rouge and then working as a Louisiana state probation and parole officer for twenty years. He and his wife have one daughter and live in Louisiana.

CONTENTS

★ ★ ★

PART ONE

THE BLADE-THIN EDGE OF DANGER

1. A Day in the Sun 11
2. The Question 27
3. Partners 41
4. Heart and Soul 57

PART TWO

THE LAST OF THE LIGHT

5. The Sycamore Leaves 75
6. Roy and Cisco 91
7. Vendetta 107
8. The City Club 125

PART THREE

TAKING A STAND

9. In the Absence of Light 143

10. Maria 161
11. Stormy Weather 177
12. Acadians 197
13. Chaplain 217

PART FOUR
NIGHTMIST AT SUNRISE

14. Elegance and Slow Grace 233
15. Ruby 247
16. Night on the Water 265
17. Friends 279
Epilogue 295

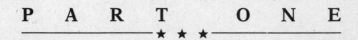

PART ★★★ ONE

THE BLADE-THIN EDGE OF DANGER

ONE

A DAY IN THE SUN

★ ★ ★

Born fifty yards from where he lay, the cotton-mouth stretched his full five-foot length on the decaying sweet gum log. He would have been virtually undetectable except for the flicking in and out of its long forked tongue, picking up the scent of blood in the water. Using the trademark of the pit viper, a dark cavity behind his slightly upturned snout, the snake detected the mammal warmth of the woman whose legs dangled idly over the edge of the bateau, pale flesh flashing against the dark water. But his hunger drew him instinctively to the stringer of bluegill that he recognized as food.

With barely a rippling of the lake's surface, the cottonmouth slid off the log, heading toward the boat with the blood trailing from the hook-ripped gills of the fish. He swam high in the water, his springlike body sinuously twisting back and forth, scarcely disturbing the glassy surface.

Catherine glanced at her husband, drowsing in the

11

willow's shade, his head pillowed on a boat cushion. She then gazed back at her red-and-white plastic cork floating on the tea-colored water, winking with sunlight. Sighing deeply, she savored the July warmth and the coolness of the water on her feet as she moved them slowly back and forth.

"Mama, I'm thirsty."

Catherine turned toward the sound of her son's voice. "Cassidy, I *told* you not to swim here. It's dangerous." She glanced at the pirogue fifty feet away where her oldest son, Dalton, sat in the shade of a huge cypress, his cane pole gleaming dully in the moss-tinted light.

"Mama!"

Catherine saw Cassidy's eyes grow wide in fear as he stared beyond the string of fish at her feet still dangling in the water. Jerking her head around, she saw the smooth serpentine motion of the big snake moving rapidly toward her son. "No!" She kicked at the cottonmouth, missed and only served to provoke it with her splashing.

Frozen in the water where he clung to the side of the boat with both hands, Cassidy gaped at the cottony white mouth of the snake, opened wide in anger three feet from his face. Its long curved fangs protruded like miniature scimitars.

With no thought for her own safety, Catherine grabbed Lane's heavy K-Bar knife from the seat behind her, holding it with both hands. She swung it at the snake's head just as it shot forward toward her son. The blade hit the open mouth at an oblique angle, clipping off the left fang and slicing on through the mouth and the spade-shaped head as far back as the eyes. The elliptical pupils went suddenly blank.

Blood spouting from its mortal wound, the great

snake writhed and twisted in the water, churning it into a reddish pink froth. Then it grew limp as though the current of life had suddenly been turned off, settling slowly downward in the dark water, its still-open white mouth catching a final flash of light.

Catherine and Cassidy, the glazed look of shock in their eyes, took simultaneous breaths of relief, both of them still at a point of fear beyond speaking.

Lane brushed his chestnut brown hair back from his eyes and sat up. He wore a pair of cutoff marine fatigues and black Converse tennis shoes. Taking his knife from Catherine's still trembling hands, he thought briefly of how he had used it in the steaming jungles of the South Pacific and the frozen, barren slopes of Korea. "I didn't know you could handle a knife like that, Cath. Guess I'd better mind my manners around you from now on."

"It—it was trying to hurt my baby!" Catherine, coming out of mild shock now, bent over and put her arms around Cassidy, still clinging to the side of the boat.

"If that knife would have been close enough, I'd have cut that snake into a thousand pieces." Cassidy, in the manner of ten-year-old boys, pulled away, trying to brush off his display of fear. "And, Mama . . . don't call me *baby!*"

"You can forget that, boy," Lane smiled. "You'll be her *baby* till you're forty . . . maybe longer. That's just the way mamas are about their youngest child."

"I can't stand that!" Cassidy muttered, climbing over the gunwales. He grabbed the gallon jug of iced tea from the bottom of the boat and poured a tall paper cup full. With a sheepish glance at his father, he turned the cup up and drained it.

Catherine stared at the gradually fading pinkish

13

tint of the water where the big snake had gone under. Suddenly she began to shake, quietly weeping as tears rolled down her pale cheeks, carrying a slight rose color from the late morning sun.

Lane moved next to her, taking her in his arms. "It's all right, Cath. That cottonmouth's nothing but turtle food now." He felt his wife's warm supple body pressing against his and in spite of what had just happened, desire stirred inside him. He had always considered it strange and wonderful that Catherine could still affect him like this, even after twenty years of marriage.

Clearing her throat, Catherine spoke in a voice drained of strength. "I was so scared, Lane! I don't think I've ever been so frightened in my life."

"But you didn't let that stop you," Lane encouraged. "You killed it anyway." *It had to be just dumb luck for her to catch that thing in the mouth with the knife blade. I probably would have missed, and I lived with that K-Bar for years*. Lane realized how fortunate they had been. The five-foot cottonmouth had enough venom to kill a horse. Their son would have been dead within minutes after those long fangs had done their work.

"I'm swimming back now." Cassidy stood on the bow of the boat, preparing to dive in and swim back to the pirogue where Dalton sat staring at them, having seen the splashing but not realizing yet what had happened.

Catherine turned quickly around, grabbed Cassidy by the arm and pulled him down on the seat. "You stay right where you are, young man. Didn't you learn anything from this?"

"Aw, Mama!"

"It's clear open water between here and the pirogue, Cath. Let him go." Lane came to his son's defense. Opening the lid of his tackle box, he lifted out the top tray, taking a Colt Woodsman wrapped in an oily cloth from the bottom. "I'll keep an eye on him."

"You're worse than he is," Catherine snapped, "and you're a grown man."

"What just happened was a fluke, Cath. Couldn't happen again in a million years." Lane pulled back the receiver of the pistol, jacking a .22 long rifle cartridge into its chamber. "Besides, I don't miss with this."

"Yeah, Mama. Don't be a spoilsport," Cassidy chimed in. "We're supposed to be having fun today."

Catherine gazed at the bright expanse of water between her and the pirogue, tied in the shady spot beneath the cypress. Feeling outnumbered, she merely shook her head.

"Coley said he and his buddies always swam out here and all over the Basin when they were growing up. They're still alive and kicking."

Catherine thought of their close friend, Coley Thibodeaux, whose camp they were staying at in the trackless Atchafalaya Basin. Slightly built and confined to a wheelchair from his wounds at Tarawa, he didn't let that interfere with his law practice or his job as State Representative in the Louisiana House. "Coley's too tough to die. If the Japs couldn't kill him with their rifles and bayonets, a snake surely couldn't."

"I rest my case," Lane grinned.

Catherine knew exactly what Lane's remark meant—that he had seen twice as many campaigns in the war as Coley had and had survived them all.

"Yes, but he's just a boy."

"He's *my* son," Lane stated as though the words imparted invulnerability to Cassidy.

"I give up." Catherine held her hands out in exas-

15

peration. "But watch him closely."

"Yipeee," Cassidy shouted gleefully, hitting an almost splashless dive off the bow of the boat.

Lane watched his youngest son swim effortlessly through the sun-sparkled water back toward his older brother in the pirogue. As he felt the balanced weight of the Colt in his hand, he wondered himself why the male of the species seemed always to have to prove something to other people. Or was it only to themselves that they felt obligated to walk for no logical reason along the blade-thin edge of danger?

★ ★ ★

"You're getting to where you can fry fish almost as good as these Cajuns, Cath." Lane sat next to Catherine in the porch swing he had hung for Coley on the little front gallery of the camp. Nestled among the giant cypress, the tiny cabin stood on pilings seven feet above the shallows and forty feet out from the shoreline of the lake.

"After all the K-Rations you've eaten, I think you'd say the same thing if I fried up some shoe leather." Catherine thought of the days and nights, especially the long nights she had spent during the months Lane had fought in Korea, and of the fact that a North Korean mortar shell had almost taken him away from her. Two wars in the past ten years were more than enough for her and she prayed that there would be no more.

"You know better," Lane chided playfully. "Even Coley says you're cooking like a native, and his mother's act in the kitchen was a hard one to follow if you can believe half of what he says about her crawfish etouffee and shrimp creole."

"I guess they weren't too bad, especially considering they were cooked on a butane stove.

"You're putting some weight back on." Catherine patted her husband's flat stomach that had been as sunken as an old man's when he had come back to her from Korea three months before.

"You can't get out of jail till you pay the money, Cassidy! Just put that little silver dog back where it came from."

"I can too! The warden gave me a pardon."

"What kind of stupid rule is that?" Dalton challenged. "It's something you just made up."

Catherine glanced through the screen door where her sons were playing Monopoly by the light of a Coleman lantern. "Can't those two get along for ten minutes without arguing?"

"I'd think they were sick if that happened." A trace of a smile flickered at the corners of Lane's mouth. "They're good kids though. You wanna know something? I don't think I'd take a good team of mules for those boys."

"I should hope not."

Lane took Catherine's face in both hands, gazing into her blue eyes. "And I wouldn't trade their mother for Marilyn Monroe and Betty Grable, even if they were sitting in a brand new Rolls Royce automobile."

"I'll bet."

"Well, I wouldn't if it was just a Chevrolet . . ." Lane leaned back against the swing, gazing thoughtfully at the dull amber glow of the lantern docked at the foot of the steps. ". . . maybe."

"No more fish for you, Lane Temple," Catherine warned. "You do your own cooking from now on."

Lane sat up quickly and lifted Catherine off the swing, plopping her down in his lap with his arms around her waist. "Never again, Cath. I won't do it again."

"Whatever are you talking about?"

"No more wars. I don't care what happens, I'm through going off to war."

Catherine ran her hand though Lane's thick hair and rested it on his shoulder. "What made you think of that?"

"I don't know. I guess I'm finally accepting the fact that I'm home again. I'm going to live." Lane stared again at the dock and the glow on the water and, farther out in the lake, the starlight gleaming on its dark surface. "I'm staying home from now on."

Catherine felt a sudden, unexpected chill at the back of her neck as though Lane's words carried an icy edge. "We just won't let anything take you away from your family again—that's all there is to it." She hurried her reply, but felt the words fall as flat and empty as pin-pricked balloons.

Out near the shoreline, a chorus of tree frogs began their nightly serenade, backed up by the deep bass of a bullfrog somewhere in the shallows.

Lane eased Catherine back onto the seat of the swing, stood up, and walked down the steps to the dock where the aluminum bateau and the handmade wooden pirogue floated side-by-side in the still water. Sitting down, he leaned back against a piling and stared out across the lake.

Catherine left the swing and went to join her husband. "How did work go this week?"

"Better."

"Brevity is for Coley and your other men friends, Lane," Catherine reminded him. "I want some of the column, not just the headlines."

Lane chuckled, stretched his legs out and folded

his arms across his chest. "Well, let's see . . . Harry Truman called and said he's *definitely* not running for president again. Ike dropped by and wanted to know what I thought of his choosing Richard Nixon for a running mate . . ."

Catherine grabbed Lane's ear, twisting it between her thumb and forefinger until he cried out in pain.

"Okay—okay! Can't you take a little kidding?"

"Sure. Now let's hear about your week."

"All right. I picked up a simple battery case. Fellow got in a fight at Dad's Bar." Lane's voice carried across the water to the shoreline and the base of a tupelo gum where a raccoon, nibbling on a small catfish he had just caught, stopped eating, turned in Lane's direction and, sensing no danger, continued his supper. "Imagine that—a fistfight in a sedate place like Dad's Bar."

"Must have been a serious breach of etiquette," Catherine chimed in with a straight face.

"Someone probably used a salad fork for the main course," Lane added, nodding his head solemnly.

"What else?"

"Some guy called from out of town wanting me to handle a land deal for him."

"Who was it?"

"Crain, I think he said. Bruce Crain." Lane gave Catherine a puzzled look. "Said he was from Chicago and wanted to invest in some timber and farmland down here."

"How'd he get your name?"

"Said a friend of his recommended me," Lane shrugged. "He didn't say who."

"Did he sound serious about it or like one of those fly-by-night characters?"

"He knew a lot about real estate. Who knows if

anything will come of it or not."

"Anything else interesting?"

"Some drunk ran a stop sign and hit one of Coley's friends. Coley wants me to handle it," Lane explained. "Says this legislative session that just ended wore him out."

"I think Coley's health is failing him." Catherine's face clouded momentarily. "He looks kind of peaked to me. Maybe he's just not eating like he should."

"I'll bet he doesn't cook very much, living alone like he does," Lane offered. "I know *I* wouldn't."

"You'd do good to open a can of tuna," Catherine added matter-of-factly. "Maybe we should ask Coley over for supper more often."

"Yeah, let's do that." Lane's brow furrowed in thought as he started to speak, then seemed to think better of it, glancing up at the pale shine of the cabin door.

His expression wasn't lost on Catherine. "Go ahead. What's on your mind?"

Lane took a deep breath. "Maybe we ought to leave Baton Rouge, Cath."

"Whatever for?"

"Well, we've had a lot of trouble here . . . haven't we?" Lane found it hard to forgive himself for the affair he had had with Bonnie Catelon, the daughter of the second most powerful political figure in Louisiana. Catherine had stood by him in spite of it all, and the guilt he carried around like an unnecessary cross now seemed a permanent part of his makeup.

Catherine knew what Lane was thinking. "'. . . forgetting those things which are behind, and reaching forth unto those things which are before, I press toward the mark.' Paul said that almost two thousand years ago, Lane. It's still good advice today."

Lane nodded his head slowly, trying to push the past back into the past where it belonged. "You're right."

"The children are finally settling down in school and making friends. Your law practice is coming back." Catherine pressed her husband's hand. "People make what they will out of *whatever* place they're in. This is our *home* now, darling."

"And there's always Coley," Lane added. "He's the best friend a man could have."

"We're staying then?"

"This is our *home*, Cath."

"That sounds so nice. I wish I'd said it."

★ ★ ★

Lane glanced up at the familiar numbers 424 as he entered the Brunswick Restaurant on Third Street. It had become his and Coley Thibodeaux's favorite lunch spot when they were handling cases in the district court in downtown Baton Rouge. Glancing around the crowded, noisy room, he quickly spotted his friend at the last booth near the kitchen.

Coley's wheelchair had been folded and leaned against the wall. Wearing his usual gray herringbone jacket, blue button-down shirt, and brown penny loafers, he sat in his favorite position—his legs stretched out on the cushioned seat of the booth, his back against the wall.

The charcoal gray slacks, replacing his usual faded jeans, and the loosened red tie dangling from his collar told Lane Coley had been in court that morning. Sipping coffee from a heavy white mug, he smiled when he saw Lane.

"You're looking mighty happy today. Judge Robichaux must have been in a good mood." Lane stared at his friend's slightly hawklike face—its prominent bone structure, thin nose, and clear gray eyes that almost matched his jacket.

"I ga-roan-tee, cher," Coley grinned, the word *cher* sounding like *sha*, as in shack, in the traditional Cajun way. "His wife must be treating him good, yeah."

Lane slid into the booth. "I think the reason you win all those cases in his court is because your names sound so much alike."

"You could be right," Coley shrugged. "What you having today?"

Lane glanced at the lunch specials on the chalkboard next to the kitchen door. "Hamburger steak. I love the way they smother it in onions."

"I'll bet you're getting squash and mashed potatoes too." Coley shook his head slowly back and forth. "Can't get away from that redneck food, can you? You better trade that pinstripe in on some overalls."

"Maybe I ought to eat something civilized like those creepy little mudbugs that crawl around in the ditches." Lane entered the fray they had carried on for six years over country cooking versus Cajun cuisine.

"I keep forgetting about your sensitive palate," Coley shot back. "'Course you only ate seven or eight pounds of crawfish bisque the last time I fixed it."

"Oh, I can eat the little rascals when they're incognito, like in a bisque or crawfish etouffee or even in one of your stews. I just can't eat 'em when they're staring at me with those big eyes run out on stems."

"Now that you mention it," Coley replied, scratching his head in a parody of thought, "I never *have* seen a crawfish that's pretty in the face."

At that moment, a skinny, harried waitress in a white uniform, with a thick ticket pad sticking out of a front pocket, slid a heavy plate holding a hamburger steak, mashed potatoes, and squash casserole onto the table, then clunked a tall glass of iced tea down next to it. "Hey, Lane. How you doin'?"

Before Lane could answer, she had hurried back toward the kitchen. He stared at the lunch he had planned to order, then at Coley. "I gotta stay away from you. You're getting to know me too well."

Coley smiled, took a swallow of coffee, and set the mug down on the table.

"Where's your food?" Lane sliced off a chunk of the hamburger steak and chewed it with obvious relish.

"Haven't got much of an appetite today," Coley drawled. "I'm just having coffee."

Lane swallowed and sipped his tea. "You need some of Catherine's home cooking, Coley. You're starting to look like a gutted rooster."

"About like you did when you stepped off the train from Korea." Coley smiled. " 'Gutted rooster.' Every time I think I've heard all your little homilies, you come up with another one. You're a walking redneck encyclopedia."

Lane had turned his attention to the plate of food before him. "Hmmm . . . boy! This squash is almost as good as my mama used to make."

Coley waved to a portly man in carpenter's overalls who was leaving a table across the restaurant, then turned back to Lane. "How'd the burglary trial go today?"

Pausing mid-bite, Lane gave Coley a sly wink. "How do you *think* it went?"

"You got him off."

Lane shook his head, his expression solemn. "Three years in Angola."

"Oh Lord, no! That boy's only seventeen years old. They'll eat him alive up there."

23

The rumor of a smile began flickering across Lane's eyes as he chewed his food.

Noticing the change in Lane's expression, Coley deliberately leaned forward, picked up the glass salt shaker, unscrewed the top, and dumped half of it on top of Lane's mashed potatoes before he could react.

"Wait a minute!"

Coley held the remainder of the salt above the squash, a puzzled frown creasing his brow. "Excuse me, did you say something?"

"Don't do that." Lane held his hand in front of him, palm outward. "I'm finished with the potatoes, but that squash is too good to waste."

Coley put the top on the salt shaker and leaned back against the wall.

"You're right. I got him off." Lane took a swallow of tea. "The judge gave him another chance because of his age and because he's supporting his mother."

"That's good." Coley leaned slightly forward, his eyes bright with pain as he rubbed his legs. "He's a good kid. Just got in with the wrong crowd since his daddy died."

"I was sure happy you gave me this case." Lane nodded his head as he spoke. "Yes sir, I can get that new mink coat for Cath now."

"How much did he pay you?"

"Hard to say." Lane rubbed his chin with a thumb and forefinger. "How much is *thank you* worth?"

Coley held Lane's eyes with his. "Maybe more than you know, partner. How about your other clients? You making any money at all?"

"Fellow coming in next week about a land deal," Lane mumbled through his last bite of squash, "and another guy after him."

Hearing Lane's voice fade toward the end of his re-

24

ply, Coley pressed him. "Who's this *other guy?*"

"Just a man needs some lawyering done."

"Michelli?"

"What if it is?"

"It's your life, but the crime boss of New Orleans may not be the best client to take on."

"*Reputed* crime boss," Lane corrected his friend. "You know I've worked for him on and off four or five years now. Everything's always been on the up-and-up. No deals cut, nobody bought off or threatened as far as I know."

"As far as you know," Coley repeated. They had had this conversation before and he could see that Lane's mind was as set as ever.

"I wouldn't be a part of anything else."

"I know that." Coley put the disagreement to rest. "When we going fishing?"

TWO

THE QUESTION

★ ★ ★

On November 30, 1894 five men and two women left the squalor of Dr. Beard's "pest house" in New Orleans. A filthy place with no heat, cracked walls, and rubbish scattered about, it deserved its reputation as a "house of disease, lost hope, and death," according to a reporter for the *Times Picayune*.

A trip upriver by coal barge brought the little group, in the middle of the night, to a lonely spit of land south of Baton Rouge where they were dumped and left to fend for themselves among the crumbling buildings of the Indian Camp Plantation, abandoned years before.

Two years later, four nurses arrived from the Charity Hospital in New Orleans to care for the patients that remained alive. Members of the Daughter's of Charity of St. Vincent de Paul, they were still there for the 1921 flag-raising ceremony marking the federal government takeover of the Louisiana Leper Home that made it part of the Public Health Service.

The order was still serving in 1941 when the hospital's director, Guy Faget, discovered the first and only effective treatment for leprosy: sulfones. The drugs stopped the disease's progress and cleared up blotches and nodules on the skin. That moment was—and is—called the "Miracle at Carville."

★ ★ ★

"I'm not so sure about this, Cath." Lane turned the black Chrysler away from the levee along the river road and onto the long drive that led toward the columned manor house where the administrative offices were located. Instead of his usual Saturday jeans and ragged tennis shoes, he wore neatly pressed tan slacks and a navy pullover shirt.

"Oh, you'll just love Homer," Catherine replied cheerfully, smoothing her pale green and white flower-print dress. "He's *such* a dear."

"I don't doubt that a bit." Lane glanced over at his wife, drinking in her blue eyes that almost exactly matched the periwinkles growing in the flower bed along their back porch. Her cornsilk-colored hair flowed in pleasant disarray along the pale, delicate skin of her slim face and neck. Back from Korea for four months, Lane still couldn't get enough of the sight of her. "It's just that . . ."

"Lane," Catherine spoke in a reassuring manner, "you're *not* going to catch anything. These people don't wear bells around their necks anymore and shout 'unclean' everywhere they go."

Looking down the long gravel drive flanked by ancient oaks that were old even when the hospital was first established, Lane mumbled, "If you say so."

"Not one doctor or nurse has ever come down with leprosy in the entire history of the hospital," Catherine encouraged. "Forget about it and enjoy your visit."

"Is that where we're supposed to go?" Lane pointed beyond the trees toward the big white antebellum structure with its lower and upper galleries.

"Yes, you can park—" Catherine stopped and pointed through the windshield. "Wait a minute. There's Homer now."

A slight, gray-haired man wearing dark brown slacks and a white dress shirt peddled a red Western Flyer bicycle in the sun-dappled shade of the driveway. Sunlight streaming down through the giant oaks touched his smile with a hint of gold as he recognized Catherine's car and waved.

"You can just park here, Lane."

Pulling over to the side of the drive, Lane parked next to a gardenia bush, its once-white blossoms now turned a dull yellowish-tan color and littering the ground. The sweet smell of decay lingered like a dream of early summer before the sun had tracked northward to its blistering zenith.

Homer peddled over to the car, got off his bicycle with some difficulty, and gingerly pushed down the kickstand with his good left foot. His right foot and hand were wrapped in socklike bandages with the numbed foot encased in a molded sandal to protect it from injury.

Catherine walked around the car toward the man who had become almost like a father to her. Giving him a careful hug, she stepped back at arm's length and beamed. "Oh, Homer! Don't you look nice today!"

With an elfin smile, Homer winked at Lane. "I think it's time you took your wife to the eye doctor, Mr. Temple."

"Call me Lane, if you don't mind." He stepped next

29

to Catherine, taking Homer's extended left hand, trying not to look at the side of the little man's head where nothing but a crusty hole remained of his right ear. "I've heard a lot about you, Mr. McCurley."

"Just Homer." He stepped back, giving Lane a quick once-over. "What a fine, strapping young husband you've got, Catherine. He *looks* like a marine."

"Not so *young* anymore," Lane disagreed. "I'll be forty next year. Catherine's two years younger."

Catherine's eyes flashed at Lane.

"Oops."

"Husbands never learn, do they, Catherine? I know I never did." Homer pointed toward several white wicker chairs beneath a pecan tree. "Let's go sit down and visit awhile. I'll leave my red chariot parked here."

"Are you enjoying the bicycle, Homer?"

"Don't know how I got along without it," he grinned. He had thanked Catherine again and again for the gift during her past three visits. "I can go all over the grounds now. We've got three hundred acres here, you know. I've seen deer way in the back."

"I see you don't have to use your cane anymore," Catherine observed, glancing at Homer's bandaged foot.

"Just once in a while. With this new sandal and my bike, I get along pretty well without it."

They walked along slowly through the pecan orchard, leaving trails in the sparkling dew-wet grass. The husks of the pecans, ripening slowly toward the fall harvest, speckled the limbs of the trees with splashes of yellow-green.

Homer sat down, resting his bandaged hand in his lap and motioning for Catherine and Lane to join him. "You've got a fine wife, Lane. She almost makes being down here at this place a pleasure."

Lane smiled, patting Catherine's hand.

"Your face is so much better now, Homer," Catherine observed. "Those lumps are almost gone."

"The 'Miracle at Carville,'" Homer replied. "If I wasn't so old, I might go back to Africa in a few years."

"Catherine told me you and your wife were missionaries there for a long time." Lane wondered how this fragile-looking man had survived in the African wilderness.

"Yep. A mighty long time. More than forty years." Homer's hazel eyes clouded with memory. "When we got there, Monrovia didn't even have a harbor."

Lane felt an inexplicable twinge of uneasiness in Homer's presence, but for reasons he could only guess at, he wanted to continue the conversation and learn more about what had shaped the man's life. "It must have been pretty dangerous in Liberia back in those days."

"Catherine's been telling you about us, I see," Homer smiled. "It was a bit risky at times, but not nearly as much as Guadalcanal or up around the thirty-eighth parallel in Korea."

Lane glanced at Catherine and smiled.

"I wanted you two to know a little bit about each other when you met," Catherine explained.

"Those were such wonderful years." Homer's sensitive, childlike mouth curved in a half-smile as he spoke.

"It must have been a pretty tough job, no matter how much you loved it," Lane remarked, leaning back in the chair and crossing his legs.

Homer gave him a puzzled frown. "Job? You know, I guess it never occurred to me to think of my work over there as a *job*. We were so busy all the time, it

31

just didn't seem like a job." He gazed out across the wide expanse of lawn at a red sports car zipping down the river road toward New Orleans. The long dark hair of the young woman driving it gleamed in the sunlight. "I guess that's a strange way to look at it, isn't it?"

"Maybe not." Lane found himself liking Homer in spite of the vague sense of uneasiness he still felt.

A hint of a smile flickered in Homer's eyes. "I guess having Jesus for a boss is what made the difference. The pay isn't so hot, but the fringe benefits are out of this world."

The sun slipped up the blue curve of the sky as Homer entertained his guests in the fragile and fleeting coolness of the pecan orchard. Soon the shade pulsated with heat as the wind blew across the open fields.

"We'd better be going, Cath." Lane glanced at his watch and leaned forward. "Jessie's probably on the verge of a nervous breakdown trying to keep Cassidy from violating big chunks of the state criminal code."

"Oh Lane, he's not all that bad! We do need to get on home though." Catherine stood up and gave Homer a quick hug. "You're such a blessing to me."

Homer merely smiled up at her from the chair, a touch of color rising in his pale cheeks.

Getting up out of his chair, Lane shook the old missionary's hand. "It's a pleasure to meet someone who actually likes his boss, Homer."

"Yep, I figure we're all like Pilate in one way," Homer responded enigmatically.

"I don't understand." Lane felt a sudden coldness in the pit of his stomach.

"We have to answer the same question that he asked that mob crying out for Jesus' blood." Homer

32

stood up, his back as erect as an eighteen-year-old's. A shaft of light falling through the swaying branches of the pecan trees struck his face, bathing it in a pale radiance.

Lane merely shrugged.

" 'What shall I do then with Jesus?' That's the question we *all* have to answer sooner or later."

★ ★ ★

"Do you think Bobby Benson will really be there, Jess?" Sharon asked with typical twelve-year-old enthusiasm as they drove along Park Boulevard. She had her father's brown hair, and her mother's intelligent blue eyes shone from behind her gold-rimmed eyeglasses.

Jessie's blond hair was the exact color of Catherine's, but she hadn't inherited her mother's willowy figure. She tended more toward well-rounded curves, and turned many a young man's eye. Her brown eyes came directly from Lane.

"Aren't you a little old for this cowboy stuff, Sharon?" Glancing over at her little sister, dressed in jeans and a red-and-white cowboy shirt with fringe on the sleeves and across the back, Jessie continued, "Bobby Benson of the B-Bar-B Ranch is just a silly radio program. I bet even Cassidy doesn't listen to it."

"I don't care," Sharon pouted. "Look at this picture of Bobby. He's *so* dreamy!"

The comment carried Jessie back to Hollywood, where she had taken her screen test the year before and had called her mother about having met Tony Vale, the latest Hollywood heartthrob. She remembered her exact words on the telephone. *He's so dreamy, Mother.*

"Don't you think so, Jess?"

Jessie glanced at the picture of Bobby Benson in his white hat with cap pistols strapped to his waist. *Look at him. He's actually wearing cap pistols.* "I didn't think you cared about boys at all, Sharon."

"I didn't until I heard Bobby on the radio. Then I got this picture in the mail."

"Well, I certainly hope you aren't disappointed."

"Oh, I just *know* I won't be."

Driving along the boulevard, beneath the ancient live oaks, Jessie stared at the stately mansions. White-columned and fronted by landscaped yards, the houses spoke of old money, musty interiors, and crusty owners. Some of the architecture ran to Tudor and Gothic pretensions with castlelike stone walls and facades boasting decorative turrets and iron grill-work.

Passing the tennis courts, Jessie turned left, pulling Lane's '39 Ford coupe up to the curb beneath the shade of one of the live oaks. "I wish we could have used Mama's Chrysler. I'm embarrassed to be seen in this ol' thing."

"I like it," Sharon beamed. "I remember Daddy driving me around in it when I was little."

Feeling suddenly ashamed of such a childish emotion, Jessie regretted that she had placed any importance on what kind of car she would be seen in. *I'm nineteen, I've been to Hollywood and to Korea with Bob Hope, and here I am acting like a kid.*

"Austin would like this. Why did he have to go up to Harvard?"

"You know he was just trying to keep peace in the family. He'd much rather be here with us and good ol' Bobby Benson." Jessie gazed beyond the trees lining the street to the huge swimming pool with its concrete island out in the middle. The tanned, wet bodies of the bathers glistened in the late morning sunlight, their shouts and laughter spilling out over the clipped fairway of the golf course.

"I thought he'd be here by now."

"I told you he had to study." Jessie had been thinking of Austin Youngblood, her high school sweetheart who had become her college beau after her disillusionment with the movie capitol. She held to the shallow satisfaction that she had rejected Hollywood, and not the other way around, like most starry-eyed hopefuls experienced.

"I mean Bobby Benson."

"Oh, *him*." Jessie glanced at the dashboard clock. "He's only ten minutes late. Maybe his horse got sick or he got ambushed by Indians."

"I don't think that's funny!" Sharon stared at her eight-by-ten glossy of the radio star.

"How's the writing coming along?"

Sharon laid the picture face down on her lap. "I'm doing a weekly column for the library's newsletter now."

Jessie's eyebrows raised in surprise. "That's wonderful. Why didn't you tell me?"

"I just did."

"Guess all those years of keeping your nose buried in a book are paying off," Jessie beamed, taking pride in her little sister's accomplishment. "Maybe you'll write a best-selling novel and they'll make a movie out of it."

"And I'll bet you know just the person to play the leading lady, don't you."

"Well, I always say it's best to keep things in the family whenever you can."

The sound of youthful voices cheering gleefully floated on the morning air.

"Oh, look, it's him!" Sharon opened the car door and leaped out, staring at a long, black Cadillac parking next to the curb half a block away.

"Settle down now," Jessie advised, getting out and walking with her younger sister toward the throng of smiling, squealing girls and the boys who feigned disinterest in the whole affair. "We've got plenty of time."

Bobby Benson climbed out of the big shiny car, waving his white cowboy hat in the air. Looking more like a precocious seventh-grader than a cowboy star, he wore a shiny blue shirt flapping with fringe and tight cream-colored trousers tucked inside white boots sporting blue swirls and flowers.

Escorting the folk hero toward a makeshift stage that had been set up beneath the nearest live oak, two men in their early twenties, wearing white paper hats bearing the slogan, *Dunkin' Donuts—Sweetest Treat in Town*, impersonated G-Men guarding their president. One carried a guitar, the other a small portable record player. With stern and practiced expressions, they shouldered a path through the crowd.

A burly man in a T-shirt and khakis, chewed on the stub of a cigar as he got out of a Dunkin' Donuts van he had parked behind the Cadillac. With the help of his two young assistants, he began unloading cartons of doughnuts and carrying them over to the platform.

Sharon took Jessie's hand as they joined in the procession of children following their colorful Pied Piper.

"He's got acne," Sharon frowned up at Jessie. "His picture doesn't show that."

"A lot of things don't show up in pictures," Jessie replied with another fleeting thought of Hollywood.

"And he's so little and skinny."

Jessie stared at her little sister's former idol. "He can't help being little, Sharon."

36

"I guess not." Sharon stared at the glittering little man, still waving his big hat as he climbed up onto the platform. "But on his radio program, he's always beating up some bank robber or horse rustler."

"Don't fret about it, sweetheart." Skirting the edge of the crowd, Jessie led Sharon up near the edge of the stage. "Let's just enjoy the show."

"I'm sorry," Sharon smiled sheepishly. "Thanks for bringing me."

Jessie squeezed her around the shoulder.

Bobby Benson called for quiet with his upraised arms. "Howdy, Buckaroos!"

"Howdy, Bobby!" The nearly all-girl chorus replied, almost in unison.

After some predictable banter back and forth with his admirers, the miniature cowboy nodded to the escort with the phonograph, who set it down on the platform and placed a record on the turntable, then waited for his cue. Taking his guitar from the second man, Benson nodded again and the strains of "Tumbling Tumbleweeds" rose on the warm air.

"I'll bet he can't sing either," the fast-becoming-jaded Sharon muttered.

As though refuting her comment, Benson began singing in a mellow baritone as he strummed his guitar.

Sharon gazed up at the platform in surprise. "He sounds like the radio. Even better!"

Amazed at the quality of Benson's voice, Jessie nodded at Sharon. "Well, I'm glad *something's* turning out like you thought it would, little sister."

As Benson was finishing his song, one of the older boys, his scalp shining beneath his blond crew cut, nonchalantly eased around to the side of the stage and grabbed a box of the doughnuts. Two of his friends who were in on the pilfering tried to snatch the box away, spilling doughnuts across the ground.

Bedlam broke loose immediately, the first doughnuts disappearing in seconds. Rushing to the side of the stage, the two escorts tried to fend off T-shirt and blue jean-clad attackers, thrown into a feeding frenzy by the sight of the Dunkin' Donuts.

Benson dropped his guitar, pulled out both of his pistols and began firing into the air. "Stop! Get away!" His voice rose to a screeching falsetto.

Sharon stood dumbfounded, staring at her radio idol, then glanced at the crowd gone berserk, storming the stage for the "Sweetest Treat in Town."

"Let the little monsters have them!" Benson muttered under his breath, running over to his stalwart escorts, still fending off the doughnut-crazed boys and a few of the more aggressive girls. "Maybe they'll choke on 'em!"

Standing close by, Sharon heard Benson's orders. Shaking her head slowly, she turned and walked away toward the car.

Jessie hurried after her. "Are you all right, Sharon? You're not hurt, are you?"

Sharon shook her head and kept walking.

When they got to the car, Sharon turned and gazed up at her big sister. "Did you see that?"

Jessie nodded. "Sometimes kids just lose control in a crowd."

"I don't mean that."

"What're you talking about then?"

"*Benson,*" Sharon shot back, her lack of respect for the idol obvious.

"What about him?"

"*Cap pistols?!*" Sharon said incredulously. "He actually shot *cap pistols* into the air like a *four-year-old.*"

Trying to suppress her laughter, Jessie glanced toward the melee, which had settled down now that the doughnut boxes were empty. Benson, obviously chagrined that the sweet treats were closer to the hearts of his fans than his singing, trudged toward his Cadillac between his two white hat-clad, surly escorts.

"Cap pistols . . ." Sharon muttered, opening the car door. "What a fool I've been!"

THREE

PARTNERS

★ ★ ★

George Newsom couldn't understand why the other children treated him the way they did. He brushed his teeth with Pepsodent and combed his hair, at least the part in front that he could see, with Wildroot Creme Oil every morning.

Because they felt comfortable that way, he wore his neatly pressed khakis four inches above his waistline, but he could never seem to get all of his shirt tucked into them properly. His teeth protruded slightly, looking much too large in his narrow face with its short, stubby nose, and his brown eyes had a glazed look about them.

Though children can be thoughtless, often cruel, George got more than his share of name-calling, teasing, and occasional punches, which were usually too hard to qualify as playful. When George transferred to Istrouma Elementary, he planned to spend recess and lunch periods hiding under the stairwell, just as he had done at other schools. He smiled with docile

41

acceptance when his classmates pointed and laughed at him, but then he met Cassidy Temple, and his life changed.

★ ★ ★

School buses, flashing bright yellow in the morning sunlight, pulled in sporadically along the street, doors opening with a swishing sound as they discharged their passengers. Laughing, pushing, and squealing down the steps, the children made their way toward the two-story tan brick building set behind a chain-link fence. Ushering in a new school year, they waved and called out to summer friends and renewed old acquaintances.

"Hey, Georgie Porgy, your shirt's on fire!" Caffey "Pancake" Sams (called so—but not to his face—because the back of his head was nearly flat) ran up behind George and pulled his shirt out of the waistband of his trousers. "Don't worry though. It's out now."

George began snuffling, jamming his shirt back into his baggy khakis. "Go away, you . . . you!"

Sams, at one hundred and twenty pounds, was by far the biggest boy in Mrs. East's fifth-grade class. He came to school barefoot except on the coldest winter days and, more often than not, mud caked the bottoms of his tattered overalls. His wiry red hair looked as though it had been cut with sheep shears and only a dark gap remained where his left eyetooth had been. "What's-a-matter, Georgie Porgy, you gonna cry to the teacher?"

"Leave him alone, 'Pancake!' "

A gasp went up from Sams' admirers, hearing the forbidden nickname used in his presence.

Sams turned around slowly, gazing down in stunned disbelief at Cassidy, who had never been one of his followers, but had certainly never openly courted destruction like this before. "I must be hearing things, short stuff."

Cassidy, a head shorter and thirty-five pounds lighter than Sams, stood his ground, lips drawn thin, his white-blond hair hanging just above blue eyes that sparked with anger. Lean in the hips and slight of build, he had yet to develop the wide shoulders and sinewy muscles that would come in late adolescence.

Taking offense not only at Cassidy's remark, but also at the sight of his crisp plaid shirt and spanking new jeans, Sams rolled his shoulders in the fashion of a bull ape and snarled, "I don't believe you really meant to say that, did you, short stuff? Why don't you try it again?"

"All right," Cassidy said flatly, his eyes narrowing as he balanced himself on the balls of his feet. He saw Sams through a red haze now. "Leave him alone, you flat-headed frog!"

Bellowing with rage, Sams doubled up his big fists and charged like a runaway bull.

Ducking under the widespread arms, Cassidy hit him a glancing blow to the right cheek.

"Oh boy!" George jumped up and down, still trying to tuck his shirt back in.

Turning around with surprising speed, Sams sized up his agile opponent. He knew Cassidy well enough to realize that he would never run away, so he walked deliberately toward him, keeping his guard up.

When Sams was almost within reach, Cassidy stepped quickly forward and jabbed him twice in the nose with his left, but felt Sams' left fist close like a vise about his wrist.

Turning his opponent sideways with his left arm, Sams rendered him momentarily defenseless and threw a heavy right that connected at the left corner of Cassidy's mouth, sending him reeling backward onto the hard-packed, grassless playground.

Landing on his back, Cassidy felt the wind go out of him. Through a gray mist, he saw Sams towering over him, reaching down with both arms. Struggling for breath, Cassidy scrambled backward, pushing with his heels and both hands.

"Don't be scared! I'm coming to help!" George ran to Cassidy, trying to help him up, but one of Sams' followers grabbed him by the waist and dragged him back away from the fight, holding him tightly.

Sams grabbed Cassidy by the right foot, but the brown loafer slipped off in his hand. Leaning over and reaching for the other leg, Sams lost his balance, stumbled forward and went down heavily on his knees.

Cassidy saw his chance and kicked Sams in the chin with his right foot, hearing a howl of pain. Jumping to his feet, Cassidy took some deep breaths and shook his head to clear his vision.

All control gone now, his jaw throbbing with pain, Sams lurched forward, tackling Cassidy at the ankles with both arms. Then he began pawing his way up Cassidy's prone body, reaching for his throat.

Cassidy immediately realized that if Sams got those big hands around his throat it was all over. Digging in his heels and flailing his arms frantically, Cassidy's right hand glanced off something slick and hard. Pulling it to him, he saw that it was a heavy dictionary someone had laid on the ground. Just as Sams reached for his throat, Cassidy, securing the book in both hands, swung it at Sams with all his remaining strength.

The hardback book slammed into the left side of

Sams' head, making a sharp slapping sound. Bellowing in pain from a broken eardrum that caused a roaring sound inside his head, he rolled to one side, holding his ear with both hands.

Cassidy felt hands grasping him underneath his arms.

"What's the matter with you two? You're acting like hooligans!" Mrs. East, her silver-rimmed eyeglasses dangling from her neck on their silver chain, her gray hair disheveled, helped Cassidy to his feet.

"I'm all right."

Dabbing at the blood on his cheek with a white lace-trimmed handkerchief, Mrs. East noticed the small cut. "Does it hurt much?"

"No, ma'am."

"Pick up your lunch bag and follow me inside then." Satisfied that Cassidy had no serious injury, Mrs. East turned to Sams, who was still writhing on the ground. Kneeling next to him, she pried his hands away from his damaged ear. "Settle down, Caffey. Let me look at it."

Sams, tears streaking his dusty face, began to calm down at the sound of his teacher's voice.

Mrs. East helped the big boy to his feet. "We'll have the school nurse take a look at your ear, Caffey. With a sidelong glance at Cassidy, she took Sams by the arms and led him off toward the school building.

Cassidy, numbed from the blow he had taken from Sams, rubbed his sore jaw. He hardly noticed the cut at the corner of his mouth, but it would leave a crescent-shaped scar that he would carry for the rest of his life.

"Let me go!"

Cassidy stared over at George, still being held by Sams' stunned accomplice. With a glance around him at his other friends, he turned George loose and ran toward the school building after Sams and his teacher.

The small crowd that had gathered at the sound of the fight dispersed, breaking up into small groups and wandering off to other parts of the school grounds.

George, jamming his shirt into his waistband, hurried over to Cassidy. "You hurt Pancake's ear." At the sound of the name, he smiled at his own boldness for using it.

"I guess so." Cassidy gazed around the school yard, still dazed from the fight.

With a smile that lit his whole face, George ran over to a wood-and-concrete bench, picked up Cassidy's brown paper lunch sack and brought it back.

"Thanks."

"Will you be my friend?"

Cassidy gazed at the soft doelike eyes of the almost gaunt-looking boy. "You got a comb?"

"Yeah," George replied, somewhat puzzled as he reached into his back pocket. "It's red. Mama bought it for me at Morgan and Lindsey."

Taking the comb, Cassidy took George by the shoulders and gently turned him around. After combing the back of his hair, he slipped the comb into the boy's pocket.

Basking in the attention he was getting, George appeared unable to stop grinning. "Are we friends?"

"You bet, partner." Cassidy stuck out his hand and shook George's limp one.

"*Partner*—I like that."

"Well, if we're gonna be partners you got to give me a better grip than that."

George squinted his eyes and squeezed.

"That's better."

"Oh, Cassidy!"

Cassidy turned and gazed at Mrs. East, waving to him at the wide glass-and-wood, double front doors. "The principal's waiting to see you."

Staring at a vulture circling at an impossible altitude against the pale morning sky, Cassidy let out a long breath. "What a way to start the year—getting sent to the principal's office on the *first* day of school."

The bell sounded loud and long, breaking up the little groups of boys and girls, drawing them with its suddenly familiar tug toward the big building.

George frowned at his new friend's unhappiness. "Want me to come with you?"

Cassidy clapped him on the shoulder. "No thanks, George. You better get on to class."

George watched his new and only friend trudge off among the other children. A warm glow seemed to rise in his chest and for the first time in his life, he felt that he belonged somewhere outside his own home.

★   ★   ★

Glancing up at the morning sunlight glinting on the windows of the Standard Oil Corporation's administrative building across Scenic Highway from his and Coley's law office, Lane pulled his '39 Ford into the gravel parking lot and shut off the engine. Across the side street, the coffee shop occupying a corner of the huge Hebert Building with its phonetic sign (a neon bear with the letter A in front of it) on the roof, was doing a bustling business.

Lane reflected fondly on that morning six years before when he had first met Coley. They had gone to Hebert's for breakfast, and Lane had ended up facing down a bear of a man he remembered only as Thurman. Coley had filed a peace bond against Thurman

47

to protect his ex-wife, and Thurman had intended to finish with his fists what the Japanese with their mortars had started on Coley's frail body at Tarawa.

Lane walked the few steps to the half-glass door of his office and entered into the dimly lit hall.

"Just in time for coffee." Rolling toward Lane from the last door of the narrow hall, which led into his tiny apartment, Coley tossed him the *Morning Advocate*, folded hard and tight, one end tucked inside the other for accurate throwing by the newsboy.

"You get a patent for blacktopping streets with that stuff of yours yet?"

"Nah." Coley leaned forward in the chair, unlocking his door. "They said it was too strong for blacktopping. Ate right on down through the gravel."

"Maybe you could sell it to the navy for washing the barnacles off ships."

"Now there's an idea."

Lane followed Coley into the office, breathed in the heady aroma of Community Dark Roast that filled the room, and set his briefcase down on the desk near the north window. As always, he found himself glancing up at the hand-lettered sign hanging on the wall:

"How much do you love me?" I asked Jesus.
"This much," He replied.
And He stretched out His arms,
And He died.

The simple little saying spoke to Lane's heart as few things had in his life, but he shook off its worrisome message in favor of more mundane conversation. "Who's gonna win the Series?"

"The Yankees." Coley wheeled over to the little homemade table he had built from weathered cypress boards salvaged from a slave cabin.

"I think Brooklyn's going to take it this year," Lane disagreed. "The Dodgers are about due."

Lifting the white ceramic French-drip pot off the hot plate, Coley poured two demitasse cups full of the rich, dark coffee. "You better be glad I'm not a betting man."

Lane sat down next to the west window in one of the two straight-back wooden chairs fitted with deer-hide seats. Scraping some crusty sugar (turned brown from a long succession of wet coffee spoons) from the sides of a jelly jar, he added it to his coffee. "How about that Jersey Joe Walcott? Thirty-seven years old and he KO's Ezzard Charles. That makes him the oldest heavyweight champion ever."

"Yeah." With something more pressing on his mind, Coley had quickly exhausted his limited interest in sports.

"Well, don't get too excited about it now. I don't want you having a stroke."

Coley took his tiny cup of coffee off the table and held it with his fingertips, leaning back in his wheelchair. "There's something I need to talk to you about, Lane—something that's been on my mind for a long time now."

"Well, whatever it is, it must be awfully lonely in there." Lane stared at him with mock concern. "Let's get it out in the open and have a good look at it."

Coley smiled wearily. "What would you think about going into politics?"

Lane stared out the window. Across the street, a young woman with long dark hair, her print skirt flouncing about her slim legs, hurried up the steps into the Standard Oil Building. "I'd put it in the same category as a ruptured appendix or sitting through a seminar on life insurance."

"I was afraid you might say that."

"Why did you ask me then?"

"Because I want you to run for my seat in the House of Representatives."

Lane turned his head away from the window slowly and deliberately, his expression one of disbelief. "You? Give up your seat in the House?"

"Stranger things have happened."

"You must be kidding!" Lane shook his head slowly without realizing he was doing it. "You'd never get away with it. The people out here in North Baton Rouge depend on you too much. They wouldn't *let* you quit."

"*Unless* they could find another man they could trust to look out for them," Coley smiled. "Somebody who wouldn't sell out to the movers and shakers down at the State Capitol."

Lane continued to shake his head, but he was well aware of doing so now.

"Somebody," Coley continued, "who's already proven he's not afraid to stand up against someone as politically powerful as André Catelon."

"That's different."

"How?"

"Give me a minute," Lane shot back, "I'll come up with something."

"The people out here *need* you, Lane." Coley continued his campaign of persuasion. "Most of them don't even have a high school education: plant workers, plumbers, carpenters, dime store clerks, rednecks from Mississippi and north Louisiana, and Cajuns from down in the swamps."

Lane sipped his coffee, glancing back out at the morning sunlight gleaming on the towers and the maze of pipes and columns of the vast Standard Oil

50

GENEVA PUBLIC LIBRARY

complex. A barefoot black boy of ten or twelve wearing nothing but a pair of threadbare overalls trudged along the gravel shoulder of Scenic Highway. Carrying a shoeshine box he lifted his voice in song. The muted sound of "Steal Away" drifted to Lane faintly through the closed window.

> My Lord, He calls me,
> He calls me by the thunder,
> The trumpet sounds within-a my soul;
> I ain't got long to stay here.

"Are you listening to me?"

"You left out the colored folks." Turning his head slightly, Lane gave his friend an oblique smile. "If anybody needs a friend in the legislature, they do."

Coley could see that Lane meant every word and felt a twinge of guilt that he had often neglected the Negro constituency in his district. "See, you're already looking out for the underdog and you're not even in office yet."

"I've got a family to support, Coley." Lane watched the shoeshine boy disappear down the highway. "Every time I get my law practice going good, the marines come up with a war for me to fight."

"You're through with all that now."

Lane finished his coffee and sat the cup down on the table. "Maybe so, but it's still going to take a while to get back to where I was when MacArthur decided to take back North Korea and throw in half of China to boot."

With Lane holding his ground, Coley decided to play his trump card. "I'm not doing this because I'm trying to dump my responsibility on you, Lane."

"I know that. I just figured you were tired of all that hot air down at the State Capitol."

"That's not it either. I just don't have the strength for it anymore."

"You're sick?"

"Not exactly. I just can't hold up like I used to," Coley said, weariness creeping into his voice. "Mainly, I think it's trying to get this chair across thresholds or curbs or finding somebody to drag me up and down the stairs. When night gets here, I'm so tired I can hardly get my shoes off."

Lane was shaking his head again. "The legislature hardly pays anything and I'll lose clients because of the time it'll take up."

"I can handle everything about your cases but the legwork from right here at the office," Coley offered. "Most lawyering is telephone and paper work anyway. I could even fill in for you at court once in a while."

Lane had suggested legislation in the past designed to help the common working men and women of the district, and Coley had managed to get some of it passed. He still had a small collection of untested ideas stored away in the dead files of his mind and thought it might be fun to reopen them.

"Well, what do you think?"

"I'd have to talk it over with Cath before I'd even consider it," Lane replied, toying with the possibility of throwing his hat into the ring.

"Good." Coley felt he had won him over already. "I'll accept that for now."

"If I didn't know you were a Christian, Coley," Lane grinned, "I might think you were trying to *con* me into running for your seat."

★ ★ ★

Wearing jeans, faded and soft from frequent washings, and a khaki shirt with the sleeves rolled up, Lane sat at his desk in the antique leather chair that Catherine had found at a small shop on Royal Street in the French Quarter. His small study, located at the rear corner of the house just off the kitchen, held a wall-to-wall shelf of heavy volumes comprising the Louisiana civil and criminal statutes, a few biographies, and a respectable collection of novels and books of poetry.

On the pecan-paneled walls hung black-and-white photographs of Lane: fading back to pass with a huge tackle thundering through the defensive line after him; breaking the tape at the finish of a hundred-yard dash; standing casually on high school and college playing fields in the company of other uniformed and youthfully confident athletes caught unaware by a photographer's flashbulb, or squinting purposely toward the lens in the slanting southern sunlight.

Bent over a legal brief, his face half-shadowed by the amber glow of a brass lamp, Lane heard the door open.

"Daddy, I need to empty the trash can."

Lane glanced over at his oldest son, wearing sweat pants and his maroon Istrouma Indians football jersey. "Come on in, Dalton. I'm about finished here."

Dalton, strongly resembling his father pictured in the old photographs, stepped over to the desk and emptied the trash can into a brown paper bag. "I made the freshman team today."

"I never doubted that you would," Lane smiled. "I guarantee you that next year you'll be the only starting sophomore on the varsity squad."

"I don't know, Daddy," Dalton shrugged. "Istrouma always gets the best players. Harry Hodges, Larry Grissom, and L. W. Alexander made All-American last year. I'll bet there ain't another school in the country that turned out three."

Lane dropped his pencil, leaning back in his chair. "Maybe so, son, but *none* of 'em have as much guts as you do."

Dalton shrugged again. "I reckon we'll find out."

"Why don't you sit down and let's visit awhile," Lane offered. "Seems like we hardly ever see each other."

"I'd really love to, Daddy, but it's nine-thirty and I'm in training."

Lane nodded. "Yep. I remember those days. Your mama didn't see me much either back then."

"I don't see a whole lot of you *these* days." Catherine leaned against the doorframe, her arms folded. Her soft robe, the color of dark roses, accentuated the pale glow of her skin, freshly scrubbed from her shower.

Lane gazed at the lamplight gleaming on Catherine's blond hair pulled back from her face and tied with a small white ribbon. "Well, let's do some catching up right now."

"Good." Catherine took Dalton briefly by the shoulders, kissing him good-night as he left. Then she walked over and sat down on the edge of Lane's desk.

Lane took his wife's slim hand in his hard brown one. He never failed to take pleasure in her touch. "I believe you're prettier today than you were on our wedding day, Mrs. Temple."

Catherine slipped down into his lap, her arms going around his neck as she kissed him warmly on the mouth. Pulling back, she smiled drowsily, her eyes a soft and depthless blue. "You found the right words."

Lane grinned. "I believe you're prettier—"

"Only works once a day." Catherine interrupted

him, placing her hand over his mouth.

"I just can't wait until tomorrow then."

Catherine took Lane's left hand in hers, tracing the thick veins with her fingertips. "I've been thinking about what Coley wants you to do."

"And. . . ?"

"And I think he might be right."

Lane tilted her chin up with his bent forefinger. "I'm barely making enough to keep us going now, Catherine."

"Coley said he'd help you any time the legislature's in session or if you had committee meetings or something," Catherine encouraged.

"I might be spending even more time away from you and the kids."

"I doubt it," Catherine replied, untying the ribbon and shaking out her still-damp hair. "After all, the sessions are right here in Baton Rouge. You'll be home every night."

Lane merely nodded, his brow furrowed in concentration as he considered Coley's offer.

Catherine took a deep breath. "I've given this a lot of thought, Lane. I think the people out here in this part of town need someone like you to look out for them."

"There are a lot of good people out here."

"But very few with your experience. Besides, you're the only one Coley will back."

"You've been talking to him, I see."

"Yes, I have," Catherine admitted. "And there's one thing I found out that he hasn't told you yet. Maybe he didn't want to put too much pressure on you."

"Well. . . ?"

"Some sort of very powerful political group is going to put up their own hand-picked candidate if Coley steps down."

"What does he know about them?"

"Not much." Catherine gazed directly into her husband's eyes. "Except that André Catelon is behind it all."

"Oh Lord! That means the end of anything good happening for the people out here if he gets *his* man in."

Catherine nodded her agreement. "That's *exactly* what Coley thinks. He's just out to expand his power base until he's got the whole state wrapped up."

Lane sighed deeply. "Why do I have to get put in this kind of predicament?"

"These are our friends and neighbors we're talking about, Lane."

"Coley told me once that holding political office was as addictive as drugs. Does that worry you?"

Catherine placed her left hand along the side of Lane's face. "Not a bit. I know you too well, Lane Temple."

"He also said that politicians will do *anything* to hold on to their power."

"What about Coley?"

"He said he'd find out about himself when it came time for him to walk away from it."

"And that's just what he's doing," Catherine added, finishing her husband's thought.

"What if I *can't* just walk away?" Lane ventured. "If I happen to get elected, that is."

"You will," Catherine assured him, "when the time comes."

FOUR

HEART AND SOUL

★ ★ ★

"You seeing the man from New Orleans today?" Coley opened the door to his office just as Lane started up the stairs.

"Ross Michelli?" Stopping on the first step, Lane glanced over his shoulder at his law partner and best friend.

"I don't mean Louis Armstrong."

Lane grinned. "I know you don't approve, Mother, but he's always been straight-up with me."

"Have it your way."

"Thanks for your permission."

"Here, you might as well take this up with you. You look like you could use it." Coley rolled backward into his office, wheeling quickly around.

Lane stepped back down the stairs and over to Coley's door. "What is it?"

In reply, Coley reappeared with a steaming cup of coffee. "You might as well be awake when you see him."

"Thanks." Lane hurried up the stairs, taking them two at a time without spilling a drop.

Entering his office filled with early, brass-colored light and deep shadow, Lane pulled open the venetian blinds and sat down at his desk. Sipping his coffee slowly, he stared out his window across three narrow alleys to the back entrance of the Hotel Bruin. A tall, angular dark-skinned man with an apron tied around his narrow waist and a white hat perched on his small head washed down the concrete with a water hose.

For five years now, Lane had watched the man in the alley. Every weekday morning and afternoon found him at his chore with the faithfulness of a cloistered monk responding to vespers. He felt a kinship for this man whose name he didn't know. His unfailing devotion to duty somehow gave Lane a feeling of comfort and reassurance.

"I don't think your friend downstairs likes me."

Whirling around, Lane stared at Ross Michelli, the reputed crime boss of New Orleans. "How in the world did you come in without my hearing you?"

Sitting in a heavy polished chair in the shadows, Michelli wore a tailored black suit with a deep red tie. He was of medium stature and, at first glance, looked as unassuming as a bank teller, but beneath his black hair, thick and going gray, his deep, dark eyes were ancient looking. A black fedora lay on his lap. "Simple. I got here before you did."

"Oh." Lane glanced quickly around his office.

"He's not with me."

Lane had never seen Michelli without the big bodyguard who looked as though someone had hit him across the forehead with an iron pipe. He didn't know his name, but he could never forget those predator eyes that fixed on him like a gunsight.

"That ought to show you how much I trust you."

"I guess it does at that." Lane flicked his desk lamp on. "Want some coffee?"

"Let's get the business over." Michelli shook his head. "I've never in my life gone to see a lawyer, and especially out of town. They always come to me."

"I know."

"That ought to tell you something about yourself too." Michelli pulled his chair over near Lane's desk.

Lane took a long swallow of coffee, as though to fortify himself. "I'm sorry about what Coley said."

The corners of Michelli's mouth crinkled slightly. "Don't be. Coley Thibodeaux's a good man. You're lucky to have him for a friend."

"You know Coley?"

"I know *about* him," Michelli corrected. "Just like I know about every other politician at the state level."

Lane knew Michelli had a point to make. He never started a conversation just to hear the sound of his own voice.

"He's one of the few who can't be bought." Michelli gazed stolidly at Lane. "And *that's* something I'm an authority on. I've had most of 'em in my hip pocket at one time or another."

Remembering his conversation with Catherine the night before, Lane decided he might get a few more facts. "What about Senator Catelon?"

"We went to school together," Michelli spat out. "But you already knew that. He has no sense of honor. I wouldn't let him clean out my dog pens."

Lane shrugged. "Well, if you don't have an opinion about him just say so."

That almost brought a smile from Michelli. He slipped a heavy brown envelope from his inside coat pocket and tossed it on Lane's desk. "It's a simple real estate transaction. I think this is all you need, but if you have any problems call me."

"You came here all the way from New Orleans just to deliver this?"

Michelli stood up, heading for the door. "I've got a little business down at the Capitol."

Lane walked around the desk and stood at his office door, watching Michelli negotiate the stair with surprising agility. *Well, he never was one for small talk.*

Coley opened his door and sat there in his wheelchair staring at Michelli just as he got down to the hallway.

"I just corrupted your buddy upstairs with an offer of honest work, Thibodeaux."

"He can't *be* corrupted," Coley replied flatly.

Glancing back at Coley, Michelli opened the front door and bumped into a tall, blond-haired man who was just entering. For an instant, Michelli's eyes blazed, then the fire abruptly died as he said, "Pardon me, my fault," and walked briskly off toward his black Cadillac parked in the side lot.

"Upstairs," Coley informed the man as he started to speak, then wheeled back into his office.

"You must be Bruce Crain," Lane called from the landing outside his office. "I'm Lane Temple. Come on up."

Crain climbed the stairs a little unsteadily, as though his equilibrium were slightly imbalanced. "My goodness, it's hot down here in Louisiana."

"And this is the cool part of the day." Gazing down at the awkward, gangly man climbing toward him, Lane felt compelled toward friendliness. "I should tell you that you'll get used to it, but you won't."

"I believe you. It gets hot in Illinois, but this humidity is killing me." Crain mopped his brow with a red handkerchief he took from his back pocket.

Crain had the tanned honest face of a midwestern farmhand. Lane liked him immediately. "I've got a ceiling fan up here, but it's still going to be warm."

Reaching the landing, Crain blew out his breath. "I reckon I'll survive."

Entering the office, Lane switched on the fan. The soft breeze stirred the papers on his desk. "Have a seat."

"Mind if I take my coat off?"

"Not at all."

Crain took a white envelope from his inside pocket, then slipped out of the tan suit coat, revealing the dark perspiration stains under the arms. Draping the coat on the hall tree in the corner, the man collapsed in the chair Michelli had used. "Does anybody down here have air conditioning?"

"Restaurants, theaters, some homes. I'm going to get a window unit up here as soon as I put a little money away."

"Well, maybe I can speed that up a little bit for you." Crain tossed the white envelope on Lane's desk. "We might both make some money."

A little surprised at the man's abrupt getting down to business, Lane took two sheets of paper out of the envelope. The first contained simple instructions with regard to forming a corporation under Louisiana civil law. The second sheet was a plat of land and the name and address of the owner. "What do you want me to do?"

"Form the corporation and buy the land."

"Why do you need me to buy the land? You can do that yourself."

"I could—maybe. But then I'm an outsider and southerners like to deal with their own," Crain smiled.

"To most people down here I'm little more than a carpetbagger."

"That's probably true in some circles." Lane found himself enjoying the man's unpretentious and forthright manner, unlike most first meetings he was used to.

"I've been buying agriculture and timberland in several parts of the country and it's like that to some extent everywhere, but a lot of people down here think that Appomattox was just a temporary ceasefire, not a surrender."

"I'm beginning to see your point," Lane laughed, glancing down at the plat. "When I go to meet the owner, I'll tell him Coley Thibodeaux is a good friend of mine."

"Coley who?"

"The man downstairs in the wheelchair. He may be the most trusted politician in south Louisiana."

"Amazing."

"What do you mean?"

"That you'd use *trust* and *politician* in the same sentence."

"You know about Louisiana's reputation, I see."

"I was talking more about Cook County, Illinois," Crain explained. "I live just south of there. You don't have a monopoly on crooked politicians."

Feeling inclined toward hospitality, Lane told Crain about some of the local history and where the best places to eat were, including a few restaurants in New Orleans. "Well, I guess I'll get busy drawing up the papers for your corporation. You want to come in and sign them in a couple of days?"

"I'll be in Des Moines tomorrow, I'm afraid."

A frown crossed Lane's face. "I don't see how we're going to accomplish anything then."

"Simple," Crain grinned. "Just put everything in your name and when you get the land deal in the bag, I'll come back down and we'll transfer everything into *my* name."

Lane glanced down at the papers, then gave Crain a skeptical glance. *There's no way I'm going to do all this work without some kind of guarantee.*

"I know," Crain began, getting up and walking over to the hall tree. "All you've got is my word and you don't want to take a chance on me."

"I see you're a mind reader as well as a business-man," Lane said evenly.

Taking another envelope, this one a lot thicker than the first, out of his inside coat pocket, Crain handed it to Lane and sat down again. "That ought to ease your mind a little."

Lane hefted the envelope, then laid it on his desk.

"Open it."

Doing as Crain said, Lane took out a thick bundle of thousand-dollar bills. Laying them one by one in a stack on his desk, he counted to forty.

"You get ten thousand for all the work. The other thirty is to buy the land. Do you trust me now?"

Lane merely nodded, dazed by the prospect of so much money for one deal. *Well, I guess even if he just disappeared, I'd be forty thousand dollars richer. I don't see how I can go wrong on a deal like this.*

With more than a touch of discernment, Crain shrugged, "The worst that could happen is I wouldn't show up again and you'd have to decide what to do with all that money. Forty thousand dollars would buy a lot of air conditioners."

One loose end bothered Lane. "How do you know you can trust *me*?"

"You've been checked out, believe me," Crain assured him. "I'm not all hayseed and horse manure. I *do* know a thing or two about business—and people."

Lane's eyes emptied of doubt. "I believe you do, Mr. Crain, and I think we can do some business."

"Good." Crain stood up and took his crumpled coat from the rack.

"Can I get you a cup of coffee or something?" Lane offered, standing up. "We usually socialize *before* we get down to business in this part of the country."

"No, thanks, I've got a plane to catch this afternoon." Crain slipped into the coat. "I'd have to give all my coats away if I lived down here."

"Oh, you'd get used to—" Lane laughed. "No, you wouldn't either."

Crain walked to the door, put his hand on the knob, then hesitated, a look of expectancy on his face. "There is *one* more thing you can do for me."

"Name it."

"Just to keep the record straight." Crain wiped a thin sheen of perspiration from his face with the big red handkerchief. "Maybe I'd better get a receipt for the money."

"Sure thing." Lane sat down and quickly wrote out a receipt and handed it to him.

Folding it up tightly, Crain stuffed it in his shirt pocket. "I'll be on the move for the next month or so, but I'll call you a couple of times a week."

"Can you give me some idea when?" Lane asked, thinking he had never had a client so easy to please. "I'd like to make sure I get the call so I can keep you up-to-date."

"I'm not sure. Sometimes I'm in places where I can't get to a telephone." Crain replied quickly.

"All right. If I'm not here, I'll have Coley take the message for me." Lane walked around his desk and shook hands with Crain, whose palm sweated profusely.

"Good." Crain wiped his hands with the handkerchief and stuffed it back into his pocket. "It's been a pleasure doing business with you."

Lane stood on the landing and watched Crain make his way carefully down the stairs. Opening the front door, he made a soft groaning sound as the humid morning air wafted across his face. He trudged out into the dazzling white light, pulling his big handkerchief out of his back pocket again.

Lane waited until the door closed, then jumped high into the air, clicking his heels together. "Hot dog! Wait until Catherine hears about this!"

Coley's office door opened slowly. He wheeled out into the dim hallway. "I take it the deal went to suit you?"

Leaning on the railing with both hands, Lane smiled down at the slight little man in the wheelchair. "You're worse than an old mother hen."

"Think so?" Coley put his hands behind his head, leaning back in the chair. "Maybe I just don't want you counting your chickens before they hatch."

Lane grinned. "This guy pays in cold, hard cash, my boy. Not like those cases you send me. If I'm lucky, I might get a dozen eggs or a homemade pie from them."

"Think of it as storing up treasures in heaven"—Coley beamed, his slim face half in shadow—"where thieves don't break in and steal and—"

"—moth and rust don't corrupt," Lane finished. "And the wolf isn't at the door and nobody pays a house note. I think He says something about *this* world too," Lane concluded. "Like rendering to Caesar. If I don't make enough money for the *rendering*,

Catherine and the kids end up in the street."

"Chalk one up for the redneck," Coley grinned, touching the tip of his forefinger to his tongue and making an imaginary mark on an invisible chalkboard.

"Now that I'll have money to pay some bills," Lane continued, walking down the stairs, "I just might consider running for your seat in the legislature—that is, if you'll buy me a late breakfast over at Hebert's Coffee Shop."

"I knew I'd get you, one way or the other," Coley gloated, pulling his office door shut.

★ ★ ★

All afternoon dark purple-and-gray clouds had been building as high as a mountain range along the western horizon. By five o'clock they had fallen across the sky. In the premature twilight, the air suddenly turned cool as a rushing wind moaned through the fallow cane fields and the marsh with its chorus of grateful frogs cheering the storm. Then rain fell in gray sheets, great drops denting the surface of the lakes and the bayous.

Lane turned off the two-lane blacktop and rattled across a bridge built of ancient creosote timbers. Beneath his tires the oyster shells covering the parking lot gleamed in the downpour. Listening to the metronomic scraping of the windshield wipers, he parked his Ford beneath a dripping oak, took a sheet of paper from his briefcase and read the name and address out loud for the second time in as many hours. "René Latiolais, General Delivery, Sorrento. Somebody around here ought to know where he lives." Lane regretted not getting better directions from the post office when he had the chance.

Rain beat loudly on the roof of the car. Through the windshield, fogged with humidity, Lane stared at the clapboard juke joint. It stood alongside a coulee rushing with new water, the long, drooping leaves of the willows growing along its banks casting a green-gold sheen in the dark air. Above the door of the ramshackle building, a purple neon sign spelled out "Home, Sweet Home." *Maybe that's just what it is for some folks.*

Lane ran to the little front stoop, opened the screen door and stepped inside. A short pudgy man with dark hair slicked straight back on his round head stood behind the bar at the far end. He carried on a conversation with a bleached blonde in a red satin dress that had probably looked good on her some twenty pounds and ten years before.

Two other customers wearing green work pants, grease-stained T-shirts, and welders' caps sat at a table against the far wall playing dominoes.

Lane smelled the chalk from the oyster shells that had been tracked onto the floor, the stale beer, the rancid grease from the kitchen, and the sharp scent of pine oil from the open bathroom door to his left. Walking over to the bar, he sat on a wooden stool and glanced at the bartender. With a weary glance at Lane, the man nodded to the woman and waddled along the duckboards down to Lane's stool.

"What'll it be?"

"A bottle of Coke and some information." Lane took a quarter out of his pocket."

"No, you don't."

"Don't what?"

"Want information. All you want is a Coke."

"I'm afraid I don't get it."

"You have to go in the back pocket for information. Front pocket money jes' get you a Coke, yeah."

"Never mind." Glancing at movement on his right, Lane saw the woman in the red dress walk over to the jukebox that sat on the bare concrete floor next to the men playing dominoes. Then he stood up to leave.

The bartender held his hands out, palms up. "Hold on. I'm just kidding you, yeah."

Lane smiled skeptically and sat back down.

The bartender held out his pudgy hand. "I'm René Latiolais. Glad to meet you."

Smiling for real now, Lane shook hands. "I won't need the back pocket money after all, will I?"

"Now I t'ink you got one on me, yeah."

"You're the man I'm looking for."

Latiolais gazed at Lane, as though trying to decide if he had ever seen him.

Lane recognized the song on the jukebox with the first few notes, Harry James' haunting trumpet caressing the melody of *Stardust*. He had expected to hear something nasal and twangy after the woman in red made her selection. *I seem to be developing a talent for misjudging people.*

"You like that song?" Latiolais could see the answer in Lane's face.

"Strange, the things a person remembers," Lane replied, more to himself than as an answer to Latiolais' question. "I heard that on a train when I was coming home after the war. A fellow was playing it on his saxophone."

"It's an old one, all right."

"Yeah." Lane looked back through the years. "It was one of my wife's favorites when we were dating more than twenty years ago." He watched the woman in red take her stool at the far end of the bar. "I guess it still is."

"You know my name." Latiolais, tired of Lane's walk down memory lane, jerked him back to the present. "Mind telling me yours?"

Lane decided to continue the game Latiolais had started. "Soon as I get my Coke."

"You catch on quick, you," Latiolais grinned. "Me, I t'ink I'm gonna like you."

Lane dropped his quarter on the wooden bar next to a cluster of cigarette burns that somehow reminded him of circling vultures. "Lane Temple."

Latiolais pulled a bottle of Coke from a galvanized tub of ice water and wiped it dry on a dish towel hanging from the back pocket of his khakis. "Temple. . . . Do I know you from somewhere, Mr. Temple?"

"Lane'll do just fine." Lane took the still-moist bottle of Coke and drained half of it. "I think this September heat is the worst. No, you don't know me."

"Yeah, September make you t'ink you oughta be cool, but you ain't."

"You might know my law partner," Lane continued, thinking that Coley might be the key to getting on the man's good side. "Coley Thibodeaux."

"Mais, yeah!" Latiolais beamed. "I don't know him personally but I hear good t'ings about him, yeah."

Lane decided to get down to business while Latiolais' thoughts were on a fellow Cajun. "I'm looking to buy some farm and timberland down here."

"Oh yeah," Latiolais replied noncommittally.

"Yeah." Lane turned up the bottle of Coke and finished it. "You got some for sale?"

"I might."

"How much?"

"How much land I got or how much I want for it?" Latiolais asked evasively.

Lane had finally grown weary of the thrust-and-parry conversation. "Why don't I just make you an offer, René, and then you can give me an answer."

"Fair enough," Latiolais nodded, "but first let me get some whiskey. I don't never do no business, me, without a shot of whiskey close by. You want some?"

"No, thanks," Lane watched him walk away on the duckboards behind the bar.

Latiolais stopped at a counter built into the far wall. Picking up a square bottle with a black-and-white label, he poured a shot glass full of amber whiskey. The lady in red batted her eyes slowly, giving Lane a smile devoid of happiness. *Heart and Soul* began playing on the jukebox.

I certainly can't fault her taste in music. Lane remembered a time in early spring when he and Catherine had lain together in the sweet green clover next to a creek bank listening to the childlike lyrics of the song playing on the car radio. *Heart and soul, I fell in love with you.*

Latiolais returned, drained half his whiskey, and made a face at the glass. "Now. How much land you interested in?"

Lane took the plat from his jacket pocket, spread it on the counter, and tapped it with his forefinger. "Three hundred acres. This tract right here."

"That's mine, all right." Latiolais sipped his whiskey, his expression giving nothing away.

"Thirty thousand dollars," Lane said evenly, tracing the perimeter of the land with the tip of his finger.

Latiolais' eyebrows raised almost imperceptibly. "A hundred dollars an acre. That's not a bad offer."

"Cash," Lane continued, using the word like a gavel slamming down on the bench. Hearing himself speak the word, he wondered why people always said that to make a point, as though paying off in bottle tops or streetcar tokens was a distinct possibility.

"What you want it for?"

"Does it matter?"

Latiolais pulled at his left ear. "It might."

"Timber—farming maybe. They tell me soybeans are the thing to get into."

"I believe we can do some business."

PART TWO

★ ★ ★

THE LAST OF THE LIGHT

FIVE

THE SYCAMORE LEAVES

★ ★ ★

"Why do we have to get up so early, Daddy?" Cassidy, pulling on his white T-shirt, plodded across the linoleum floor to the back door, gazing out into the yard through the half-glass door. "Look at this. It's not even daylight yet!"

Wearing his favorite Levis and khaki shirt, Lane stood in front of the white enameled stove, breaking eggs into a big skillet of hot bacon grease. "We've got a lot of work to do. It'll probably take all day."

"But it's Saturday," Cassidy grumbled, turning toward his father as he rubbed the sleep from his eyes.

"Give us a break will you, Cass?" Dalton took two pieces of brown toast from the toaster, lay them on a white plate bordered with blue flowers, and spread butter on them liberally from the matching butter dish. "Why don't you do something besides stand there grumbling?"

"All right," Cassidy shot back, pulling out a heavy chrome chair from the table and plopping onto it. "I'll sit down and grumble. I want to go back to bed. It's too hot in here. That light's too bright. I don't like—"

"Shut up, you little sheep-headed creep!" Dalton turned on his brother.

"Don't call me a sheep!" Cassidy pushed back in the chair and stalked over to his brother.

At fourteen, Dalton looked more like a seventeen-year-old with his wide shoulders and heavy biceps. "You wouldn't last two seconds with me."

Cassidy doubled up his fists, staring up into his brother's face. "I'll bet that's just what Goliath told David."

Trying not to laugh, Lane lay the spatula on the side of the skillet and stepped between them. "He just called you a sheep because your hair's almost white, Cass. Your mother and Jessie both have hair like that. Nothing wrong with it."

"Oh."

"Don't worry," Lane grinned down at his youngest child. "There's nothing *else* about you that's like a sheep."

"Okay then."

"You boys shake hands," Lane ordered.

"I don't want—" Cassidy caught himself when he glanced at his father's expression, then reached for Dalton's outstretched hand. "Don't think I'm scared of you though. If—"

"That's enough, Cass!"

"Yes sir!"

Lane returned to his eggs while Dalton set the bacon on the table, saw to the toast, and poured the coffee. Cassidy sipped his milk-whitened coffee with his head down and did the grumbling for all three of them.

Taking a final bite of bacon and eggs, Lane washed

76

it down with coffee and grinned over at his youngest son's glum face. "Boy, that was good! Makes a man happy he's got a hard day's work ahead of him, doesn't it, Cass?"

Cassidy mumbled into his half-eaten breakfast.

"I thought you'd feel that way." Lane stood up abruptly, sliding his chair back noisily. "C'mon, boys, let's get going. It's almost daylight."

After putting the dishes in the sink, Lane stepped out onto the wide back gallery, followed by his sons. He listened to the musical sound the fountain made as water flowed from one tier to another. A mockingbird sang high in the top of the live oak as the first pink glow touched the horizon. Off in the starlit darkness, a rooster crowed.

Walking down the brick path to the garage, Dalton rolled up the sleeves of his Istrouma jersey. "It's hot already."

"You oughta be used to it after four weeks of football practice." Lane walked around to the back of his Ford and opened the trunk. "Bring the signs on out here."

Dalton and Cassidy began carrying the campaign signs from the garage out to the car. White with a red border, they proclaimed "Lane Temple for State Representative" in bold blue letters beneath an American flag.

Cassidy dumped a load of signs into the truck. "How come your picture's not on these things?"

"Too expensive." Lane stacked the signs neatly in the rear, making room for more. "Besides," he crossed his eyes and stuck out his tongue. "You think this face is gonna make anybody vote for me?"

"Mama likes it," Cassidy said absently, turning back toward the garage.

"Your mama's a strange woman."

After loading the signs, they climbed into the car with Cassidy claiming "shotgun" and sitting on his heels with his elbow poking out the car window.

Leaving the driveway, Lane turned left on Evangeline and left again when he came to Scenic Highway. At 3682 he turned into the front lot of Peterson Chevrolet, got out of the car and opened the trunk. "Okay, boys, let's get busy. Bring two of those biggest signs over here."

Taking a key ring from his pocket, Lane opened the front door and went into the showroom. While his sons held the signs for him, he taped one to each end of the huge expanse of plate glass. "Good job. Now let's get rolling."

Piling into the car, they drove three blocks south and repeated the procedure at Hunt's Flowers and Istrouma Laundry, its valentine-shaped sign telling customers it was "The Laundry With a Heart." Four blocks farther on, Hollabough-Seale Mortuary soon sported one of the signs in its front window, and afterward another decorated Gully and Poor Realtors.

Turning left on Choctaw, Lane drove past St. Anthony Catholic Church and turned left again. Ten minutes later, Ourso's Grocery and Department Store told everyone passing on Plank Road that Lane Temple was the man to vote for.

"Daddy, where did you get the keys to all these places?" Cassidy had climbed into the backseat when his father told him to let Dalton sit by the window awhile.

"The owners let me have them when I told them we'd be putting out signs before they opened for business." Lane sat with the engine idling, staring over the backseat at Cassidy, his blue eyes holding another question.

"Ain't they afraid you might steal something?"

"Nope."

"Oh."

"I'll drop the keys off Monday when I go in to the office," Lane explained, anticipating his son's next question.

Lane glanced at the narrow brick building across from them where Chippewa dead-ended into Plank Road. "Tony's Do-nuts, 1946" was inscribed in concrete above the door. A single plate-glass window revealed little of the shop's dimly lighted interior.

Cassidy followed the direction of his father's eyes. "Can we get some doughnuts?"

"You just had breakfast an hour ago."

"Look at all the hard work we done though." Cassidy got up on his knees, leaning over the backseat to make his point.

"Maybe you're right. I could use a cup of coffee." Lane was thinking of the warm, sweet softness of Tony's doughnuts. They had a taste like no other he had ever eaten. "Tony said we could put a sign in his window so we have to go in there anyway."

Dalton turned to his father, asking in a voice slightly tinged with guilt. "You think it'd be all right if I had just *one*, Daddy, even if I *am* in training?"

"No."

"Well, okay," Dalton agreed halfheartedly.

"I think you oughta have *two* . . . or *three*. Nobody can eat just *one* of Tony's doughnuts."

At the end of the long day, Lane pulled into his driveway and sat staring through the windshield at the sanguine afterglow. To the west, beyond the river, the sky looked as though great fires were burning on the far side of the horizon.

Cassidy, who seemed to gain energy as the day wore on, peered over the backseat at his brother. "Looks like Dalton pooped out on us."

Lane glanced at his son, curled up asleep. "Yep. You boys put in a hard day. I'm proud of both of you."

"Did I work hard?"

Lane nodded. "Hard as the rest of us."

"I could do some more."

"I didn't think you were going to make it out to the car this morning."

"Me neither." Cassidy glanced at his brother again. "I guess morning is Dalton's time and night is mine. I don't hardly feel tired at all now."

Feeling reluctant to let the day end, Lane felt a deep sense of contentment at merely sitting in the company of his sons, even if one of them was lost in dreams. "You will when you get your bath and hit the sack."

"You know something, Daddy?" Cassidy gazed at the sky, which was turning a deep blue as the last of the light began to fade. A single star glimmered at the trailing edge of an oak limb.

"What's that, son?"

"I like this."

"The sunset?"

"No, the work."

His eyebrows raised in astonishment, Lane stared at Cassidy. "You do?"

"Yep."

"Well, you sure worked hard today."

Cassidy turned toward his father. "Oh, I didn't like it much when I was doing it. It was hot and I got thirsty and tired, but now—I don't know how to tell it, I guess."

Lane knew his son had touched on a truth that some people never learned. "You feel good about yourself. You're tired, but it's a kind of happy tiredness."

Cassidy thought it over. "Yeah. I think that's it. It makes you feel tired and good."

"Well, right now I'm good and tired," Lane admitted. "Let's go in and see if your mother's got some supper ready for the workingmen in the family."

★ ★ ★

Prussian blue carpet and smoke-gray leather chairs studded in bronze decorated André Catelon's plush office, located in the southeast corner of the Capitol building. Wearing his pinstripe suit tailored to make his short, stout body appear slimmer, he stood at the tall southern windows that looked out on the formal gardens with their one-hundred-year-old live oaks shading azalea bushes that would flame with pink, lavender, and white blossoms come spring. Beyond, lay the downtown business district and, in the hazy distance, the LSU campus.

In the early morning sunlight, the statue marking the grave of Huey Long cast its shadow across the walkways and clipped hedges, reaching toward the long brown sweep of the Mississippi, winding finally down to the Gulf.

Catelon's thoughts turned toward Bonnie, his only child. Beneath his black hair, flecked with gray and combed straight back from his low forehead, his obsidian eyes burned with a cold and remote light.

A light knock on the door pulled Catelon from his thoughts. Walking over to his massive desk of walnut and Australian laurel wood, he reclined in his custom-made leather chair. It irritated him that his feet didn't touch the floor, but making the chair shorter would only have put him at an intolerable level below the top of the desk. Sticking a thin cigar in his mouth he clenched it between his teeth. "Come in."

Bonnie Catelon, her dark shoulder-length hair glistening in the early autumn light streaming in the windows, entered the office and walked slowly over to the desk. "Hey, Daddy."

"You look nice today, baby." Catelon nodded at the pale green silk dress that matched the color of his daughter's eyes. "Is that new?"

"Yes," Bonnie replied in a hushed, almost formal tone, easing into one of the leather chairs.

"How about going to eat with me at Giamanco's tonight?" Catelon offered. "You know Charley sets the best Italian table in town."

Bonnie glanced up, her full lips turned slightly downward. "No, thanks."

"Bonnie, you're just going to have to snap out of this, you hear?" Catelon's face colored as he stood up abruptly. "It's driving me *crazy* to see you acting like this."

Bonnie wanted to cry, but felt she had lost the capacity for that too.

Catelon paced behind Bonnie's chair. "It's been almost *three* years. It's time you found someone else!"

"I've dated a lot of men, Daddy. There's no way to change what I feel inside."

Stopping next to his daughter, Catelon took her hand in both of his, squeezing firmly. "You know what I always say when things are going badly?"

Bonnie knew, but played along with her father, taking the easy way out.

"A little *revenge* always makes a man—or woman—feel a whole lot better."

"I don't want revenge on anybody, Daddy," Bonnie sighed, closing her eyes, their long lashes dark and curving against her pale skin. "I'd just like to have some reason to get up in the morning, that's all."

"What kind of talk is that?" Catelon began his pacing again. "You've got all the clothes anybody could want, plenty of money, a nice house, and a red convertible that I'd have given anything for when I was your age."

"I wish Mama was still alive."

"She's been dead fifteen years," Catelon almost wailed, incensed that Bonnie had added another dimension to her grief. "You oughta be over *that* too."

Bonnie stood up and walked over to the east windows, pulled back the drapes, and stared out at the play of light and shadow beneath the trees, and the sun rays glinting on the roof of the old walled arsenal.

Walking around behind his desk, Catelon unrolled a big map, holding it in place with brass paper weights and two copper ash trays. "Come over here and take a look at this. Maybe it'll make you feel better."

Bonnie glanced over her shoulder. "I'm not interested in any of your deals, Daddy."

"Get over here!"

With a downcast look, Bonnie strolled over and gazed down at the thin white paper with its myriad lines and curves and numbers. "What is it?"

"The river parishes—from Baton Rouge to New Orleans." Pointing with a gold fountain pen to a shaded area that curved from the top to the bottom of the map, Catelon's lips formed an insidious smile.

"So what?"

"See this long, thin shaded area?"

Bonnie nodded.

"That little curving line is the answer to your prayers, honey—and mine."

Catelon sat down, rocking in his big chair, his feet touching the carpet, pushing him back and forth like a child in a playground swing. "Our president, the honorable Dwight D. Eisenhower, who won World War II singlehandedly, is also a man of vision in peacetime."

Bonnie knew her father wanted to draw her into his little scenario of dropping information on her bit by bit like crumbs from a rich man's table. As a child and for years afterward she had played along, a trained puppy fetching the master's stick, but now she just didn't care.

"Are you listening to me, Bonnie?" Catelon's voice held an edge of anger.

Walking back over to the window, Bonnie spoke in a hushed tone. "Yes, Daddy."

Catelon grew peevish, the voice that he had trained so diligently listening to men like Huey Long, whose fiery speeches he fashioned his own after; the voice that commanded attention and respect in the Senate, now carried a slight whine. "Don't you want to look at my map?"

"I saw it. A map's a map."

"Not *this* map," Catelon objected, forcing the proper timbre back into his voice.

Bonnie finally relented, glancing back at her father. "Okay. What's so special about your map?"

Gleefully, Catelon began to explain. "This is the proposed route of Eisenhower's interstate system— the part from Baton Rouge to New Orleans. It's going to be named I–10."

"How did you find out about it?"

"It pays to have friends in Washington, baby," Catelon gloated, tapping his stubby forefinger on the map—and I've got some in the right places."

Intrigued now by how her father planned to use this information to his advantage, Bonnie still could not bring herself to ask him any more questions.

Catelon tried to pique his daughter's interest with another crumb. "The interstate highways are going to revolutionize travel in this country."

"I guess so."

Even more puzzling now to Bonnie was Catelon's mention of revenge. *I just know Daddy's got some sort of political vendetta in mind. But how in the world would Eisenhower's interstate highway system have anything to do with that?* She was to find out in the next twenty minutes.

As though reading his daughter's mind, Catelon began to explain precisely the sort of revenge he had in mind, the tone of his voice rising and falling with the emphasis of a fanatic as he drove home his points.

★ ★ ★

Half an hour later, Bonnie stepped off the elevator and walked across the polished hardwood floors toward the main entrance, the sound of her high heels echoing in the lofty recesses of the vast Memorial Hall. Glancing at the bronze doors sculpted with scenes of Colonial Louisiana that led into the Senate, she thought of the times as a child she had sat in the visitors' gallery with her nurse, watching her father's commanding presence as he stood at the podium engaged in fiery rhetoric.

Outside, at the bottom of the grand staircase, Bonnie got into her MG convertible, revved up the engine, and sped down the sloping concrete width of State Capitol Drive, skidding right onto North Third with a screeching of tires. Driving on past the lake, she took Chippewa to Scenic Highway and turned north. A block south of Hebert's, she turned onto a side street, parking beneath a sycamore tree.

Bonnie killed the engine and rolled down the window. A freshening breeze fanned her hair out across her face. Pushing it back, she sat staring at the dry sycamore leaves scraping along the street. *My life is as dry and dead as they are. Why do I feel so hollow and cold . . . and empty?*

Leaving her car, Bonnie glanced at her watch and walked around the corner to Hebert's Coffee Shop. She nodded to the slim man behind the counter who parted his hair in the middle. He had tried to get a date with her the first six or eight times she'd come into the shop. Now, nine months later, he had finally gotten the message and learned to content himself with a longing glance.

Bonnie took a table next to the plate-glass window that looked north across the gravel parking lot behind Dad's Bar to the small two-story brick office building. She thought back on the dozens of times she had come here at this same hour hoping for a glimpse of him.

"Here's your coffee, sugar." The waitress, wearing her white name tag with "Juanita" printed in red block letters, gazed down at Bonnie with faded blue eyes. Her hawkish nose bent slightly over the thin red line of her lips.

"Thank you," Bonnie said in a hushed, polite tone, her voice rasping slightly.

"Can't even talk just thinking about seeing him, can you?" Juanita clicked her teeth.

"Pardon me?"

Juanita wiped her hands on the dishcloth hanging from the side pocket of her black dress with its row of big white buttons. "I been serving you a long time now, ain't I?

Bonnie nodded.

"And I ain't never said nothing but 'Good morning' and 'Will there be anything else?'—stuff like that."

Shrugging, Bonnie agreed, "I guess so."

"You're throwing your life away, honey." Juanita glanced at the brick building beyond the parking lot. "He's married and he's got four children and he's happy."

Bonnie started to protest, then wilted under the truth of Juanita's words and the concern in her eyes.

"You're just as pretty as you can be and you're still young. Find somebody else."

"You don't know how I *feel*." Bonnie hung her head, staring at the steaming coffee.

"Yes, I do."

Bonnie gazed up at Juanita, seeing the bright unshed tears in her eyes.

"I waited and hoped and even prayed—for years," Juanita said, wiping her hands nervously, "back when I was still pretty . . . and young. Now it's too late for me."

"I'm so sorry."

"But it's not too late for you, sweetheart." Juanita nodded at a bearded man in overalls who had motioned for her. "You find somebody and make a good life for yourself."

Bonnie watched Juanita hurry over to her impatient customer holding his coffee cup aloft.

Sipping her coffee and staring out the plate-glass window, Bonnie watched a white-haired man in neat gray trousers with blue suspenders walk along the sidewalk with his companion, a slim woman about his age who wore a simple lavender dress with a certain elegance and style.

Bonnie could see that the couple shared the kind of familiarity that comes with years of being together. At the end of the block, they stopped in front of a house where blue and gold and white wildflowers bloomed outside an unpainted wooden fence. The man stooped down a little awkwardly and picked a small bouquet, handing it to his wife.

Admiring her colorful gift, the woman stood up on tiptoe and kissed her husband on the cheek. The tall man, his smile almost as bright as the flowers, slipped his arm around his wife's waist as they disappeared around he corner.

With her coffee growing cold, Bonnie stared at the flowers along the fence for a long time. She thought of the nights she had spent alone in her father's apartment in the Pentagon, trying to read or watching the ship traffic out on the Mississippi until the dawn tinted the muddy water with a rose-colored light.

A flash of sunlight on chrome caught Bonnie's eye as she turned and watched a black Chrysler pull into the small parking lot next to the brick office building.

The man in the front seat leaned over and kissed the blond woman behind the wheel, then got out of the car. Reaching inside the back window, he ruffled up the almost white hair of the ten-year-old boy who swung at him playfully as the car backed out into the street.

The man, his tan suit slightly loose on his lean frame, walked across to the building and with a final wave disappeared through the front door.

"You want a refill, sugar?"

Bonnie gazed up at Juanita, who stood with her coffeepot ready. "No thanks. I'm just leaving."

As she turned toward her other customers, Juanita left Bonnie with a final thought. "Remember what I told you, sweetheart."

Bonnie felt a slow, insidious pain building inside her heart. In recent weeks it had been happening with more frequency as though it were becoming a permanent part of her life. With a glance at the front door of the office building, she found herself giving in to bitterness. *Why should you be so happy when I'm so miserable? Maybe Daddy's right. Maybe revenge is sweet. I've hoped and prayed for so long now. . . . Why didn't you just die in Korea? Then I'd have you out of my life forever!*

SIX

ROY AND CISCO

★ ★ ★

Dalton took a towel from the team manager and wiped the sweat pouring from his face as he paced the sidelines with Junior Varsity coach Tommy McCoin. Glancing up at the scoreboard, he read the numbers for the third time in forty-five seconds: Istrouma–7, Jesuit–13. The clock read eleven seconds left in the game. "Coach, let me take the punt."

McCoin, a dark scowl beneath his crew-cut blond hair, growled back, "You've played every minute of the game and scored our only touchdown, Temple! Take a breather."

"Please, Coach. I know I can do it."

"We've got to hold 'em first." McCoin stared out at the field where the quarterback of the New Orleans team barked signals on his own nineteen-yard-line. Rather than taking a chance on fumbling with a hand-off to one of his backs, he tucked the ball against his stomach with both arms and followed his center in a quarterback sneak straight up the middle of the field as the Istrouma line slammed into the Jesuit's with a popping of leather, holding them to a three-yard gain.

The Istrouma band broke into a resounding rendition of the "Indian Fight Song," with the crowd rising to their feet and singing along.

Go, Indians, go.
Your power shows.
Fight on
A little bit, more a bit, lots a bit—
Indians, go!

Out in front of the band along the sidelines the cheerleaders did cartwheels, their legs flashing against their pleated gray and maroon skirts.

"Fourth down, Coach." Dalton strapped on his helmet, confident that he would go back in. "They gotta punt now!"

McCoin stared at Dalton, seeing the sweat dripping from his nose, his body as taut as a coiled spring and the fierce light of competition in his eyes. "Cannon's gonna take it. He's quicker."

"Billy's too skinny!" Dalton complained, watching his teammate out on the field brush his hand across his sandy crew cut.

Ignoring Dalton, McCoin turned to see the Jesuit team shift into punt formation, the center snapping the ball crisply back to the quarterback. He laid his foot perfectly into the ball, sending it spiraling high against the nighttime sky.

Never taking his eyes from the punt, Cannon dropped back ten yards farther, taking the ball on his own forty-eight-yard-line. Following his offensive line straight up the middle, he took advantage of a block by Carroll Debenedetto, the quick, agile guard who could always be counted on to open a hole, and found himself on the Jesuit forty, heading for the sidelines.

On the twenty-five, seeing two defensive backs in position to cut him off, Cannon stopped abruptly, letting one of them rush past, grabbing wildly for his jersey. Spinning quickly, he stiff-armed the second back and sprinted for the goal line. He had reached the eight when the quarterback, who had been following the flow of the play, blind-sided him, sending him crashing to the ground on the six-yard-line.

The Istrouma fans cheered wildly, jumping up and down and stomping their feet on the wooden seats, ringing cowbells and waving their pennants.

Coach McCoin called time out, waving to his team as he knelt with a clipboard in front of the band, their cymbals and horns drowning out his voice.

As his teammates trotted off the field, Dalton glanced at the scoreboard. Five seconds remained on the clock.

The Istrouma team bunched around their coach. He called the play that everyone in the stands as well as the Jesuit team knew he would.

Two minutes later the teams faced each other at the six-yard-line, the players digging their cleats into the turf for better footing. The Istrouma quarterback took the snap from center and stepped back quickly, spinning to his right with the ball held outward in both hands.

Dalton exploded from his three-point stance, felt the ball snap into his midsection, and cradled it tightly with both hands clasped over its ends. In a quick blur of motion, he saw Debenedetto cut the legs out from under the right tackle.

Anticipating the call, the linebackers as well as all three defensive backs had shifted to positions in front of their own left-tackle position.

Jesuit's big left tackle roared in ahead of the other linemen. Dalton feinted to the outside, throwing him slightly off-balance, then lowered his head and slammed his helmet directly into the big lineman's solar plexis. His face went white, his breath leaving his lungs in a whooshing sound as he collapsed.

Dalton, seeing a wall of Jesuit defenders directly in front of him, knew his small victory was short-lived. His legs churning and his head lowered, he rammed into them with all the power he could muster, feeling the weight of their combined bodies, the strength of bone, muscle, and sinew crushing him to the ground.

A loud moan rose from the Istrouma stands at the same time the Jesuit supporters across the field broke into pandemonium.

Untangling himself from the pile of bodies on the damp, mangled earth, Dalton stared at the scoreboard, watching the long second hand sweep past zero for a final time.

★ ★ ★

After the game every Friday night during football season, Hopper's Drive Inn swarmed with teenagers walking among the bumper to bumper cars and dodging the carhops as they whizzed by, making their appointed rounds. They gathered in small groups around car windows, shouting across the parking lot at their friends. Some crowded inside the brightly lit building behind the big plate-glass windows, at the counters and booths, talking too loudly with the animation and energy of youth.

Many of the cars held families who had come to this unofficial gathering place of North Baton Rouge to celebrate an Istrouma victory or drown their defeat in thick, rich malts served in heavy glasses or in cherry Cokes. These were accompanied by home-made hamburgers between soft Holsum buns, topped off with tomatoes, lettuce, and grilled onions.

"Here you go, Mr. Temple." Before Lane could turn around, Nick Landry, the short, wiry head carhop who always drove himself at full speed during his entire shift, had hurried off to another customer blinking his lights as a signal that he was ready to leave.

"Don't take it so hard, son." Lane served his family from the tray that Nick had attached to the car win-dow. "You played your heart out tonight. That's all anybody could ask. Give this to your mother, Sharon."

"I shoulda scored," Dalton, wearing his JV letter jacket, his hair still damp from the locker-room shower, mumbled from the backseat.

Sharon, her gold-rimmed glasses glinting in the bright neon lights running along the eave of the build-ing, sat in the front seat between Lane and Catherine. She handed the Coke to her mother, then took the tall, heavy glass, beaded with moisture and drank from the two straws standing upright in the thick chocolate malt. With a sigh, she proclaimed, "I could drink a hundred of these."

"You've never been able to finish one yet, sweet-heart," Catherine smiled.

"Where's my hamburger, Daddy?" Cassidy, his pale hair hanging just above his eyes, leaned forward over the seat, looking around his father at the tray.

"Here you go." Lane handed him two thick ham-burgers wrapped in wax paper spotted with grease. "Give the other one to your brother."

"I ain't hungry."

"Can I have his, Daddy?"

"No you can't, greedy gut." Lane handed the cold

glasses toward the back. "And be careful with this Coke. Your mother'll tan your hide if you spill it in her car."

Dalton took his hamburger and Coke and held them in his lap, staring at them sullenly.

"Come on now, son. Cheer up." Lane took a big swallow of his malt directly from the glass.

"We lost."

"I'm glad you hate to lose, Dalton. That's what it takes to make a winner, but you still have to shake the losses off and think ahead to the next game."

"I guess so." Dalton's voice carried the sound of resignation laced liberally with hope.

"If you can't do that, you might as well hang up your cleats right now." Lane took another big swallow. "Besides, the varsity team won 13–7."

"You're right. I gotta learn to shake off the losses. That's what Coach told me." Dalton unwrapped his hamburger and took a big bite.

"Aw, I liked it better when he was disgusted," Cassidy mumbled through a mouthful of his sandwich. "I coulda had his hamburger."

From the outside loudspeakers, the distinctive voice of Teresa Brewer sang "Till I Waltz Again With You."

"Oh, I just love that song." Sharon stared out through the windshield toward the speakers at something or someone only she could see.

"You don't have to worry about anybody waltzing with you, 'Four Eyes,' " Cassidy teased from the backseat. "No boy in his right mind's gonna look at you in them goofy glasses."

"That's enough, Cassidy." Catherine brushed Sharon's soft brown hair away from her face. "You're as pretty as anybody. I think the glasses just make you look intelligent, even sophisticated."

"Where's Jess tonight?" The hamburger and Coke had begun to siphon away Dalton's doldrums of defeat. "I thought she was coming to the game."

"She wanted to . . . she really did." Catherine glanced back at her oldest son, thinking how very much he looked like his father. "But she had to stay out at LSU and practice. She's got the lead in South Pacific."

"Aw, she gets the lead in *everything*," Cassidy chimed in. "This is kid stuff compared to Hollywood. I don't know why she didn't stay out there and get in the movies."

"She didn't like it," Catherine said succinctly. "And I'm *glad* she didn't."

Cassidy slurped the last of his Coke and protested. "But I could tell everybody my big sister's a movie star."

"Some things aren't worth the price you pay for them, Cass." Lane glanced over at Catherine, then leaned over and kissed Sharon on the top of her head.

"Why don't you tell the children your good news, Lane?" Catherine suggested.

"Well, I wasn't going to say anything until the deal was officially closed."

"Oh, go on."

"All right." Lane turned his heavy glass up, taking his time swallowing the rest of the smooth, rich chocolate malt.

"C'mon, Daddy, tell us!" Cassidy jumped forward, leaning over the seat. With a clinking of ice against glass, the Coke fell off the seat onto the floor.

"Cassidy! Your daddy told you to be careful!" Catherine took a handful of napkins from Lane, handing them to her son. "Hurry. Clean it up!"

97

"Aw, Mama," Cassidy protested. "It was just a little ice. I finished the Coke."

"Wipe it up anyway."

Grumbling under his breath, Cassidy bent down and cleaned up the mess.

Cassidy had distracted everyone but Sharon. "What's the surprise, Daddy?"

"Dum . . . da-dum-dum," Lane replied enigmatically in a deep bass voice.

"That's 'Dragnet'!" Cassidy cried out from the floorboard. "I seen it on television in the window of Durham's Hardware Store over on Weller Avenue."

"Are we getting a television, Daddy?" Sharon asked in a hushed tone.

"We sure are, baby."

"Oh boy!" Cassidy bounded off the floorboard, clanking the glass against the side of the back door.

"Settle down, Cass!" Catherine warned.

Bouncing up and down on the backseat, Cassidy cheered. "I can watch 'The Roy Rogers Show' and 'Gangbusters' and 'The Cisco Kid' and 'Dragnet' . . . Dum . . . da-dum-dum, and—"

"Hold on, Cass," Lane interrupted. "Somebody else might want to watch something too."

Catherine glanced at Lane, shaking her head slowly while Cassidy continued to bounce on the backseat. "This could be a *big* mistake."

"Can I watch 'Your Show of Shows,' Mama?" Sharon asked, leaning close so she could be heard over Cassidy's running dialogue. "I heard Imogene Coca's real funny."

"Why certainly you can, sweetheart."

Lane turned around toward the back, resting his arm on the seat. "You're mighty quiet, Dalton. Don't you want to watch anything?"

"They have any football on television?"

"I think so. Maybe not a whole lot now, but there'll probably be more on in a year or two," Lane remarked. "The pros are getting pretty popular."

"Ya'll finished?"

Lane turned to see Nick Landry standing at the window, his hair shining with oil and his teeth bright in his dark face. "I ain't tryin' to rush you now."

"We're ready, Nick." Lane collected the glasses from his family and dropped two one-dollar bills on the tray. "You just get faster and faster, Nick."

"Gotta hustle to make money in this business," Nick called back over his shoulder. "And thanks for the tip."

Lane backed carefully through the maze of cars and pulled out into Scenic Highway. Heading north toward home, he noticed the columns of white smoke rolling up against the dark sky. Tall yellow flames shot upward from other towers, roaring in the distance like the sound of giant waterfalls.

Sharon had dropped off to sleep, her head pillowed on her mother's lap. In the backseat the boys were arguing over what television shows they were going to watch.

"Catherine. . . ." Lane looked over at his drowsy wife, her face that of a young girl's in the soft light.

"Yes, darling." She turned her head, resting on the back of the seat, toward him.

"There's some news I didn't get a chance to tell you yet."

"What is it?"

"We're closing sale on the land Monday."

"I thought Mr. Crain couldn't make it back to town for a couple of weeks yet."

"He called again. Said it might be a month now, so

I should go ahead and close the sale and put everything in my name until he gets here."

"That means we'll have the money to pay off all the bills we ran up while you were in Korea."

Lane nodded.

"Oh, darling, that's wonderful!"

★ ★ ★

Lane stepped out the door of the Piccadilly Cafeteria onto the sunlit sidewalks of Third Street. "Well, that certainly was a good meal!"

"I'm glad we finally got to have a Sunday dinner without the children." Stepping out of the way of the people going in and out of the doorway, Catherine looked into the mirror of her gold compact and applied lipstick. "I thought the pastor preached a good sermon today."

Giving a noncommittal grunt, Lane took off his gray suitcoat, hung it over his shoulder and loosened his deep red tie. "Maybe we oughta go see *High Noon* next week."

Catherine glanced at the marquee of the Paramount Theater directly across the street. "Let's do. They say Gary Cooper might win an Oscar for this one."

Lane put his arm around Catherine's shoulder as they walked north on Third Street. "It *is* nice to get away from the kids once in a while."

The bright October sunshine cast the buildings and sidewalk on the opposite side of the street into deep shade and glinted on the tall windows and business signs that Lane and Catherine walked past. Mild weather had enticed people to stroll the downtown business district after their church services and Sunday dinners and the sidewalks were almost as crowded as on weekdays. Children squealed with delight as they playfully eluded parents down side streets or played chase among the Sunday strollers.

"Looks like things are finally getting straightened out for us, Cath." Lane took her hand as they crossed Florida Street, continuing north toward the Capitol.

"I'm *so* happy, darling!" Catherine squeezed her husband's hand. "I know how hard you've worked."

"I never would have made it without you," Lane admitted, his voice slightly husky.

"That's why we're together," Catherine smiled. "It takes both of us to get by in this old world. Us and the children. I can't *imagine* a world without them."

"I can imagine one with a little more peace and quiet . . . without a certain little white-headed boy."

"Oh, Lane, that's awful!"

"You know I'm only kidding." Lane pulled Catherine aside as a freckled-faced boy on a blue-and-white bicycle whizzed past them. "Cassidy's like the Tabasco on red beans and rice. It adds flavor—if you don't get too much."

"I'm not sure I like that analogy."

Lane changed to a somber tone. "I truly believe Cassidy's going to do something unusual with his life. Let's just hope it's heading in the right direction."

As they crossed Main Street, a boy of about three wearing red overalls burst through the heavy glass doors beneath the Sitman's Rexall Drugstore sign. Lane grabbed him, holding him around the waist as he giggled and twisted to get free.

The boy's young but haggard-looking mother rushed out after him, sighing with relief when she saw that Lane had corralled her wayward child. "Oh, thank goodness you caught him. He's worse than a jackrabbit."

101

Hefting the boy in his arms and handing him to the woman, Lane remarked, "I know the feeling. I've got one that was just like him at that age."

"Does it get any better?" The mother asked, holding the boy on her hip.

"Sure it will," Lane replied, in a tone that skirted the farthest boundaries of sincerity.

Continuing on their journey toward the Capitol, Lane and Catherine crossed Boyd Avenue and strolled through the formal gardens. Walking along a sidewalk lined with crepe myrtle, they came to a stone bench and sat down. The October sunlight held little warmth, but turned the capitol grounds into a bright patchwork of pale gold splashes and deep shadows.

"What kind of television do you want to get?" Lane's face brightened with the prospect.

"I haven't really thought about it," Catherine shrugged, gazing at the last pale pink blossoms scattered along the sidewalk from the overhanging myrtle trees.

"You don't sound very happy about the whole thing. Don't you even want one?"

"Not especially," Catherine answered, then patted Lane on the hand, "but I know you and the children do."

"We don't *have* to get one."

"No, it's okay."

"Fine," Lane beamed, thinking of weekend football games with his sons, accompanied by big bowls of popcorn and tall glasses of Coke. "I think we'll get a Philco."

Catherine picked up a pink petal at her feet, holding it up to the light.

"I saw a twenty-one-inch console over at Durham's Hardware," Lane continued. "It cost—"

"Hello, Lane." André Catelon walked toward them, accompanied by two young men in business suits who were obviously trying to outdo each other in their attempts to impress the good senator. "Mrs. Temple, *my*, you look radiant this afternoon! Your husband's a lucky man."

Stunned into silence, Lane watched his wife calmly and politely return the greeting.

"Why, thank you, Senator," Catherine smiled. "You're looking well yourself."

Not bothering to introduce his companions, Catelon straightened up to his full five-foot, five-inch height. "Just taking my afternoon constitutional from those mountains of paper work in my office. We public servants can't even take a Sunday off when there's work to be done."

"I guess dedication is what it takes to be a true servant of the people, Senator," Catherine remarked sweetly, her serene gaze fastened on Catelon's darting eyes.

"Yes, ma'am, I reckon it does." Momentarily distracted by an errant breeze blowing Catherine's hair into a swirling brightness about her face, Catelon lapsed accidentally into the aphorisms of his north Louisiana counterparts. "I—I mean, it does take a certain dedication."

Lane stared at the small man framed by the towering limestone walls of the capitol building behind him. Glancing at Catelon's young toadies, in awe of their mentor, Lane marveled that people were so easily fooled. He thought of his own involvement with Catelon and of how he had barely escaped becoming a very wealthy and completely miserable human being.

Uncomfortable as always in the face of silence, Catelon broke it. "I hear you're considering a run for the House seat in the northern part of the parish, Lane."

Lane merely nodded, enjoying the unease he detected in Catelon.

"Well, politics is an interesting business. It's certainly been good to me."

"I'm sure it has," Lane agreed, recalling a few of the secret deals that Catelon had cut.

Catelon's eyes registered the meaning of Lane's words. "Well, I want to wish you luck in your first political race. Maybe we'll be seeing each other at the Capitol."

"Word has it that you've got your own man in the race, Senator."

"Rumors are always circulating about me every time an election rolls around." Catelon twisted his right earlobe between thumb and forefinger. "I may decide to endorse someone—and then again I may not."

"Coley's backing Lane," Catherine said cheerfully. "Everybody in the district likes him. A lot of people say he's the only—uh, the most honest politician in Louisiana."

"He's a good man, all right." Catelon's eyes had darted at his two companions as Catherine spoke. "Well, I guess we'll be going along now. Nice seeing ya'll."

Lane watched Catelon walk hurriedly off down the myrtle-lined walk. "He certainly took off when you mentioned Coley, didn't he?"

"I wonder why he did that?"

Lane remembered Coley's stories about some of his and Catelon's confrontations when Coley had managed to block some of the senator's special-interest legislation. "I think maybe Coley is the only man in the House or Senate that he can't intimidate . . . one way or the other."

"Well, he certainly doesn't seem to be holding a grudge against *you* now."

"Coley says there's one thing you need to know about a man like André Catelon."

"What's that?"

"You can't rely on *one* word he says."

"Maybe Coley misjudged him," Catherine protested mildly. "How could he be so friendly if he's still carrying this vendetta against you?"

"Beats me." Lane glanced at Catelon, walking briskly out of sight behind a stand of cedars. "All I know is that Coley said once you cross him, you're his enemy forever."

SEVEN

VENDETTA

★ ★ ★

Turning off the Ford's ignition, Lane rolled down the window and stared at the deep red leaves of a sweet gum in the backyard of a house behind the office. Late October had brought the first cold air mass down from Canada and with it, the stirring up of his old memories of squirrel hunts with his father in the rolling forests of Mississippi.

Lane lost himself in the smell of woodsmoke on those early chill mornings as they downed breakfasts of country ham and homemade biscuits—crusty, with light fluffy insides, and rich with freshly churned butter. Then came the wooded hills and hollows of the farm, shrouded with soft gray mist like a forest in a dream of hunting.

And afterwards, they would sit beside a fire, warm and weary and as happy as a father and son could be together as they drank coffee and spoke of the morning's hunt and told again the old familiar stories of hunts long ago.

Still wrapped in the past, Lane got out of the car and walked over to his office. As he entered the dimly lit hallway, a sudden, jarring iron grip from behind on his upper arms jerked him back to the present.

"Lane Temp—"

Lane automatically dropped to a crouched position—years of marine training and combat taking command of his body. He stomped his right heel down on the instep of the man still holding onto him from behind. With a howl of pain, the shadowy figure released Lane's arms and stumbled backward.

Lane had already spun around, driving forward from the hips, slamming his wedgelike fist directly toward the big man's throat. The downward thrust of his chin deflecting the blow prevented Lane from crushing his windpipe.

"Lane—stop!"

Only the familiar sound of Coley's voice prevented Lane from delivering the death blow by driving the heel of his left hand into the base of the man's nose, causing broken bone and cartilage fragments to penetrate his brain.

With his hand frozen halfway through the final blow, Lane shook his head, glancing around and coming slowly back to reality. He glanced down at the bulky uniformed policeman, slumped now against the wall.

"Man-oh-man! I never saw nothin' like that before in my life!" A second officer, his eyes wide, his right hand on the butt of his holstered revolver, stood at the top of the stairs outside Lane's open door.

Wearing a gray business suit, another man, tall and broad-shouldered with a shock of wheat-colored hair, stepped out of Lane's office. He stared down at the little scene playing out below, a smug grin spreading across the clean features of his face.

"You okay, partner?" Coley sat in his wheelchair in the hall just inside the front door.

Lane glanced over at him. "I guess so. Sorry, I didn't mean to do that."

"*Semper fi*, Mac." Coley used the old catchall marine slogan that in this instance meant *Take it easy, marine. It wasn't your fault.*

The young crew-cut officer began a careful walk down the stairs, his hand still on his gun butt, the leather strap unsnapped. "We don't want no trouble now."

Coley glanced beyond him at Harlan Hinton, the first assistant with the District Attorney's Office, who still stood on the upstairs landing. He knew Hinton would never enter Lane's office without a search warrant. *It must be something pretty important for Harlan to come out here himself.*

A moan rose from the shadows across the tiny foyer as the burly officer who had grabbed Lane from behind tried awkwardly to get up.

Lane stepped over to him, took his arm, and helped him to his feet.

"Back off—now!" The crew-cut officer had gained the bottom of the stairs and had his revolver trained directly at the center of Lane's chest.

Lane looked around at the other officer just as Coley's left arm flicked out in a blur of motion and snatched the pistol out of the man's hand.

"Are you crazy?" the young man blurted out. "You're interfering with an officer in the line of duty."

"No, I'm not," Coley said flatly, holding the pistol by its barrel. "I'm just trying to help keep the two of you from doing anything *else* stupid!"

"I've got a warrant for this man's arrest!" He

snatched a folded paper from his chest pocket, waving it wildly at Coley, then over at Lane.

"I'll have a look at it then. I'm his attorney. Put this thing back in the holster," Coley shot back, handing the man his gun and taking the warrant from his hand, "and start acting like an officer of the law instead of like somebody playing Dick Tracy."

"Better listen to him," Hinton called out from above, "he's also a state representative."

Scowling, the young man held his tongue and holstered his pistol.

Seeing he had nothing further to fear from Lane, the big policeman limped over and joined his friend. He stood next to him, his dull eyes revealing a brain still slightly addled from the force of Lane's blow.

Coley ignored Hinton altogether, knowing that it would only serve to give him additional leverage if either he or Lane reacted to his taunts. After a cursory look at the warrant, he handed it back to the scowling policeman.

Hinton, seeing that neither Coley nor Lane could be drawn into his little trap, turned and disappeared back into the office.

"What's it say?" Lane stared at Coley from the shadows, his eyes flickering with a primal light. His mind whirled with disconnected thoughts like leaves blowing outside in the autumn winds. *What's happening here? I haven't broken any laws. Somebody just made a mistake.*

"He's right." Coley glanced at the two men in uniform. "They've got to take you in."

"What for?"

"Theft by fraud."

"That's all it says?" Catelon's professional smile flashed across Lane's mind. He could almost see the

110

little man's teeth gleaming in the sunlight that day on the Capitol grounds when he had turned his syrupy charms on Catherine.

"I'll know all the details in about ten minutes," Coley assured Lane.

"You ready to go?" The crew-cut officer slipped a pair of handcuffs from their leather case on his heavy belt.

"You won't need those," Coley snapped, his patience running thin.

"Standard procedure," the man grinned. "I ain't got no choice about it."

"Who's the duty judge?"

The big officer, who seemed to be regaining use of his faculties, pulled a blue spiral-ring notebook from his back pocket. "Judge Robichaux."

Coley nodded.

The man with the cuffs walked over to Lane, motioning for him to turn around.

Lane complied, placing his hands behind his back.

After snapping the cuffs on Lane, the crew-cut officer smirked, "Just thought you'd like to know: I'm charging you with resisting arrest."

Coley made no protest, knowing it would accomplish nothing but please the man. "I'll have your bond ready before they get you downtown."

"Thanks."

"And don't worry," Coley encouraged. "We'll have this mess straightened out in no time."

"One more thing."

"All right!" the officer snapped. "Quit stalling! We ain't got all day here."

Coley turned on the man, his gray eyes holding a stony gaze. "What is it, Lane?"

"Don't tell Catherine yet." Lane's voice cracked

111

slightly. "I want to do that."

"No trouble. I'll have somebody pick you up and bring you straight home."

Lane nodded.

Coley turned to the two policemen. "Take him out the back door, will you?"

The man with the crew-cut snarled, "We'll take him out any door we—"

"No," the burly officer cut in. "We got some bad information on this man. He's not anything like they said he'd be. He'll go out the back way."

"But he—"

"That's enough!" The burly officer snapped. "We've made a big enough mess here as it is."

Coley thanked the man with a nod of his head, then watched as Lane walked away between the two officers down the narrow hall and out the back door. Sitting disconsolately in his chair in the shadowy foyer, he listened to the noise upstairs.

Hinton and someone else were having a good time digging through drawers and files, shuffling papers around and dropping things on the floor. Finally he stepped out onto the landing and stared below as though he knew Coley would still be where he had left him.

Coley stared back, his gaze never leaving Hinton's smirking face. He could hear the other man putting things back in place inside the office.

Holding a sheaf of papers out in front of him as though he had just won a trophy, Hinton spoke in his best courtroom voice. "I knew we'd find something like this."

Coley stared at Hinton until his smile vanished and he stepped back into the office. As he wheeled around to go back into his own office, Coley made a mental note to file a motion of discovery at the first opportunity.

★ ★ ★

Catherine felt a heavy dull ache in her breast as she glanced at the headline of the *Morning Advocate* spread on her kitchen table: LOCAL ATTORNEY DISBARRED—LAND PROBE CONTINUES.

Coley, his gray eyes dulled from long hours poring over lawbooks and making contacts in his effort to clear Lane before the case went to trial, folded the newspaper carefully and tossed it over on the cabinet. "There's only one thing I'm absolutely sure of in this whole mess."

Lane pinched the bridge of his nose between thumb and forefinger, then rested his chin on his clasped hands as he gazed wearily at his best friend. "What's that?"

"Catelon set it all up."

"But there's no evidence." Catherine's voice sounded thin and fragile as though it were on the verge of cracking. "You said so yourself."

"I don't *need* any evidence," Coley said deliberately. "He might just as well have put his signature on it."

"What do you mean?"

Coley gazed across the table at Catherine, noticing again the purplish shadows beneath her eyes that spoke of worry and lack of sleep. "What cinched it was when you told me how nice he was to you and Lane that day at the Capitol."

"He was a real peach, all right," Lane added, remembering how syrupy sweet Catelon had been.

"That's the way the game's played." Coley didn't try to hide the contempt in his voice. "If he's got you all

113

set up, he comes on like your favorite uncle. You're safe as long as he treats you like last week's garbage."

"Well, we can sit here all night and agree what a thoroughly disagreeable fellow Catelon is, but we still don't have anything at all we can use in court," Lane said with finality. "We might as well go to bed."

Coley recognized the flat sound of resignation in Lane's voice. "Don't give up on me now. We'll beat this thing if we stick together."

Lane felt an icy chill in the pit of his stomach, but nodded and forced a smile for Catherine's sake.

"We've got a lot of friends out there who are behind us all the way, Lane." Catherine reached across the table and took her husband's hand. "All the phone calls and letters of encouragement—that's a lot to be thankful for."

"She's right." Coley tried to sound hopeful in spite of the irrefutable and bothersome evidence in the case against Lane. "I hear the *North Baton Rouge Journal* is calling for an investigation by the Attorney General's Office."

"And most people are keeping your campaign signs up in their businesses and yards."

Lane stared thoughtfully at a painting of The Last Supper on the opposite wall. "It's finally sunk in."

"What?" Catherine asked.

"Latiolais' got to be in cahoots with Catelon to make this whole thing work."

Catherine glanced at Coley. "Who's that?"

"The man who sold Lane the land," Coley answered, seeing Lane still working things out in his mind.

"It *has* to be."

"Keep talking, you might be onto something here," Coley encouraged.

114

Lane got up and walked over to the stove. "It's the *only* way it would work. Catelon set this up with Latiolais so he could ruin me *and* make money on the right of way."

"You're right!" Coley agreed, slapping the flat of his hand on the table. "Catelon's in the perfect position to have known where the interstate was going to be built."

Pouring a cup of coffee, Lane finished Coley's thought for him. "And instead of buying up the land and making all the money for himself—"

"And taking a chance on a fraud charge *himself*," Coley interjected.

"Exactly. He brings Latiolais in on the deal, splits the profit with him, and nails me to boot."

Coley stared at Lane as he sat back down at the table. "Now all we have to do is prove it."

"You saw Crain that day he came to the office. I know it's only hearsay, but couldn't we use it somehow?"

Shaking his head, knowing that Lane knew the rules of evidence as well or better than he did and he was just grasping at straws, Coley explained, "I've gone over it a hundred times and every way I look at it, it's still hearsay. I could only testify to what *you* told me Crain said or did. There's just no way to make anything else out of it."

"And Crain's one man we'll never see in this town again. We'll just have to hit it from another angle, I guess." Lane stared again at the painting, focusing his thoughts on the man at the center of the table. He remembered that this man too was brought before the magistrates for trumped-up charges and wondered if he himself would have the strength to endure. *What-*

ever happens, it won't be that bad—they can't crucify me!

For the past few moments, Catherine's thoughts had turned again to her children. She spoke her heart as though there was no one else in the room. "I wish there was some way to protect them from all this."

Knowing who she was talking about, Coley asked, "How are they doing so far?"

"I think Sharon's taking it the hardest," Catherine replied softly. "She's almost quit talking altogether. Jess and Dalton are both strong. It's not going to be easy, but they'll make it."

"What about Cass?"

Catherine sighed and turned to Lane, seemingly unable or unwilling to answer for her youngest child.

"Cass doesn't suffer fools gladly, I'm afraid." Lane almost smiled, his voice laced with a touch of his old easygoing confidence. "He had two fights at school yesterday with boys kidding him about his ol' man being a jailbird. That boy hasn't got sense enough to know he's supposed to be afraid of boys who are bigger and older and stronger than he is."

Catherine knew where Cassidy had gotten the trait, that iron will that was central to his character and that would eventually become true courage. Combat in the South Pacific and Korea had documented this same trait in his father. In spite of this, she sensed somehow that Lane would need more than his own courage to make it through what lay ahead.

★ ★ ★

Pale winter sunlight streamed through the high windows of the courtroom, reflecting off the polished marble floor and the blond hardwood tables and chairs. The austere judge's bench stood in front as a lofty centerpiece of justice. Twelve ordinary men and women sat in the jury box, contemplating the murmuring crowd, and a few stragglers pushed their way toward the remaining vacant seats. At the two tables directly in front of the bench, the prosecution and defense polished the final details of their strategies.

Suddenly, from a door in the left corner of the room, a short, stocky man, middle-aged with his dark hair thinning noticeably in front, walked briskly toward the bench. His long black robe swirled and flapped, displaying the energy of its wearer.

"The court will come to order. Everyone rise." The little gray-haired and uniformed bailiff spoke out in a surprisingly strong baritone, calling the courtroom to order.

The murmuring stopped as though a silence button had been pushed, everyone doing the bailiff's bidding.

"Oh, yay—oh, yay—oh, yay," the bailiff continued, using the "olde English" vernacular. "The Nineteenth Judicial Court is now in session, Honorable Alton J. Robichaux presiding."

After surveying his domain with a professional eye and apparently satisfying himself that all was in order, the judge sat down.

"Everyone be seated," the bailiff finished, then limped over to a chair at a side table and sat down to await the first recess and his next brief performance.

After the charges were read and the other preliminaries taken care of, the first act began.

Harlan Hinton, his right hand clasping the lapel of his carefully fitted pinstripe coat in a practiced manner, walked deliberately over to the jury box. Leaning on the carved wooden rail, he cast his eyes over the courtroom, let them fall briefly on the jury, and then fixed them on Lane.

A juror coughed, temporarily breaking the spell Hinton was so judiciously trying to weave.

Glaring at the offending juror, Hinton continued, pointing at Lane with the carefully manicured nail of a scrubbed forefinger. "That man, Lane Temple, has violated the oath that attorneys have taken in this state for generations; the sacred trust that you the people have placed in this honorable profession since Caesar ruled in Rome."

Trying to keep a straight face, Coley felt his stomach turning over at the sound of Hinton's pomposity.

As though reading Coley's mind, Hinton turned on him. "And you will find, ladies and gentlemen, that we have an airtight case against this man. Our chain of evidence tracing his fraudulent and insidious scheme is clearly unbroken and untainted."

Coley held Hinton's gaze.

"I supervised the execution of the search warrant myself," Hinton continued, giving the jury the benefit of his mirror-perfected smile.

"He's got us dead to rights, but if he keeps talking, he might aggravate the jury enough to sway them in our direction anyway," Coley whispered, leaning toward Lane.

After some grandiose phrases mixed with the proper seasoning of legalistic metaphors, Hinton concluded his opening remarks. "There will be no 'Fruit of the Poisoned Tree' in this courtroom today, Mr. Thibodeaux."

Coley's defense centered around Lane's reputation for honesty in his profession and his standing in the community. He leaned heavily on Lane's being a decorated veteran of two wars, as well as upon a long list of character witnesses.

From time to time Hinton shook his head sadly while Coley spoke, as though in sympathy for the lack of credibility in his presentation.

Coley faced the jury for his final comments. "The evidence against Lane Temple is as Mr. Hinton has described—airtight and perfect."

A murmuring ran through the crowd.

"Too perfect!" Coley suggested adamantly. "Lane Temple is a good lawyer and an intelligent man. Too intelligent to establish his own guilt by putting the bank account, the corporation papers, and all the real estate transactions in his name, knowing that it was only a matter of time before the interstate project became public knowledge."

Hinton continued to shake his head slowly, smiling with a smug satisfaction.

"My client is the victim of an onerous as well as obvious conspiracy. I believe you will see that the case against him is little more than a well-written legal script and that you will have no choice but to find him not guilty."

Hinton proceeded with the state's case against Lane, which amounted primarily to introducing the legal documentation. Latiolais took the stand to testify that Lane had mentioned no one else when he negotiated to buy his land, and Hinton's assistant documented the papers found in Lane's office.

Coley did some cursory cross-examination, but there was virtually nothing in the prosecution's case that could be objected to or weakened.

Finally, Hinton rose from the table, holding an engineering map which he unfolded, displaying the blue section squares and the topography of the area where

Latiolais' land was located.

Turning to Lane, Coley whispered, "This is the critical point in the whole trial and I can't think of one earthly way to refute the evidence."

Lane nodded, remembering the long hours he and Coley had pored over the case since Coley's motion for discovery had produced a copy of the same map that Hinton was now displaying to the jurors.

"Ladies and gentlemen of the jury," Hinton began, holding the map as though it would lead the jury directly to tons of gold located in the Lost Dutchman's Mine, "we have proven everything in this case that any reasonable man—or woman"—he grinned toward the back row at a sophisticated-appearing, champagne-blond woman wearing a white silk blouse—"would need to convict the defendant of fraud."

"Here it comes," Coley whispered, "and he's going to make the most of it."

Pausing for effect, Hinton spread his arms and snapped the creases out of the paper with a popping sound. "Everything but one, that is."

"Make your point, Harlan," Judge Robichaux interrupted. "We've got other cases today."

His face coloring slightly, Hinton rushed ahead. "Intent. That's the missing element. We've got to prove that Lane Temple knew ahead of time exactly where the Interstate right-of-way would be located."

Some of the jurors leaned forward, squinting at the outspread map.

"Here you are, ladies and gentlemen. I'm going to pass this around so you can get a good look at it."

The map passed from hand to hand slowly along the two rows of jurors, each gazing at it intently in turn.

As the map made its incriminating rounds, Hinton supplied the monologue: "As you can see, the shaded portion of the map is the proposed route that Interstate 10 will follow between New Orleans and Baton Rouge."

Having already examined the evidence, Coley had no choice but to remain a spectator.

"Anyone in possession of such a map would be in a position to buy up property from unsuspecting landowners for resale to the federal government at a tidy profit." Hinton gazed at the lofty ceiling, tugging at his right earlobe. "Now, how do you suppose this map came into our possession?"

Robichaux began tapping his pencil loudly on the sharp edge of the bench.

Hearing the sound of impatience behind him, Hinton hurried to conclusion. "This official Department of Highways map was located in Lane Temple's law office when a search warrant was executed on said premises."

The last juror handed the map back to Hinton, as a few of the others cut their eyes over at Lane.

With an expression of smug satisfaction, Hinton returned to his table.

"Any questions, Mr. Thibodeaux?" Robichaux asked abruptly, glancing at his watch.

"None, Your Honor."

The judge turned his stare on Hinton. "Has the prosecution finished its case?"

"Almost, Your Honor," Hinton replied with obvious deference. "We have one further bit of evidence."

"Very well. Proceed."

Hinton slipped a single sheet of paper out of a manila folder and walked toward the jury box.

"Your Honor, I was under the impression that all

the evidence had been submitted." Coley wheeled his chair out from behind the table.

Robichaux turned toward Hinton. "Would you like to explain this to the defense?"

"Yes, sir, Your Honor," Hinton agreed magnanimously. "This is something that just came to light."

"I'd like to examine it, please." Coley stopped in front of the bench, motioning to Hinton.

"Certainly." With an apologetic smile at the jury, Hinton walked over to the bench.

After a quick perusal of the single sheet of paper, Coley said bluntly, "I strongly object to this being admissible evidence, Your Honor."

"If I were representing your client, I'd do the same thing, Thibodeaux."

"That's enough, Mr. Hinton," Robichaux warned, taking the paper from Coley.

"Yes, sir."

As the judge looked over the sheet of paper, Coley continued. "This is totally irrelevant to the charges against my client and has absolutely no bearing on this case."

"Mr. Hinton."

"Not so, Your Honor." Hinton spoke in tones calculated to be heard by the jury members. "The defense's whole case is based on the sterling character of Lane Temple. I submit that this proves otherwise."

"Very well. Objection overruled."

Having heard the conversation at the judge's bench, Lane felt he knew what was on the sheet of paper. He regretted now that he had ignored all of Coley's warnings.

Holding his sheet of paper like a victory banner, Hinton returned to the jury box. "Ya'll have heard Mr. Thibodeaux's Hollywood movie script about the life of

Saint Lane of Evangeline Street."

"We've had enough of your theatrics today, Mr. Hinton," Robichaux warned.

Acting as though he hadn't heard, Hinton got down to the business at hand. "I have in my hand a summary of Saint—excuse me—of Mr. Temple's legal transactions for one of his most favored clients."

"I object, Your Honor."

"Objection sustained," Robichaux declared. "You'll refrain from judgments regarding the status of Mr. Temple's clients, Mr. Hinton. Unless you can prove one of his clients received favored treatment over another."

"Yes, Your Honor."

Coley felt no pleasure in his small victory.

"I have here," Hinton corrected, "a list of legal transactions for one of Mr. Temple's clients going back four or five years. I think the amount of work speaks for itself."

As the jury foreman took the paper and began to read, Hinton said almost as an afterthought, "Oh, one other thing: You might be interested in noting who this particular client is. His name is in the upper right-hand corner of the paper—Ross Michelli."

EIGHT

THE CITY CLUB

★ ★ ★

Catherine sat next to Lane in the bustling lunch-hour crowd of the Piccadilly Cafeteria. Lawyers, accountants, secretaries, dime store clerks, state employees, and a few politicians shoved through the doors and joined the twin serving lines or walked about the crowded dining area looking for a clean table. The muted clattering of dishes and pans from back in the kitchen area and the chattering of the good-natured women on the serving line joined with the din of fifty different conversations, giving the place the feel of a large family reunion.

Thinking of the many times she and Lane and the children had enjoyed their after-church dinners here, Catherine tried to put the awful burden of the trial out of her mind. "How long do you think the jury will be out?"

Coley, his tie loosened and his gray jacket limp from its countless trips to Tip-Top Cleaners, shook his head slowly. "An hour, a week—who knows?"

Lane showed little interest in Coley's opinion as he gave his full attention to devouring a double helping of collard greens, a chicken-fried steak almost as big as the platter it was served on, mashed potatoes and gravy, and four pieces of cornbread. Two thick, tempting pieces of pecan pie waited on their separate dishes in the background.

Catherine merely nodded at Coley's answer, gazing with sorrowful eyes at her husband. She knew that his years spent with too much blood and butchery and random death had produced in him a survival instinct honed to a fine edge. Most men in his situation would be too distraught to even think of eating, but not Lane Temple. She knew that Lane, just as he had done at Christmas and Thanksgiving on the front lines, was taking full advantage of what might be his last decent meal for a very long time.

Lane's actions meant to Catherine that he had given up completely on any chance of acquittal and was enjoying to the fullest these last good hours before he was sentenced to prison for a crime he didn't commit. She prayed silently for a miracle as they ate, knowing that nothing less would bring her husband home with her when the jury reached their verdict.

"You trying to put all your weight back on in one sitting?" Coley tried to brighten the tone of conversation, feeling there would be plenty of time for darkness later on.

Lane forked the first chunk of pecan pie into his mouth and chewed it with relish before replying. "I'm back up to 180 now. That's my old playing weight."

"You still working out?"

"Running three or four times a week, push-ups, sit-ups, chins—the same old routine we always did in all those years of football," Lane mumbled through another bite of pie.

Avoiding the subject of the trial altogether, Coley pressed for happier times. "We oughta have a good crawfish season down in the basin this year."

"Yeah," Lane said absently, sipping his strong black coffee. "Maybe we'll spend a few days at the camp. Run the traps and drown some worms."

"Sounds good to me," Coley agreed amiably. "'Course we got to get all the cold, wet weather out of the way first."

"You make it sound like spring's just around the corner. We haven't even had Christmas yet."

"March," Coley said, as if pronouncing some far-away mystical month.

"March," Lane repeated, sliding his second piece of pie over in front of him, "for the crawfish. But it's still going to be cold out on that water."

Coley nodded, dumped a teaspoon of sugar into his coffee and sipped it slowly.

"April." Lane held onto the last syllable with a sound like an April breeze blowing across open water. "I can just feel that warm sunshine and smell the sweet olive trees blooming all along the edge of the lake."

"Hey," Coley's voice sang with good times and sweet memories, "you remember that time we stayed up all night long running trotlines and—"

"I know just what you're gonna say," Lane broke in. "—and all we caught was three choupique."

Catherine gazed at Coley's smile and thought she could see him as a boy, healthy and sound and running through a sea of spring clover on the levee.

"Yeah, that's the time," Coley laughed, his gray eyes gleaming with remembrance. "The only thing biting that night were the mosquitoes. I thought I was gonna have to get a blood transfusion when I got back to town."

"And the very next night—"

It was Coley's turn to interrupt. "—we caught thirty-eight blue cat using the same trotline and the same kind of bait, Lazy Ike. Whew! I can still smell that stuff."

"I bet it smells like Evening in Paris to a catfish." Lane scraped the last of the pie off his saucer, finishing it with a sigh of satisfaction.

"Or maybe a piece of pecan pie," Coley added.

Lane nodded, washing down the last of the rich, sweet filling and flaky crust with coffee.

"I think I outdid myself cooking those blue cat that night," Coley continued. "And the hush puppies I fixed would have made my mama jealous."

"We've got to do it again this spring," Lane said, as though he was waiting for Nick Landry to bring him a chocolate malt at Hopper's rather than a jury to bring back a decision that could send him to Angola. "I'll untangle that mile of line I've got out in the garage and we'll get a five-gallon bucket of chicken guts for bait. We can both take a whole week off and. . . ."

Catherine felt the sharp pain of separation and the deep longing for Lane's return as though he had already been convicted and taken off to prison. She recalled Lane's telling her of the times in combat when things looked the most hopeless, when terror and desperation sat on the shoulders of his men like twin vultures. During those dark and troubled times, the men created among themselves places of peace and beauty and safety, using the only tools available to them: their imaginations and their words.

Gazing at Coley and her husband, listening to

them talk of the Atchafalaya Basin as though it had become a wetlands Garden of Eden, she knew they had both fallen back into the old habits they had picked up in combat; knew that both of them had accepted the fact that Lane would be found guilty and were living in a world without juries and bailiffs and bars for the brief span of time left to them.

As though reading Catherine's mind, Coley's voice took on a somber tone. "If things don't go our way today, ol' buddy, I'll come up with some new evidence to turn things around for you. You can count on it."

"Thanks." A smile flickered at the corners of Lane's mouth, then vanished.

"I think the jury might be on our side," Catherine offered, stepping into a fantasy of her own.

Lane turned to her; the numb acceptance of a situation totally beyond his control clouding his deep brown eyes jolted her back to reality. "You remember where the bankbook and my will are?"

Catherine felt like sobbing. "Lane, you act like you're already on your way to—"

"Listen, Cath." Lane took her hand and squeezed gently. "This may be the last time we'll have to talk for a while. Coley knows everything about our business, so if you have any problems at all, call him first."

"But, Lane—"

"I've already showed Dalton how to start the old Ford on cold mornings in case Jess has any problems with it. Once it gets warmed up, it's all right."

★ ★ ★

The City Club faced to the south toward the long alley of ancient live oaks lining North Boulevard. Built in 1895, the Renaissance Revival building with its Corinthian columns, stone arches, and extensive

129

terra-cotta ornamentation served as Baton Rouge's main post office until 1933 when it became the City Hall. Later, as a privately owned club, the elegant old building catered to those citizens of the capital city whose likenesses graced the front pages of the society section of the *State Times* or *Morning Advocate*, and those who gained admission to this privileged enclave through money or charm or good looks.

Directly across from the wide front steps of the City Club in the median of North Boulevard stood a statue of Hebe, clad in a flowing robe and holding her cup out in front of her like an offering. Daughter of Zeus and Hera, she was known in Greek mythology as the wine-bearer to the gods. The Women's Christian Temperance Union presented the statue to the city of Baton Rouge in 1914.

★ ★ ★

"Bring us another round of drinks, Jackson." André Catelon, his gray sharkskin suit catching the dim light of the City Club's lounge area, lifted his martini glass toward the tall, distinguished-looking Negro waiter.

"Yes, sir." Jackson, wearing a black morning coat and bow tie, made for the bar.

Catelon glanced at the two young men who had been with him the day of his encounter with Lane and Catherine on the Capitol grounds and who had just gotten up from his table and headed toward the bar behind Jackson. "Well, Bonnie, what did you think about their report?"

Bonnie recalled the look of glee on the faces of the young men, carbon copies of each other in their dark suits, starched white shirts and perfectly knotted ties, when they had given their account of the morning trial of Lane Temple. "I think that innocence or guilt has very little to do with decisions made in a courtroom."

Catelon gazed thoughtfully at his daughter. In her white silk blouse and charcoal skirt, she presented the picture of the young businesswoman, but she had never shown interest in anything remotely resembling a career. Idleness seemed her only true passion—idleness, and a succession of male companions since her divorce three years earlier. "I disagree, my dear. Innocence or guilt has *everything* to do with courtroom decisions. It's just that neither may have any connection with the *outcome*."

Bonnie finished her whiskey sour and set it on the linen napkin in front of her. "Isn't that the same thing?"

"Not at all. The two are worlds apart," Catelon smiled knowingly. "Decisions about guilt or innocence are made on the facts presented, but facts and truth often part company in the halls of jurisprudence."

"Here you are, miss." Jackson, his smile as white as the bar towel draped over his arm, placed another whiskey sour in front of Bonnie.

"Thank you."

Moving efficiently around the table with Catelon's martini, Jackson executed his little ritual with the precision of the picture-perfect catches he had made for the Grambling University football team. "Will that be all, sir?"

Catelon glanced up and dropped a dollar bill on the tray. "You're a good man, Jackson."

"Thank you, sir, but my tip's already on your bill." It was a game Jackson always went along with. It got him an extra dollar and Catelon got something in return. Jackson had never been able to figure out exactly what.

Staring at his daughter's downcast eyes, her lashes long and dark against the smooth skin beneath them, Catelon felt a slight prickling of resentment. "You're not getting an attack of conscience about this Temple character, are you?"

"Conscience?" Bonnie glanced at her father. "I don't think so. Not at this stage of the game."

"Good. A man like that *has* to be stopped."

"Why?" Bonnie wondered what he had to be stopped from doing but didn't ask. "Because he's honest?"

Catelon, intending a smile that didn't quite become one, bared his teeth. "Honest? You think he gave his wife a daily report when he was having his little fling with you?"

Bonnie's face colored slightly. "No."

"Nobody's honest." Catelon sipped his martini, his eyes narrowing.

"What about Coley Thibodeaux?"

Having no answer that wouldn't negate the point he was trying to make, Catelon ignored his daughter's comment. "It's just that some have a higher price than others."

Bonnie knew she had won points in this round, but also that her father would never concede them to her. "Well, what about Lane? He backed out of your deal when he could have stayed in and made a lot of money."

Catelon's eyes flashed with anger as he thought of the millions Lane had cost him with the state oil leases in the Atchafalaya Basin. "That wasn't *honesty*. He just got cold feet—a boy trying to play a man's game."

Although she remembered how Lane had refused to go along with the oil lease scheme in spite of all her father's threats to ruin him, Bonnie knew better than to confront Catelon with the facts. "Maybe you're right."

"Certainly, I am," Catelon assured her, savoring his victory. "But you have to get players like Temple out of the game or they can be a real nuisance."

Bonnie smiled, a sad light coming to her eyes. "Well, if he gets sentenced to Angola today, I guess that'll get him out of the game for a while."

"What do you mean, *if*? He's as good as—" Catelon glanced at a sudden brightness across the room. "We'll soon get the news from the horse's mouth."

After the glare of day, Harlan Hinton squinted in the dimly lighted lounge area. Sighting Catelon and his daughter, hc waved and headed for their table.

"Have a seat, Harlan," Catelon greeted him with genuine enthusiasm, "and give us the lowdown on the Thibodeaux-Temple dog-and-pony show."

"That's what it was, all right," Hinton laughed, sliding into a leather and mahogany chair. "Thibodeaux didn't have a leg to stand on . . . if you know what I mean."

"Hey, that's a good one, Harlan," Catelon grinned. ". . . 'a leg to stand on.' I like that."

"Yes, sir, we've got a reason to celebrate." Hinton glanced suspiciously at Bonnie.

"You can feel safe to say anything in front of my daughter, Harlan."

Hinton peered furtively around the lounge area. "Maybe we shouldn't be seen together at all."

"Nonsense!" Catelon brushed the suggestion away with a flick of his hand. "We've been friends for years. It's only natural that we get together for a drink now and then. If we break our patterns—*that's* suspicious."

Hinton shrugged and leaned toward Catelon. "I've already taken care of the evidence."

"Good, good." Catelon sipped his martini. "You're tying up all the loose ends I assume."

"I'm going to put my ten thousand in a safety deposit box. Latiolais' going to do the same. It'll be years before the money's missed, if at all, and by then it'll be virtually untraceable."

"Virtually?" Catelon's dark eyes held Hinton's with a cold light. "I like things a little tidier than that, Harlan. I'm afraid *virtually* isn't good enough. You're getting ten thousand dollars of *my* money to make absolutely *certain* nothing goes wrong."

Hinton laughed nervously. "Just a slip of the tongue, Senator. I told Thibodeaux we'd hold the money until the appeals process is exhausted. By then, someone will have mysteriously absconded with it. It's not all that unusual for evidence to get misplaced—especially after a few years go by."

"That takes care of *your* money and Latiolais'."

"Almost forgot," Hinton apologized with a sheepish grin as he took a thick brown envelope from his inside coat pocket. "Here's the other twenty thousand."

With a satisfied smile, Catelon took the envelope and tucked it back inside Hinton's jacket.

"What's that for?"

"I might need your services again before too long, Harlan," Catelon replied, his voice flat and emotionless. "Consider this an advance payment."

Hinton reached inside his jacket, taking the envelope halfway out. "But . . ." Without finishing his objection, he slowly pushed the money deep inside his pocket.

"How are you going to handle the safety deposit box?"

"I thought I'd use the name Rock Hudson."

"Who?"

"Rock Hudson," Hinton repeated, waving for a drink. "He's a new actor. A real *man's* man."

"Whatever you say, Harlan."

Hinton gave Bonnie a sidelong glance. "I really appreciate this, Senator."

Catelon acted as though he hadn't heard Hinton express his gratitude. "Thirty thousand. Not bad for one morning's work, I'd say."

Sipping her drink, Bonnie watched her father and Harlan Hinton work out the final details of their plot, gloating over their victory. She had no inclination to join the conversation, content in the knowledge that Lane Temple was going to suffer for spurning her. Her long nights of grief and tears would finally be avenged.

Bonnie thought this news would bring some happiness into her life after three years of terrible loneliness, a life as cold as the light in her father's eyes. *I've got to snap out of this. I've got what I wanted now.* She tried to smile at a remark Catelon made, but her lips refused to form one. *Something's wrong with me. It must be the whiskey making me feel so numb.*

"Well, now that Temple's out of the race for state representative, you can go ahead and throw your hat into the ring, Harlan," Catelon declared.

"No conflict of interest now, is there?" Hinton clarified. "It would've been a little awkward if I had announced a couple of months ago and then had to prosecute the man I was running against."

Catelon nodded his agreement. "You'll get elected in the first primary. Thibodeaux won't back anybody but Temple and nobody else out in that part of town has any political clout."

"I'll call next week and have them start working on the campaign signs."

"That's fine," Catelon nodded, his eyes bright with alcohol. "I think you ought to wait for another month or two before announcing your candidacy though."

"Maybe you're right. We don't want to look too obvious, now that everything's going so well."

Catelon turned toward his daughter. "You're mighty quiet today, Bonnie."

Bonnie stared at her drink, running the tip of her little finger around the edge of the glass. Then she tapped the side with her polished nail, making the dinging sound of a miniature elevator alerting its passengers to another floor.

"I guess that's better than total silence." Catelon winced at his daughter's minor rebuke. "I can see you're in no mood to celebrate with us."

"Well, *I* think we need another round," Hinton suggested. "I'll go have the office phone me if the jury comes in early. It's only a two-minute walk."

As Hinton walked off in the direction of the bar, Catelon gave his daughter a perplexed look. "What in the world is wrong with you *now*?"

Bonnie dinged her glass again.

Catelon fought to control his anger. "I don't know what it's going to take to make you happy."

Her green eyes taking on a slightly yellowish tint in the muted light of the lounge, Bonnie gazed at her father. She felt that there was an unfathomable distance between them. "I don't know either. I wish I did."

★ ★ ★

"There, there, baby." Catherine sat on the edge of her bed holding Sharon in her lap, rocking gently back and forth. "It'll be all right. You'll see."

As inconsolable as she had been since the moment Catherine had broken the news to her children, Sharon lifted her head, turning her swollen red eyes on her mother. Her voice, racked with hoarseness, plumbed the depths of sorrow. "But they took Daddy away from us! They didn't even let him come home to tell us goodbye."

Catherine brushed the tears away from her daughter's soft cheeks. Then she gazed into her sad eyes, the deep blue color of the evening sky. "I know, sweetheart. But your daddy didn't do anything wrong so we're believing that he'll be back home with us very soon."

"Why did they take him away, then?" Sharon gasped. "He's not a bad man."

"I know that, baby." Catherine longed for the right words, some way to end her daughter's pain, but all she could do was hold Sharon in her arms, and rock her slowly back and forth as she had done when she was a small child.

"I want Daddy to come back home." Sharon's voice was growing weaker, burdened with the feeble huskiness of her immense sorrow.

As Catherine held her child, feeling helpless to console her, she found herself singing the words to the old, old song that she had first heard as a child herself in the tiny clapboard church standing like a beacon of light in the piney hills of Mississippi. While she sang softly in the growing darkness of the bedroom, the words themselves seemed to burst forth with light. She sang them again as tears rolled down her cheeks.

Through many dangers, toils and snares,
I have already come;
'Tis grace hath brought me safe thus far,
And grace will lead me home.

"Mama, are you all right?" Standing at the door, Jessie peered into the darkened bedroom.

Catherine motioned for her to come in as she began singing the last verse.

Jessie walked softly over to the nightstand and turned on the lamp. "Is she asleep?"

Catherine nodded as she finished the song. Then she pulled the bedclothes down, lay Sharon's head gently on the pillow, and tucked her in. "I'm going to let her sleep in here tonight. She's so exhausted, I doubt she'll be able to go to school tomorrow."

Jessie smiled down at her little sister, her small hand placed against the side of her face as though she were about to utter an exclamation. "Well, it certainly won't hurt her to miss a day or two. She never makes anything but A's."

"How are the boys doing?"

Sitting on the bed next to her mother, Jessie stared out the French doors that led onto the balcony. Above the dark treetops, a thin moon fixed a curve of pale light against the night sky. "Dalton's frustrated because he knows his daddy's being sent off for something he didn't do."

"He'll weather the storm," Catherine said with conviction. "He's got that same iron will as his daddy. I can even see it in the set of his jaw—just like Lane."

Jessie continued to stare out the window, her eyes as blank as panes of glass.

"What about Cassidy?"

Rolling her eyes toward the ceiling, Jessie threw up her hands and groaned.

"That bad, huh?"

"Murder and mayhem," Jessie said to the ceiling. "That's what's on *his* mind."

"Well, at least the child's consistent."

Jessie leaned toward Catherine, lowering her voice as though to tell some dark secret about her little brother. "You want to know what he told me?"

"I'm afraid to ask."

"He said he wished that he could have been in that courtroom with a flamethrower and a whole bunch of hand grenades—and he meant every word of it."

Catherine's eyes filled with alarm momentarily, then she shook her head slowly. "No, he didn't, Jess. Cass just—well, you know how Cass is. Besides, he's just a little boy."

"I don't know, Mama," Jessie said doubtfully. "There's always been something different about him. First of all, he's never been afraid of anything or anybody."

"It's just his way of handling this thing, Jess," Catherine dismissed her concern. "We all have to get by somehow. Are you doing all right?"

"I miss him so much already," Jessie confessed, her face slack with grief. "I always feel so safe as long as he's around. You know, like nothing could ever go wrong just as long as Daddy's there to take care of everything."

Catherine put her arms around Jessie, laying her head against her shoulder. "I know, sweetheart. But we've still got each other . . . we're still a family."

PART THREE

TAKING A STAND

NINE

IN THE ABSENCE OF LIGHT

★ ★ ★

"You got a raw deal, Lane." Corporal J. E. Ball, his bulky frame crammed behind the steering wheel, drove his Plymouth sedan north up Highway 61. An East Baton Rouge Parish Sheriff's Deputy, he had drawn the dubious distinction of transporting Lane Temple to the State Penitentiary at Angola. "I'm sorry about them cuffs, but they'd skin me if I took 'em off you."

"Don't worry about it." Lane sat in the backseat behind the wire screen, his wrists cuffed to the steel rings of the heavy leather transport belt cinched around his waist.

"I've known you three years now—long enough to know you would never do nothin' like that." Ball turned his pie-shaped face around to take a quick look at his prisoner. "You done that work for me when I didn't even have grocery money and didn't charge me one red cent for it. No sir, a man like that don't take to cheating other people like they say you done."

"Thanks, J. E." Lane shifted on the seat to ease his cramped hands. "It's good to know that not everybody in town thinks I'm a crook."

"You got more friends than you think, Lane." Ball trained his pale blue eyes straight ahead as a rabbit flashed across the road in the bright beams of the headlights. "Ain't nobody I know believes you done nothing wrong."

Lane had lost all desire to defend himself anymore or to even agree with Ball, who was so obviously on his side. The ten years he faced behind Angola's tall wire fences had drained him of hope. He felt dead inside, his mind as blank as the car window with nothing beyond but darkness.

Ball turned left onto a gravel road. "Here it is— Highway 66. Twenty-two miles of hills and curves, and it finally deadends at Angola. What a place!"

Lane rode in silence while Ball made encouraging remarks or droned on about the latest football scores. Occasionally they passed a farmhouse set back off the road, rectangles of yellow light marking its windows.

Suddenly, around a sharp curve and at the end of a short straightaway, Angola State Penitentiary stood before them like a nightmare of drab block buildings and high fences topped with barbed wire.

Ball pulled the Plymouth up in front of a squat guard shack outside the main gate. A man in his sixties with a face like a shaved cocker spaniel opened the door and walked at a snail's pace over to the car. His uniform hung on his thin frame like a pair of well-used pajamas.

Getting out of the car, Ball opened the back door and gave Lane a hand. "Here you go," he said, holding out the brown folder of legal paper work.

144

"Kinda late, ain't you?" The man turned his rheumy eyes on Lane.

"I don't decide when to take people up here," Ball snapped. "The sheriff does."

"Don't get your dander up. I jest ain't used to checking many in this late." The guard glanced at Lane's shackled hands and motioned for him to follow.

"You want this paper work?"

"Oh yeah." He turned around, took the folder, and started to walk away.

"Ain't you going to look at it?"

"What fer?"

"To see if everything's in order."

The guard shrugged. "Wouldn't do no good. I can't read a word."

"All right if I take this off now?" Ball pointed to Lane's shackles.

"Shore. He ain't goin' nowhere now. Ain't no place to run but the woods, swamps, and the river."

Ball uncuffed Lane's hands, then unbuckled the transport belt behind his back.

Rubbing his wrists, Lane stared at the glare of neon inside the little shack.

"You look out for yourself now, Lane," Ball urged as he opened the car door. "And don't forget that you still got a whole lot of friends on the outside."

Lane stared at the curved block letters above the main gate: *State Penitentiary*. Built above the small office at the right side, a square tower rose on cantilevered pillars. An iron ladder led up to it through the roof.

Leaning over the iron railing of the tower, the bony-looking tower guard cradled his .30-caliber carbine in the crook of his arm. When Lane looked up, the man spat a gob of tobacco juice that landed in the dirt next to Lane's foot.

Lane remembered the blurred faces and forms of men he had seen down the sights of a rifle identical to the one the guard held so casually.

"Don't pay him no mind," the spaniel-faced man advised. "He don't like nobody. Not even his own mama."

"I'm Lane Temple. What's your name?"

The little man seemed stunned by the question. "Berry. Modell Berry."

Lane held out his hand.

Berry glanced furtively around, then fixed his sad eyes on Lane's.

"What's wrong?"

Berry leaned close and whispered. "Don't *never* do that in this place."

Lane wanted to ask why, but thought better of it and followed Berry into the little office.

Berry sat down in a folding chair with its wooden seat splintering away. "Take off yore clothes."

"Why?"

Turning his head toward a heavy glass partition reinforced with wire, Berry nodded. "'Cause you don't want them boys in there to come out here and do it for you."

Glancing at the two beefy guards on the other side of the partition, Lane began taking off his clothes. When he got to his shorts and shoes he stopped.

"All the way," Berry advised cautiously. "Then take yore stuff and go in there."

Lane finished undressing and walked over to the door that led into the next office.

One of the guards, a night stick hanging on a metal ring at his belt, walked over and unlocked the door, motioning for Lane to come through.

As Lane stepped into the room, the other guard, his dark greasy hair cut in white sidewalls, motioned Lane against the opposite wall.

"You don't have to do that," Lane said in an even voice. "They searched me down at—"

WHACK!

Lane felt a sudden burning pain on his right hip, the shock of it collapsing the leg, sending him sprawling on the floor with his clothes scattering.

The guard who had let him in stood above him, pointing with his nightstick to a white sign on the wall. Bold black letters warned Lane too late—SILENCE.

After he had been searched and allowed to put his clothes back on, the guard who had almost broken his hip with the nightstick, picked up the receiver of a heavy black telephone and dialed a four-digit number. He said, "pickup," and dropped the receiver back in place. It was the only word spoken in the forty-five minutes Lane was in the room.

Then Lane found himself in the back of a pickup, chained to an iron rod that ran along the sidewall from the tailgate to the cab. He played over in his mind the strange experience with the two men in the office next to the main gate. After searching him—humiliating him as though he were nothing but an animal—they totally ignored him as they sat at a scarred gray table playing gin with a deck of cards that looked like colored pieces of scrap paper.

Leaning back against the sidewall of the truck, Lane stared up into the vast black dome of heaven. The stars glittered with a cold hard light, as cold as the December wind blowing off the Mississippi River, which formed a great sweeping bend around the western edge of the eighteen-thousand acres of Angola Prison.

As the truck bumped along a rutted gravel road, Lane thought of Catherine. *How will she have the strength to survive this? It was hard enough on her when I had to be away from her and the children fighting in two wars. But this! This may be more than she can bear!*

Calling up the memory of Catherine's face, Lane gazed at it for what seemed like a long while. Then he pictured the faces of each of his children one by one, and heard again their voices and their laughter until he could no longer stand it.

Lane felt a terrible loneliness fall across his soul. He could almost sense some great beast brushing its hard, scaly body against him as he lay on the cold metal floor of the pickup, and for the first time in his life he wanted to lie down and go to sleep and never wake up again.

The pickup pulled over to the side of the road and stopped. Lane squinted into the star-brightened darkness. A low, flat-roofed concrete structure no more than eight-by-sixteen feet stood in an open field next to the road.

Berry, who had driven Lane away from his two reticent tormentors at the front gate, climbed down from the cab of the pickup and walked around to the back. Taking a huge ring of keys off his belt, he unfastened the padlock that held Lane chained to the long iron rod.

Lane climbed down and held his wrists out while Berry took the handcuffs off. "What's this?"

Glancing at the little building with its three doors and three lengths of pipe protruding from the roof, Berry answered almost apologetically, "It's the isolation cells. Everybody jes' calls it 'The Hole.' "

Lane thought of the guard pointing to the SI-LENCE sign on the wall in the cramped little office next to the front gate. "What'd I do to get put in here?"

"Nothin'," Berry mumbled. "You jes' got here too late at night. That's all."

Lane followed Berry, who had produced a flash-light from his back pocket, over to the building where he opened the door on the left.

"It's jes' for tonight." Berry shined the light inside the tiny room. "They'll put you in one of the regular camps tomorrow morning."

In the harsh beam of light, Lane saw a four-by-seven-foot concrete cubbyhole. A metal bucket par-tially eaten away by rust provided the only furnishing. "Do they really put people in these things?"

"Only when they do something real bad," Berry ex-plained, "like talking back to a guard."

"There's no bed."

"Usually a feller gets two blankets in the winter-time, but nobody expected you to come in so late."

"I guess I can handle it for tonight."

Berry looked back toward his truck. "Hang on fer jes' a minute."

Lane watched the gnarled little man walk stiffly to-ward his truck. He opened the passenger-side door, reached in, and took out something that looked like a pile of colorful rags.

"Here you go," Berry said almost cheerfully, hand-ing Lane a tattered and filthy quilt.

Lane accepted the quilt with gratitude, thinking of the cold, tomblike space where he would spend the rest of the night. "Thanks."

"It ain't much," Berry went on, "but it's all I got. I

use it when I have to be out in the truck a lot, like to-night."

"Maybe you'd better keep it then." Lane felt that Berry's kindness was a rare thing indeed at Angola.

"Naw. I'm going back and sidle up against that lit-tle space heater back at the gate."

"I appreciate it."

"Shore." Berry almost grinned, then mumbled at his feet. "I got to lock you in."

Taking one last look at the star-crowded sky, Lane nodded and stepped into the little concrete box. He heard the heavy door slam behind him and the key turn in the lock. The darkness was so thick, he felt he could hardly move inside it.

"I'll pick you up when I find out what camp they're sending you to." Berry's voice came through the con-crete walls, thin and muffled.

Lane stepped closer to the door.

"You got about two hours to get some sleep."

"Two hours," Lane said out loud after Berry had gone. "I'm so exhausted I can hardly move now."

After a few seconds, it occurred to him. *I've been in here less than a minute and I'm already talking to myself. How can any human being stand this for days on end?*

Spreading the quilt on the bare concrete floor, Lane sat down on part of it and pulled the rest across his shoulders for the meager warmth it offered. With-out understanding why, he could not bring himself to lie down. Then it occurred to him that to do so would somehow be a sign of giving up, of letting the cold and the dark and the loneliness get the best of him.

As Lane stared out into the infinite darkness, thoughts of Catherine and their children returned un-bidden. It became an almost unbearable torment as he saw their bright faces in the absence of all light.

Bowing his head, his arms clasped around his chest, Lane felt as though he were sinking inexorably, then falling at great speed into a cold, bottomless pit—a place without light, without hope. "God help me!"

Lane felt the terrible plunge come to a halt. He found himself merely sitting alone in the little concrete room. "Lord, I know I don't deserve Your help. I just ask You to take care of Catherine and my children. They need You."

A great weariness fell over Lane. He rolled slowly over on his side, his legs pulled up against his folded arms, and dropped down into a deep and dreamless sleep.

★ ★ ★

"Hold that thang over here, boy," the old convict working the serving line yelled at Lane. "If you ain't hungry, move on and let somebody else git some."

Shuffling along with the other convicts in the noisy, dimly lit chow hall, the heavy, black-and-white striped work pants and shirt chafing against his skin, Lane shook his head, trying to rid it of the cobwebs of fatigue and disorientation.

"You eatin' or not?"

Lane blinked his eyes at the grizzled head with its bloated red face, then held his tray toward it.

The convict dropped two heavy biscuits the color of raw dough onto a plate. "Move on! Move on!"

Staring at the biscuits, Lane moved toward the huge cauldron of boiling coffee. *How can these things be so hard and not even be brown?* he thought.

"C'mon, gimme that cup."

Lane picked up the tin cup on his tray and shoved

it in the general direction of the cauldron. A hairy hand poured the cup full of hot, black coffee.

The crowded mess hall bustled with men in horizontal stripes. Some carried trays to the long, crude wooden tables; some carried them toward the far side of the kitchen, where they dumped them on a counter to be scraped and cleaned by silent men in white aprons and T-shirts.

Stumbling wearily to an open seat on a long bench, Lane clanked his tray down on the table and sat in front of it. Holding the tin cup with both hands, he drank slowly. The hot coffee burned all the way down, helping to drive out the chill that had seeped into his bones during his two hours in The Hole.

Pouring blackstrap molasses onto his plate from a gallon jug that sat on the table, Lane dipped a biscuit into it and took a bite. Tasteless and dry, it crumbled like bits of soft concrete. Using the syrup and the coffee to wash them down, he managed to eat the two biscuits. When he looked up, he saw a man in his late twenties staring at him.

The man scratched his head and glanced quickly around at the closest guards, who were occupied with their own conversation. "Don't I know you from somewhere?"

The voice sounded vaguely familiar. Lane stared at the lean face, suddenly recalling its deep tan from the last time he had seen it. Now the skin was sickly pale, tinted with a reddish flush from days out in the wind and the pale winter sunlight. "You were playing 'Stardust' on your saxophone . . . heading down to New Orleans to make it big in the music business."

"Yeah! I made it big, all right. You can tell by these tailored clothes and this fancy French cuisine." The man's face brightened as the memory came back to him. "It was on the train coming home at the end of the war. You were in the marines, right?"

Lane nodded, taking a furtive glance at the group of guards. *Looks like I'm picking up the survival techniques already.* "And you were 101st Airborne."

"You got a good memory."

"Not for names."

"Joe Buckels."

"Lane Temple." Lane restrained the urge to reach across the table and shake his hand.

"How long you been here?"

"Since last night. You?"

"A week." Buckels shook his head sadly. "Seems like all my life."

Lane noticed again the chalky pallor of Buckels' skin and the hollow, vacant look in his dark brown eyes. "What'd you do to get sent up here?"

"I'm a musician," Buckels muttered. "Does that give you a clue?"

"Drugs?"

Buckels nodded. "You?"

"I'm a lawyer and I'd tell you if we had three or four weeks after breakfast."

"A lawyer?" Buckels moved his eyes from side to side, then leaned forward slightly. "I thought you boys was all too crooked to end up in a place like this."

Lane almost laughed, but it came out a grunt instead. "I made a politician mad at me."

"Oh," Buckels exclaimed under his breath, as though that explained everything.

Almost everyone had made it through the serving line. A few stragglers hurried in, the men behind the counter snapping their curses at them like mule-skinner's whips. The men savored these last few minutes

153

over their coffee before their long day in the fields began.

Feeling the last swallows from his own cup bring a soothing warmth to his stomach, Lane ventured: "What'll they have us doing?"

Buckels moaned softly, staring at the floor. "I wish you hadn't asked that."

"Come on. It can't be all *that* bad." Lane had grown up on a farm and hard work held no mystery or fear for him. Having met someone he knew, even if remotely, had made prison seem more bearable already.

"Clearing new ground."

"I've done that before. I can do it again."

Staring at Lane with his dark, hollow eyes, Buckels groaned, "Maybe you can help me get through the day, then. This work is killing me."

"Sure."

"They give you a shovel and a dull axe and point to a stump the size of a Greyhound bus," Buckels moaned. "Then if you ain't got it dug out when they think you ought to, they come at you with the leather straps."

"Don't worry." Lane tried to drag Buckels up out of his despair and in the process his own troubles seemed lighter. "We'll show 'em we can cut it."

"Everybody out!" Seemingly from nowhere, the voice boomed across the mess hall.

With no wasted motion and a scraping of chairs and clattering of trays and cups, all the men filed quickly out of the big hall and into the early morning chill.

In the gradually lightening darkness, Lane found himself trudging down a dirt road in a long double file of convicts. The ground gave way slowly as they moved out of the hills toward the bottomlands, closer to the muddy westward curve of the Mississippi.

Rainwater stood in the shallow ditches on both sides of the road, its dark sheen catching the muted pink-and-orange hues glowing along the horizon behind them. Glancing upward, Lane's sharp eyes sighted several vultures circling high in the bone white sky, their black wings glinting in the first long, slanting golden rays of sunlight.

Buckels, his shoulders as thin and stooped as an old man's, walked directly in front of Lane.

Lane leaned his head slightly forward toward the man, keeping an eye on the guard cradling a .30-.30 Winchester in his arms as he rode the flanks of the long lines of men astride a bay stallion. "How much farther?"

Turning his head away from the guard, Buckels spoke just loudly enough for Lane to hear. "You don't want to get there, believe me. Just enjoy the walk."

Buckels proved to be right. He and Lane and the others worked until noon digging and chopping huge oak and beech and sycamore stumps out of the ground, making it ready for another field of crops to feed the inmates.

The lunch truck arrived with huge pots of greens, boiled potatoes, long pans piled high with cornbread, and several jugs of blackstrap molasses. The men picked up their tin plates and cups and formed the ubiquitous long lines common to all prisons. Sitting in small groups on the bare ground near their stump holes, they ate and rested for thirty minutes. Many of them managed to drop off for a much needed twenty-five minutes of sleep before the whistle shrieked, summoning them back to their shovels and axes.

★ ★ ★

"That's the guy you got to watch out for," Buckels whispered over the edge of the top bunk. "He's the king of Camp E—maybe the other ones too."

Sitting below on his thin striped mattress, Lane gazed down the long row of bunk beds put together from rough-cut two-by-fours, four-by-fours, and sixteen-penny nails. A single naked sixty-watt bulb hanging from the ceiling by a black cord gave the dormitory a hazy appearance.

A barrel-chested brute of a man, six-foot-three and weighing no less than two hundred and fifty pounds, swaggered down the aisle between the double row of beds. He wore nothing but three ragged green towels knotted together about his belly. Not a single hair grew on his huge head, but he sported a bristly, black briar patch of a beard. His pale eyes, almost colorless, looked strangely out of place in his dark face, brown as bark.

Still in his filthy prison garb, Lane unlaced his muddy brogans and dropped them on the floor. "What's his name?"

"Brister Hogeman," Buckels whispered with a kind of reverence. He glanced back to see Hogeman leaning on a bunk talking with one of his toadies. " 'Hog-man' when he's not around to hear it."

"I'll be sure to remember that." Lane lay back on his bunk, opening and closing his blistered and calloused hands to keep them from getting stiff. He had almost dropped off to sleep when a sudden jarring brought him back.

Hogeman stood above him, his thick lips drawn back from his green-and-yellow-stained teeth in a look that once could have been a smile. "You got the duty!"

Lane sat up on the side of the bunk, rubbing his eyes. "What duty?"

"You'll find out soon enough," Hogeman growled, pointing to a heavy galvanized bucket of water and a mop at the end of Lane's bunk before he stalked off.

Glancing up at Buckels, Lane felt groggy and unreal, as though he had awakened into another level of dreams. "What's he talking about?"

Buckels slid off the top bunk and sat down beside Lane. Shaking his head sadly, he glanced at the big man as he walked away. "I hoped this wouldn't happen."

"What are you talking about?"

"Sometimes the Hog-man picks out a new man for the mopping duty."

"So what?"

"That's just his way of putting his mark on him."

"For what?"

Buckels' dark eyes registered fear as he turned them on Lane. "For anything he wants to do to you."

"He try anything with you?"

Shaking his head, Buckels snorted, "Nah. Guess he figured I wasn't worth fooling with."

Lane had seen men like Hogeman before. Usually the marines managed to cull them out, but one or two always managed to slip through. Men who were somehow lacking the essential quality of humanity: who had no sense of anyone's suffering or pain or sorrow but their own—whose every waking thought concerned only gratifying themselves. And Lane knew there was only one way to deal with such men.

Seeing Lane still sitting on his bunk, Hogeman's face took on a black scowl. With a knowing look at the men around him, he stalked deliberately over to Lane's bunk.

"You got to let him know where you stand . . . right now!" Buckels warned, climbing back onto the top bunk.

"Get up and get this place mopped!" Hogeman folded his massive arms across his chest.

Without a word, Lane stood up, splashed water from the bucket onto the bare wooden floor, and began mopping it.

From the safety of his top bunk, Buckels, mumbling under his breath, stared down at Lane. "Oh, Lord. He'll never last a week here."

As Lane bent over to wring out the mop, he felt a sudden blow from behind that sent him sprawling on the floor.

Hogeman stood with his hands on his hips, roaring with laughter. "Come on now, little lady. You got to do a better job than that."

Lane got up and walked back to the bucket. Bending down, he took the heavy mop wringer by its edge, noticing the sharp flanges and crosspieces as he loosened it slightly from the rim of the bucket. Gripping one end of its iron crossbar with both hands, he suddenly thrust upward with his legs and whirled around. In a single blur of motion, forcing all the strength of his shoulders, back, and arms into the swing, he slammed the wringer directly into Hogeman's laughing face.

For just an instant, Hogeman's dark eyes registered what was about to happen. Then they went completely blank to the dull cracking sound of his cheek and nose bones caving in. The swarthy skin of his face split from his lips to a point just below his left eye. Most of his front teeth fell back into his mouth.

With a heavy thudding sound, the big man dropped to the floor and lay utterly still. The raspy

158

stertorous breath escaping from his ruined nose and mouth and the soft popping of frothy red bubbles were the only sounds in the long, dusky room.

Lane picked up the mop and bucket and left them at the side of the aisle, then walked past Hogeman, back to his own bunk, without a glance at the man.

The others, who had been standing around enjoying Hogeman's nightly performance, went about their business with nothing more than a few mumbled remarks.

His mouth open, his eyes as yet uncomprehending the magnitude of what had happened, Buckels climbed slowly down from his bunk and walked over to the spot where Hogeman lay. Then with a half-smile, he glanced back at Lane. "I guess he knows where you stand, all right."

Lane lay back on his bunk staring at the ceiling. He felt a strong urge to get up and see if he could help Hogeman, but knew that it would be seen as nothing more than weakness and would break down the wall of safety he had just built between him and Hogeman's followers—and most anyone else in the prison with thoughts of testing the new man.

In combat, Lane had tried to keep loss of life to a minimum, to take every precaution for the men around him in the deadly business of war. In the new battleground of Angola, nearly everyone was a potential enemy. Compassion and ordinary decency were luxuries he could not afford.

TEN

MARIA

★ ★ ★

A front had moved up from the sun-warmed waters of the Gulf of Mexico, bringing several days with temperatures in the seventies. Some of the trees had started to bud out and patches of new grass sprang from the winter earth. Soon another cold air mass would creep down from Minnesota and the thermometer would hover near the freezing mark in the early morning hours, but for now the false spring brought a welcome relief from the usual January wind and chill.

Cassidy, wearing only a T-shirt and jeans, bounded down the stairs, across the short stretch of hall, and into the kitchen. "Hey, Uncle Coley. Mama, can me and George and Pancake have some pie?"

Catherine poured water from the teakettle into the top of the drip coffeepot. "I guess so. Then I want you boys to go outside and play. It sounds like a war going on up there in your room."

161

"It ought to, 'cause that's what we're playing—war," Cassidy explained.

George Newsom stood at the kitchen door, his slightly glazed brown eyes staring with innocent wonder. As always, his khakis and cotton shirt were neatly pressed and his hair combed down, even the part in back.

Looming in the shadows behind George, Caffey "Pancake" Sams looked awkward and out of place. Combing his wiry red hair down with both hands, he glanced at his tattered overalls and bare feet spattered with mud, then back down the hall as though plotting his escape route out of the house.

Catherine smiled at the unlikely pair that Cassidy had chosen as friends. "Come on in, boys. I've got a pecan pie that's just dying to snuggle up inside your stomachs."

With a cherubic grin, George walked slowly over to the table and climbed up into a chair.

Pancake lumbered after George, plopping down next to him and giving Catherine a suspicious glance. More accustomed to screaming and swearing in his own kitchen, he felt uncomfortable in the warm glow of her hospitality.

Coley pushed up the sleeves of his faded marine fatigue jacket, leaning his slim, muscular forearms on the table. "Who's winning the war up there, boys?"

"The marines," Cassidy, who was taking a knife out of a cabinet drawer, yelled from across the kitchen. "We're fighting the Germans and we're kicking their bu—"

"Cassidy Temple!" Catherine interrupted just in time. "You know better than to use language like that!"

"Yes ma'am." Cassidy grinned at Coley while he

cut three pieces of the rich brown pie and placed them on saucers.

As Catherine got coffee cups out of the cabinet she watched Cassidy carry the pie over to his friends, noticing that Pancake's piece was twice as big as the others.

After serving his friends, Cassidy sat down next to Coley with his own piece of pie. "Uncle Coley was a real marine just like my daddy."

Catherine took a quart bottle of milk from the refrigerator, pulled the tab up on the cardboard top, popped it out, and poured three glasses full. Carrying them over to the table, she watched Pancake shoving the last of his pie into his mouth with his hands. After she had put the glasses down, she took his saucer and cut him another big piece.

Pancake stared up at her in amazement as she placed it before him. "Th—thank you, Mrs. Temple."

"You're quite welcome, Caffey." Catherine patted him on the shoulder.

George looked up at Catherine with his placid smile. "Pancake eats like a mule, don't he?"

"No, George." Catherine kept her laughter inside. "He just has a healthy appetite.

"See, smarty, I'm just healthy," Pancake broke in, gazing up at Catherine.

"It's a real compliment to see how much you enjoy my cooking, Caffey," Catherine continued.

Pancake gave her his missing-eyetooth smile and began wolfing down his second helping.

After watching Catherine play the gracious hostess, Coley began to entertain the boys. "Cassidy's right. His daddy and I were both in the marines, but I only made it through part of one war. Lane fought in the South Pacific *and* in Korea."

"Did ya'll kill any bad men, Mr. Coley?" George held his fork halfway to his mouth, anticipating a war story.

"I did a lot of shooting, George," Coley explained, "but I don't know if I ever hit anybody or not."

"They musta hit you good," Pancake mumbled through his pie as he glanced at Coley's wheelchair.

Coley laughed at the boy's guileless response. "They sure did, son. I thought the whole Jap army was shooting at me for a while there."

"Tell us about it, Uncle Coley!" Cassidy shoved his saucer aside, his eyes wide with anticipation.

"You've already heard this story, Cass."

"Yeah, but *they* ain't," Cassidy insisted, pointing to his friends, "and, besides, it's good enough to hear again."

Coley noticed that even Pancake had stopped eating. "Okay, boys. Well, to start with, the name of the place was Tarawa and it was the biggest one of the Gilbert Islands."

"That's a funny name, *Tara*," George said, a frown of concentration on his narrow face. "But it seems like it's another war and not the Japs."

Surprised that George had made the connection with the Civil War by mispronouncing the name, Coley decided that a compliment would be better than a detailed explanation. "Yeah, it is a funny name, George, and you're right—there was another Tara in another war. You're a real smart boy."

George grinned and looked around at Cassidy and Pancake, proud of his knowledge.

Coley continued his story. "Our airplanes bombed that island for a week and then the big battleships shelled it for hours before we made our landings."

"I bet there wudn't many of them Jap sojurs alive

164

after all that," Pancake said, shoveling in the last of his pie.

"That's what we *all* thought, Pancake," Coley replied. He could almost hear the roar of the big marine engine as the landing craft thundered in toward the Tarawa beachhead. "But we were dead wrong."

"What happened then?" Cassidy asked, leaning forward on the table.

Coley took a deep breath, surprised that retelling the story should bother him after almost a decade had passed. *Maybe it never really leaves you.* "The boys in the Amtracks made it to the beaches all right 'cause they could climb right over the coral reefs that ran around the island."

"Like a tractor?" Cassidy asked, remembering what the Amtracks were from a previous telling.

"Yep, like a tractor," Coley agreed. "But a lot of us in the next wave didn't make it to shore."

"Why not?" Lost in the story, George spoke through a piece of pie he had forgotten to chew.

"We were in Higgins boats. They had flat bottoms and got hung up on the reefs, so we had to wade a real long way through the ocean to get to the shore."

"Was it too deep?" Pancake asked, his appetite temporarily assuaged.

"No, but it took us a long time, and the Japs hit us with everything they had—artillery, mortars, and heavy machine guns—while we were trapped out there in the water with nothing to hide behind."

George's eyes grew wide, his mouth slightly open. "That's when you got hurt?"

Coley nodded, hearing again the rushing freight train sound of the shells coming in. "That's when I got hurt, George. I didn't even get past the beach."

"Who won the war?" Pancake pushed forward on the edge of his chair.

"We took the island"—Coley's eyes narrowed in thought—"but it took us four days and 991 marines got killed doing it." He could almost see the bodies washing against the reef, arms and legs banging limp and lifeless against the sharp coral.

"Yeah, but look at all the Japs ya'll killed," Cassidy almost shouted. "How many was it?"

"Four or five thousand—something like that, Cass. I don't remember exactly. I *do* remember that only seventeen were taken prisoner."

Catherine saw the thin sheen of sweat on Coley's face and the shadows filling his eyes. "All right, boys, that's enough. Give Coley a break."

"Let's go play war outside!" Cassidy vaulted out of his chair, heading for the stairs. "I'll go get the guns. Ya'll wait right here for me."

A half-minute later, Cassidy bounded down the stairs carrying a toy M–1 rifle, a look-alike Army .45, and two gleaming cap pistols. "C'mon outside, Uncle Coley. You and George can be the Japs and me and Pancake'll hit the beaches."

"Your uncle Coley might not feel like playing right now, Cass," Catherine suggested with a glance at Coley.

"Sure, I do. Somebody's got to help me down the steps, though. This ol' wheelchair is worse than one of them Higgins boats trying to get over a coral reef."

"Here, take these." Cassidy handed the weapons to George and Pancake. Opening the kitchen door that led onto the back gallery, he waited for Coley to wheel himself through it and over to the edge of the steps.

"Let me help," George offered.

"Naw, I got it," Cassidy protested. "I do this all the time, huh, Uncle Coley.

"Yep. You do a good job of it too."

Taking a firm grip on the wheelchair's handles, Cassidy propped his foot on the bottom brace and rocked the chair back so that the front wheels were suspended in the air. Then leaning his weight backward, he let the chair bump easily, one step at a time, down to the brick walk at the bottom. "See, I told you."

Catherine watched from the kitchen door as Coley, brandishing a gleaming cap pistol, wheeled down the walk behind the yelling boys.

★ ★ ★

"Well, I managed to get the appeals process underway." Coley, his face pale from his backyard warfare with Cass and George and Pancake, sipped his coffee from one of three cups left in a set Catherine had gotten for a wedding present. He stared at the delicate grapevine pattern running around the rim. "I'm not much on cups, but these surely are pretty."

"I've always thought so," Catherine nodded, the sight of the cup, as always, bringing back some memory of her wedding day. This time it was the touch of Lane's hand as he slipped the ring on her finger.

"Now," Coley said with finality, "we've got to plan the strategy for our own brand of warfare—the legal type. I think I'd rather shoulder an M–1 any day."

"What else can we do?"

Coley's gray eyes filled with an intense light. "I don't know for sure. Whatever it takes to get Lane out of prison—and the sooner the better."

Catherine sat across the table from Coley, her milk-whitened tea before her on the table. "Here, I always think better with one of these."

Taking one of the tea cakes Catherine offered him, Coley munched it absently as he gazed through the half-glass door at the boys playing in the backyard.

"My mother used to make these for all the church socials, and when somebody special was coming over to visit." Catherine held one of the tea cakes between a thumb and forefinger.

Coley knew how painful it was for her to discuss anything relating to Lane's being sent to prison and that she was now calling up childhood memories to wall out the sorrow. "Maybe you'd rather not talk about this now, Catherine. I can go on back to the office and work on it there."

Catherine steeled herself. "No, we'll do it together. I won't let you shoulder *my* responsibility too."

Biting into a cake, Coley chewed slowly, then swallowed it. "First of all, let's put down what we know for sure." Coley began writing with a number-two pencil on a yellow legal pad Catherine had gotten from Lane's study.

"We know Lane's innocent," Catherine offered.

Coley merely nodded and continued writing, then glanced up at her. "Number one—Catelon's behind the whole thing."

"You know that for sure?"

"I know that for sure," Coley repeated, his voice sounding hard and flat in the quiet kitchen.

If Catherine had had any doubts before, Coley had just dispelled them.

"Next—Bruce Crain, or whatever his name is, was hired by Catelon. But we'll probably never see him again, and even if we do we can't prove anything.

"René Latiolais is part of the conspiracy." Coley scribbled on the pad. "But I don't know yet how we can prove his part in this, or his connection with Catelon."

Catherine nibbled her cake, thanking God that He had sent her and Lane a friend like Coley Thibodeaux.

"I can almost guarantee that Hinton is in on the deal somehow—probably something to do with that search warrant and the papers from the highway department that somebody planted in Lane's office—which means we won't get any cooperation at all from the DA's office."

Coley turned the pencil over, tapping the eraser on the tablet. "I know for a fact that Judge Robichaux *isn't* part of the conspiracy—he's been a friend so long I know he's not capable of something like this—but it would be an ethics violation for him to help us. So," Coley turned the pencil over and began to write again, "I'll just go to his law clerk and see if there's anything in their files that I might have overlooked."

"Sounds like a good plan to me," Catherine offered, handing Coley another cake.

"Mama used to make 'em just like these," Coley smiled, taking the tea cake from Catherine. "They always made me feel better back then too."

"There must be something *I* can do, Coley!" Catherine almost demanded, rubbing the back of her neck with both hands. "This waiting around for some kind of miracle to happen that'll get Lane out makes me feel so *useless*."

"You can drive me down to the courthouse in the morning after you take the kids to school," Coley offered, brushing crumbs from the corner of his mouth.

"Is that all I'm good for?"

"There's nothing anyone can do, Catherine." Coley stared out into the backyard. "Except what I'm going to do, and that's to start digging and hope I run across some leads that will help us get to the truth of what really happened."

"I guess you're right."

"You just take care of your children—and pray. Let me handle the rest."

★ ★ ★

Breathing heavily, Coley wheeled into the outer office of Judge Robichaux's chambers. Glancing around the deserted room with its gleaming tile floors and neatly stacked magazines, he called out, "Anybody home in here?"

A young woman in her early twenties walked in through a side door. She wore a gray skirt and a lavender blouse. Possessing a trim figure, she stood scarcely over five feet tall and had the face of a Titian madonna. Her large brown eyes were filled with light and her dark hair fell in pleasant disarray about her shoulders. "Why are you huffing and puffing?"

Stunned by the young woman's sudden and striking appearance, Coley blurted out the first thing that popped into his mind: "The better to blow your house down, my dear—unless, of course, it's made of brick."

The woman's shapely brows raised slightly. Giving Coley a skeptical look, she glanced about the office as though she were about to summon the judge's bailiff.

"No—it's all right," Coley assured her, "I just have a problem sometimes getting over curbs and thresholds in this rubber-tired chariot. Besides, I'm a lawyer."

"Now I'm *really* worried," the young woman shot back. "I thought you were only a mugger."

Coley laughed, then broke into a coughing spell.

"Let me get you some water."

"No . . . no. Really, it's okay." Coley held out his

hand. "I'm Coley Thibodeaux. The judge is a friend of mine."

The tension left the woman's face as the light in her dark eyes softened. "Maria Genero. The judge's told me a lot about you." She took Coley's hand.

"Well, he never told me a *thing* about you." Coley held on to Maria's hand, the sensation so pleasant that he found himself reluctant to let it go.

"Probably because I've only been here a week."

Coley knew there would be more. For some reason, people usually told him all about themselves.

"I graduated from Tulane Law School, and Judge Robichaux hired me as his law clerk until I can take the bar exam—or maybe I should say, until I *pass* the bar exam."

"You'll pass it."

"How can you tell?"

"Oh . . . I know about these things." Coley placed the tip of his forefinger against his left temple. "It's a gift."

Maria glanced at Coley's faded jeans and slightly rumpled herringbone jacket. "Are you sure you're Coley Thibodeaux? The judge said he's a state representative."

"Well, I usually don't admit to being a politician." Coley glanced around suspiciously. "It's bad enough when people find out I'm a *lawyer*."

"I guess you are who you say you are, all right." Maria held Coley's eyes with her own, wondering what it was about them that held an attraction for her. *Serenity!* It came to her almost like an epiphany. Such a serene assurance lay in their clear gray depths. "The judge told me you were a bit . . . unusual."

"Kind of him to say so." Coley found himself so absorbed with Maria, he had almost forgotten the reason he came to the office. Lane's case flitted around the edges of his mind. "So you're from the 'City that Care Forgot,' huh? I think that phrase might have applied back at the turn of the century."

"I didn't say I was from New Orleans," Maria corrected him. "I only said I graduated from Tulane."

Coley gave her a knowing smile.

"The accent, huh?"

"Not as heavy as most, but it's still got that touch of Brooklyn about it."

Maria leaned back against the walnut receptionist's desk. "I always heard when I was growing up that New Orleans had the prettiest girls in the country— that is, until they opened their mouths. So, what can I do for you this morning, Mr. Coley Thibodeaux, State Representative?"

Coley made a face at her at the sound of the title and wheeled his chair closer. "Must be getting senile. I almost forgot why I came down here."

Maria found herself staring at Coley's intelligent gray eyes, their lashes as long as a girl's.

"I'd like to go over the transcript of the Lane Temple trial and take a look at the evidence."

"Transcript's no problem," Maria shrugged, "but the DA's office has all the physical evidence."

Coley grunted.

"Won't they let you see it?"

Shaking his head slowly, Coley said, "If I got an order . . . maybe, and then they could use delaying tactics until it'd be too late for it to do any good, I'm afraid."

"Why would they do that?"

"It's a long story."

"Well, I guess I can see their point."

"What's that supposed to mean?"

"A man like this Temple character. He's the kind that gives lawyers a bad name."

Coley felt a warmth rising in his face and pushed the anger back down. "Is that so?"

"Well . . . sure," Maria declared bluntly. "He used all that stolen information about the interstate right-of-way to cheat that poor man out of his land."

"Tell me all *you* know about Lane Temple, Miss Genero." Coley's eyes narrowed in anger.

"Well, I read most of the minutes of the trial."

"And . . ."

"It was an open-and-shut case."

Coley took a deep breath. "Just like Boston Blackie on television, right? Lane Temple would have to have the IQ of a Bartlett pear to do the stupid things that the evidence in this case says he did."

"Well—"

"Let me tell you a little about the man you're sitting in judgment on, Miss Genero." Coley gave Maria the abbreviated biography of Lane Temple, including his service record with medals of valor won in two wars, his family, and the years he had worked free for people who had been turned down by every other lawyer in town.

Maria listened in wide-eyed silence, then as Coley finished, replied softly, "Oh."

"I thought you'd say that."

"You have to admit the prosecution had a picture-perfect case against him."

"*Too* perfect."

"And the kind of man you just described doesn't sound like the same man in that court record."

"Exactly."

Maria caressed her left earlobe with thumb and forefinger, her head tilted at a thoughtful angle. "The judge never would comment on this case, but I could tell he had some serious doubts about the way it was handled—just too perfect. The jury's verdict didn't leave him with much choice though."

Coley seldom made quick decisions about people, preferring to let the passage of time show him their true nature, but in this instance he made an exception to his rule. "You want to help me get Lane out of this mess and back with his family?"

Just as Maria started to reply, a bass voice boomed from behind Coley.

"Hey, Maria. You 'bout ready to put on the ol' feed-bag?" Harlan Hinton, his square jaw pointed down at Coley, crossed the room in five strides.

Coley glanced at Maria, wondering what she could possibly have in common with Hinton and thinking that perhaps there really was no substitute for the passage of time, after all. *Maybe she just goes for guys who look like Kirk Douglas.*

"Morning, Thibodeaux. How 'bout some break-fast?" Standing purposely close to the wheelchair, Hinton positioned himself so that he gazed down on the top of Coley's head.

Coley shook his head, refusing to crane his neck upward to see Hinton. "Could you back up just a little, Harlan? It's kind of chilly down here in the shade."

Maria glanced toward the window behind her, suppressing a giggle.

Hinton, seeing Maria's reaction, decided to go on the offensive again. "I reckon I *am* as tall as a tree to some people. How tall are you, Thibodeaux?"

Coley rubbed his chin, still refusing to look up. "A little less than a foot."

"What? You gotta be taller than that."

"Height is a vertical measurement, Harlan," Coley

explained. "When I'm in my natural position, like you are now, the biggest measure of me is horizontal."

"What are you talking about?"

"Now, if you asked me how *long* I am, it'd be somewhere around five feet, ten inches."

Hinton felt things going wrong, but couldn't quite figure out why. He glanced over at Maria, who was biting her lip to keep the laughter in.

"I'd be happy to let you measure me—that is, if you want to know for sure."

Hinton began backing slowly away from Coley. "Nah, that's all right."

"You could find out real easy, Harlan." Beginning to enjoy himself, Coley rolled his chair after Hinton. "It'd be kind of like measuring a fish in a boat, except I wouldn't do nearly as much flopping around."

Hinton headed toward the door. "Maria, you ready to go to breakfast?"

"Just let me get my purse, Harlan." Unable to control herself any longer, Maria burst out laughing and hurried into the side office.

Coley eased his chair around to face Hinton, who stood across the room next to the door that led out into the hallway. "Maybe I *will* have some breakfast with ya'll."

Glancing at the door Maria had just disappeared through, Hinton said almost in a whisper, "I just asked you along to be polite, Thibodeaux."

"You mean you really don't want me to go to breakfast with you, Harlan?"

Hinton's eyes bulged slightly as he raised his voice. "No! I don't even like you, Thibodeaux! You're—"

Maria, her purse hanging on her crossed arms, appeared in the doorway watching Hinton.

175

Hinton cut his words short. "Uh, Maria! I didn't see you. You ready?"

Maria nodded, her right eyebrow raising slightly.

Coley continued to smile benignly at Hinton. Then he watched Maria walk across the room.

Stopping at the doorway, Maria turned back. "Feel free to use the files. I'll be back in a little while."

"Thanks."

Just before Maria disappeared through the door after Hinton, she turned her head and gave Coley a smile so warm and genuine that it made him think her taste in men probably wasn't so bad after all.

ELEVEN

STORMY WEATHER

★ ★ ★

Rain fell on the city. Streets and buildings glistened with a wet sheen. The clouds hung so low and dark that 10:00 A.M. looked like dusk and drivers turned on their headlights. Out on the river, boat captains sounded their foghorns as they nudged the long lines of barges through a gray mist that hung above the surface of the muddy water.

Coley sat at the tall windows, staring through the rain-streaked glass. Behind him on a long, blond hardwood table, the files of Lane's trial lay neatly stacked. An antique clock, slightly charred at the base and brought home by the judge from Dresden after the war, ticked the seconds away with its meticulous, metronomic rhythm.

"Lord, we've got to have some help with this." Coley spoke in the conversational tone he used when he and Lane were discussing a particularly complicated legal problem. "You know we both did our best to win the trial, but things were just stacked against us. I don't understand why Lane has to go through so much. He loves Catherine and his children and he works hard for them . . ."

The rain hissed faintly through the window as time sped by with its precise, measured beat.

"Jesus, You've never let me down. You know my heart—You know I trust You, but right now I'm just so down and discouraged about my friend, I don't know which way to turn. I ask that You'll set Your angel over Lane to protect him in prison and that You'll give me the help I need to get him out of this mess."

Lost in prayer, Coley didn't hear the hall door open and close. "I just give this whole business to You, Jesus, 'cause I can't see any way out of it."

Maria stepped into the judge's law library and glanced around. She had overheard Coley and had supposed at first that someone else was in the room with him before she realized that he was praying. Even then, she almost felt the presence of another there with him.

Her own experience with prayer had been mostly listening as a child to the Sunday-morning rituals in church. She had pictured God as a huge, white-bearded figure—cold, distant, remote—somewhere off in the clouds.

Even though his eyes had been closed and his head bowed, Coley sounded as though he had been talking with someone he knew very well—a friend. At that instant, Coley took on another dimension for Maria, one that intrigued her and at the same time gave her a feeling of uneasiness.

Maria hung her purse on a clothes tree standing in the corner. "How is it going with the research?"

Coley looked back out at the rain.

"You haven't even started yet," Maria observed, glancing at the files.

"I gave 'em a cursory look," Coley replied, still staring out the window.

Maria walked the length of the table, pulled out a green-cushioned chair, and sat down next to him. "You don't sound very enthusiastic about your chances."

"About *Lane's* chances," Coley corrected. "This is just a starting place. Whatever I find to clear Lane won't be found in *any* official files."

"Maybe *I* can help."

Coley looked away from the rain. He noticed the fine wet tendrils of hair curling about Maria's neck and the soft delicate lines of her ears. "You have the time?"

"Things have been slow since I got here," Maria answered. "Besides, the judge is off for a couple of days and I've already finished the things he left for me to do."

"How was breakfast?" Coley was bothered by the tone of his voice and wished he could have taken the words back. *That sounded almost like jealousy.*

"Okay," Maria replied noncommittally. "Where do you want me to start?"

"Huh? Oh, yes. I guess we'll just start at the beginning and go right on through."

"What a novel idea."

Coley felt a warmth rising from his neck up into his face. "That *did* sound kind of dumb, didn't it?"

"A little." Maria had begun to find that Coley's shyness was somehow disturbingly attractive. She knew of his reputation as a tenacious fighter and articulate speaker on the floor of the House for the people he represented, but he seemed almost backward in her presence.

Coley took a deep breath. "I guess maybe it's because for the first time in a long while I'm afraid that the bad guys are going to win this one, hands down."

Maria opened the first file and handed it to Coley. "You start with the minutes."

"That sounds logical."

"And I'll start with the depositions." She opened another file and began to sort though the papers.

"And I'll be in Scotland 'afore ye."

Maria smiled at Coley and began to read.

★ ★ ★

"Thanks for the lift." Coley pulled the seat forward, reached behind him, and lifted his wheelchair out.

"Just a minute, I'll help you." Maria got out on the driver's side of her '48 Plymouth coupe, opened her umbrella, and walked around the car, stepping over puddles.

Coley had already set the chair down on the ground and pulled it open. He slid into it just as Maria reached the passenger door, holding her umbrella over him.

"That's pretty quick."

"I've had a lot of practice." Coley wheeled around the car and up the walk to the office building with Maria walking along beside him.

"That's a good idea. They should put these everywhere." Maria glanced down at the little wooden ramp that led up to the level of the front door.

"Lane built it for me." Coley opened the door and glided into the dimly lighted hallway.

Maria stood on the little stoop, staring at Coley with an expression of mild surprise.

"Did you want to come in?" It had never occurred to Coley that she would want to spend any more time with him. "I could fix us some coffee."

Shivering slightly, Maria glanced at the chilly January rain beating steadily on the sidewalk just behind her. Across Scenic Highway, the huge columns and towers of the Standard Oil Refinery were lost in the gray mist. "I could stand something hot inside me— if it's not too much trouble."

"No trouble at all," Coley said quickly, unlocking his office door. "I just didn't think you'd . . ."

Maria reached around him and opened the door, then took the handles of the wheelchair and pushed him inside. "It's okay to let someone help you once in a while, Coley."

Coley merely glided across the pine flooring of the office, switched his desk lamp on, and turned to face Maria. "It's not much. But it's dry and warm."

"Sometimes that's a lot," Maria smiled as she slipped out of her raincoat.

Coley made coffee on the single-burner hotplate while Maria sat next to him on a straight-backed wooden chair with a deer-hide seat. Pouring from the white ceramic pot, Coley noticed Maria's slim, graceful hands as they held the cup out toward him.

"This looks strong enough to be New Orleans coffee." Maria scraped sugar out of an old jelly jar with pictures of Bugs Bunny and Elmer Fudd on its sides.

"No chicory though—too bitter for my taste," Coley explained, watching Maria with his makeshift sugar bowl. "I'm sorry there's no cream. I don't entertain much."

"This is fine."

Coley found himself at a loss for words in Maria's company. *What's wrong with me? I'm acting like a six-*

181

teen-year-old on his first date.

Maria sat back in her chair, sipping the coffee slowly and with obvious pleasure. "Hmmm . . . this is delicious. How'd you learn to make it so smooth?"

"My mother."

"Do you see her much?"

"She's dead."

"Oh, I'm sorry. I didn't mean to—"

"It's all right. It happened a long time ago." Coley began telling Maria the story of his parents' deaths without intending to. "I came home from school one day and . . ."

Maria held her cup with the fingertips of both hands, staring over its rim into Coley's eyes. "It's okay if you'd rather not talk about it."

"I don't want to bore you."

"You may be many things, Coley Thibodeaux," Maria said softly. "*Boring* isn't one of them."

Coley told her about how he had found his parents murdered in their home and that the killer had never been caught. A passerby had seen a stocky man with a limp crossing the front yard shortly after the time of their deaths, but he was never located.

"I hated that man for a long, long time," Coley admitted. "Thank God, *that's* over."

Maria continued to gaze into Coley's eyes as he spoke and saw no sign of hate or desire for revenge in them, only deep, lingering memories of the past that somehow seemed to hold much more joy than sorrow. "I'll bet they'd be proud of you if they could see how you turned out."

Coley stared out at the rain. Cars hissed by on the wet pavement, their headlights flashing through the lead-colored afternoon.

"Are you all right?"

182

"Sure," Coley smiled, still gazing out through the window. "I was just thinking about Mama and Daddy. We sure did have some good times in that little shack on Bayou Grosse Tete."

Maria sipped her coffee, strangely content just to sit in the cluttered little office watching the rain.

"Well, Ike gets inaugurated next week." Coley returned from the past. "Think he'll make a good president?"

"Who knows?" Maria shrugged. "He helped hold the country together during the war. Maybe he can do the same thing during peacetime."

"I remember during his campaign he said, 'Our government makes no sense unless it is founded in a deeply felt religious faith. . . .'" Coley took his eyes from the window. "Let's hope that wasn't just political rhetoric."

"I've enjoyed the day, Coley," Maria said brightly, a hint of a smile lifting the corners of her mouth.

Coley shifted uneasily in his chair, finding her directness disconcerting; wondering why words had deserted him again. "Thanks . . . uh, I mean, me too. I really did, Maria."

"It's okay, Coley. I believe you."

Blushing slightly, Coley turned his thoughts back to Lane. "I think the next thing we—maybe I should say I—oughta do is go see Latiolais."

"*We'll* do it then."

★ ★ ★

"Looks like it's raining all over the world." Coley stared out the window of the blue Plymouth. Slender cattails along the bayou next to the road were bending in the wind. Sacalait and chinquapin broke through the water's dark, rain-dented surface as they fed among the islands of lily pads.

"I heard on the weather that the front's stalled." Maria watched the sweep of the windshield wipers and beyond them the blurred white line in the middle of the blacktop. "This might last another day."

"It's a wonder we all don't grow gills down here," Coley mused out loud. "And look at this. Mosquitoes in January." He clapped one between the palms of his hands, stared at it, and brushed it off onto the floor.

In the misty gray distance, Maria sighted the glow of a purple neon sign. "I believe that's Latiolais' place over there," she said, pointing it out.

Coley could barely make out "Home, Sweet Home" through the car window.

Maria turned the coupe off the road, clattering over the wooden bridge and across a layer of sodden dark leaves that covered most of the oyster shell parking lot. Pulling beneath the stark, leafless branches of an oak, she stopped, put the gearshift in reverse, and killed the engine.

"You think he leaves that sign on all the time?" Coley wondered how much business a beer joint like this out in the middle of a sea of cane fields and rundown clapboard shacks could do at ten o'clock in the morning.

Maria buttoned her black raincoat. "You ready to go in?"

Coley listened to the rain drumming on the tin roof five yards away. Water poured off the eaves and spattered below in a shallow trench. "I don't think it's going to let up."

By the time Maria had opened her umbrella and splashed around the car, soaking her blue tennis shoes and the bottoms of her jeans, Coley had his wheelchair out. She held the umbrella for him while he opened the chair, locked it, and lifted himself in, bending over to adjust his legs on the foot rests. Coley wheeled himself over to the little stoop, and backed the chair against the first of the two low steps.

"Hold this." Maria handed him the umbrella, grabbed the handles of the wheelchair, and bumped Coley up onto the rickety wooden floor.

Peering through the screen door, Coley saw the glow of a jukebox standing against the far wall and a neon Pabst Blue Ribbon sign on the wall behind the bar to his left. "Well, let's see if the owner's around."

"He's probably getting things ready for the monthly meeting of the Ladies Garden Club." Maria opened the screen door and followed Coley inside.

Coley wheeled over to a table near the bar and called out, "Anybody home?"

Someone coughed behind a door at the end of the bar. In a few seconds, a short, pudgy man, pulling his elastic suspenders over his shoulders with both thumbs, opened the door and stepped into the gloom of the barroom. Squinting into the gray light filtering in through the screen door, he mumbled, "We ain't open yet."

"Door's open." Coley pointed behind him.

The man slicked his dark hair down on his head with both hands. "You drinking this early?"

Coley noticed the gleam of recognition light Latiolais' dark eyes. "Nope. Just wanted to ask you some questions."

Latiolais trudged over behind the bar, popped the cork on a bottle of whiskey and poured a shot glass full. He took in Coley's jeans and rumpled jacket. "You're that state representative, ain't you?"

"Yep."

Latiolais ran his sullen eyes over Maria standing

next to Coley, her hand on the back of his chair. "You don't dress like no politician *I* ever knew."

"You know a lot of them?"

Latiolais flinched slightly, then turned the shot glass up and drained it. "Nah."

Coley decided to make Latiolais swing for the fence or back away from the plate. "André Catelon . . ."

Latiolais' puffy face abruptly darkened. He grabbed his bottle and poured another drink. "Never heard of him."

Coley could almost see Latiolais back off, and knew for certain then that he was part of the conspiracy. "A man who's been a state senator for over twenty years—and you've never heard of him."

Downing his drink, Latiolais slammed the glass down on the scarred wooden bar. "I said I don't *know* him. Don't you come in here putting words in my mouth, no!"

"Sorry. My mistake." Coley didn't want to end it just yet. "I don't want to make a fellow Cajun mad, no. We need to stick together, us."

Latiolais' scowl slowly drained from his swollen face. "Yeah, you right about dat, cher. Especially when one of us got his name in dat big room up in de Capitol."

Coley smiled. "How 'bout some coffee?"

Latiolais' dark eyes narrowed suspiciously, then blinked as he seemed to reach a decision. "Might as well."

"One sugar," Coley said.

"You want some, uh—" Latiolais squinted at Maria.

Maria opened her mouth to reply, but found herself cut off by Coley.

"A friend." Coley winked at Latiolais. "Two sugars and some cream."

Latiolais nodded slightly. He poured coffee into small white cups from a heavy metal pot that sat on a hot plate behind the bar, added the sugar and cream, and brought them out to the table. Then he went back to his bottle, poured another drink, and brought it back with him.

"What kind of crawfish season we gonna have this year?" Coley sipped his coffee.

Glancing at Maria, who sat next to Coley, Latiolais nudged his glass back and forth on the table with a stubby forefinger. "Oughta be pretty good, yeah. Hope so, anyway. I'm ready for two or t'ree gallon of bisque, me."

"I bet you make a good one, you."

"De best in Ascension Parish."

"The fishing any good? I know where to go out in Grosse Tete, but I haven't been much down here."

Latiolais downed his whiskey, his face now flushed and relaxed as he basked in an alcohol glow. "Mais, yeah. Jes' take Blind River into Maurepas and fish in dem cypress knee next to de shore all the way to the Amite. . . . You gonna catch a icebox full of dem big sacalait, you."

After a few more minutes of local gossip, Coley tried a high, hard one. "How'd you come out with your land?"

"Oh, I done sold dat, cher. Made me some big money too." Latiolais' face slowly clouded over as he realized too late what he had just said.

Coley tried to allay Latiolais' suspicions. "Just curious. I wondered what happened to it."

"I t'ink you ain't interested in no fishing, Coley Thibodeaux," Latiolais said coldly. He got up and went behind the bar. Reaching beneath the cash register, he came up with a sawed-off baseball bat, the handle wrapped in leather. "Get outta my place and don't come snooping around here no more, you!"

Coley held Latiolais' stare until he glanced down at the bat he was slapping softly against the palm of his hand.

"Let's go, Coley." Maria stood up and stepped toward Coley's wheelchair to take the handles.

With a nod of his head, Coley motioned her away. "I guess we might as well. Looks like we've worn out our welcome here in 'Home, Sweet Home.'"

Maria headed toward the door, glancing back at the burly man behind the bar.

Wheeling his chair over closer to the bar, Coley stared up and across it directly at Latiolais' darting eyes. "You're going to Angola, Latiolais."

"You must be crazy," Latiolais growled, "coming in here and talking to me like dat."

"One or two of the others might slip out of it somehow, but not you," Coley continued evenly as though Latiolais hadn't said a word. "Any amount of money you made on this deal isn't going to be worth the time you spend up there."

Latiolais slammed the bat down on the wooden counter. A highball glass fell over on its side, rolled off onto the concrete floor, and shattered. "Shut you mouth!"

"Coley, please!" Maria stood just inside the screen, her left hand to her throat.

Giving Latiolais a placid smile, Coley turned toward the door. "Thanks for the hospitality."

★ ★ ★

"Let's not go back to town just yet." Maria turned

onto Highway 22 toward the Mississippi River.

Coley shrugged, listening to the sound of the rain falling through the trees that hung over the road like a canopy. "Fine with me. I'd hate to waste such a nice day."

"It *could* be a nice day," Maria ventured.

"You're right," Coley admitted. "Sorry I'm not fit company. I don't usually let things get me down, but thinking about Lane shut away up there and all that Catherine and the kids are going through, well . . ."

Maria reached over and squeezed Coley's hand. "You're doing the best you can."

Coley felt the warmth of Maria's hand. It seemed to flow up his arm and into his chest like a current. He tried to speak, but found his throat constricted. Clearing it and swallowing, he said, "Let's *make* it a good day. Turn left here on 44 and we'll go down to Hymel's for some corn soup."

"I've never been there. Is it good?"

"The best in south Louisiana."

Maria gave him a skeptical glance. "Remember, I'm from New Orleans. We've got the best restaurants in the country—maybe even the whole world."

"We won't know till you taste it then, will we?" Coley remarked. "You need to try something new anyhow. There *are* people who can cook outside 'The City.' "

"I believe that," Maria agreed readily. "They just don't cook as *well*, that's all."

"Maybe . . ." Coley *had* begun to enjoy the day, in spite of his encounter with Latiolais. He glanced at Maria. The pleasant shape of her face and the soft sheen of her hair in the muted light filtering through the windshield made him think of old portraits he had seen in the antique shops of Royal Street in the French Quarter.

Maria drove in silence for a while, seemingly content just looking at the drenched countryside. Then she pointed off to the left. "Oh, look how beautiful!"

Coley gazed at the raised Greek Revival cottage set back off the road among the live oaks and azaleas. With its elaborate wrought-iron-trimmed galleries and ornate friezes and medallions, it spoke of days long past; of garden parties and gracious living before the corridor between Baton Rouge and New Orleans began to blossom with petrochemical plants. "That's Tezcuco Plantation."

"All my life I've lived within an hour's drive of these old plantations along the river road and the only one I've seen is Oak Alley." Maria slowed down, staring out at the elegant old home, white and shining in the rain. "Do you know when it was built?"

"One of the last plantations built before the Civil War," Coley answered. "Around 1855, I think."

Maria turned her eyes back toward the long, gradual curving of the road. "Maybe we could take a day or two in the spring and visit some of these old places."

"I think I'd like that."

Twenty-five minutes later they turned into the shell parking lot of Hymel's Restaurant. As they entered the main dining area, Maria glanced to the left through the open doorway that led into the bar. "Goodness! That looks like a zoo without cages."

Coley gazed at the paneled walls, crowded with the mounted heads of deer, bear, coyote, bobcat, and other animals indigenous to the surrounding wilderness. Smaller creatures such as squirrels, snakes, and birds assumed lifelike poses on shelves and perches. "It is a bit *different*."

Square tables made from weathered cypress and set with red-and-white checked place mats and napkins stood about the dining area. A white-haired couple in casual clothes occupied a table in the near corner next to the door leading back to the kitchen. The others were vacant.

After they had seated themselves and ordered, Maria watched the couple as they ate together in a way that made you know they'd been doing it for a very long time. "They look so happy, don't they?"

Coley nodded, his mind having returned to the scene in *Home, Sweet Home*.

As though she sensed this, Maria asked, "Do you think you know who all the people are that may be involved in this business with Lane?"

"Catelon, the man who called himself Bruce Crain, our hospitable friend Latiolais, and one or two others." Coley purposely left out Hinton, knowing of Maria's relationship with him, though not yet knowing the nature of it.

The short, thin waitress, wearing a dress that matched the napkins, looked almost as old as the building itself. She set two large bowls of corn soup on the table in front of them, along with sliced French bread still warm from the oven. "Ya'll gonna want dessert?"

"Whatcha got?" Coley asked, unfolding his napkin and reaching for a spoon.

"Bread pudding, served with a special sauce from a secret recipe that's been in the family for five generations." The waitress gave the description as though from long acquaintance.

Coley smiled at Maria. "With that kind of tradition

behind it, how could we refuse?"

The waitress nodded and walked back toward the kitchen area, stopping to chat with the other couple.

Maria glanced at the soup, then gazed across the table at Coley. "Well, now that you've found out who's involved, what's our next move?"

Coley broke off a piece of French bread and spooned up some soup. "I thought maybe we'd *move* some of this soup from these bowls into our bellies."

"I agree wholeheartedly," Maria laughed, taking her first bite. The rich, spicy broth full of kernel corn and succulent shrimp fresh from the Gulf made her sigh with pleasure. "Hmmm. . . . I hate to admit that you're right about this, but you are. There's not a restaurant in New Orleans that can touch this."

"Yep, some things out here in the provinces are tolerable, I guess."

Maria ate the warm, crusty-outside, soft-inside French bread with the soup and felt the dreariness of the day fade like her hunger. "Tell me about yourself, Coley."

"Grosse Tete to Tarawa to Dixie," Coley said, after swallowing a chunk of bread.

"Grosse Tete's in the bayou country twenty miles west of Baton Rouge, and anybody who's heard of World War II knows about Tarawa," Maria responded, "but there's nothing unique about Dixie. We're *all* from Dixie down here."

"I mean that little area out in north Baton Rouge that grew up around the Standard Oil refinery—where my office is," Coley explained. "I lived there after I finished my pre-law courses and got accepted to law school at LSU."

"Why way up there when you could have lived out near the campus?"

192

"It was so much cheaper. Besides, I had to work, and south Baton Rouge didn't have much tolerance for us ignorant Cajuns coming up out of the swamps." Coley smiled at the memory of his college days. "Those rednecks out there didn't think they were any better than we were."

"And now you're a respected politician."

Coley savored a bite of the soup, then smiled, "Those are mutually exclusive terms, Maria."

"How long have you lived out in Dixie?"

"Two years of law school before the war, then after Tarawa I came back and finished up and just stayed there." Coley felt himself tremble slightly as he pronounced the name of the island that he barely returned from.

"How'd you get elected in a district where you lived such a short time?" Maria asked. "Down in New Orleans a man has to live in the same neighborhood just about all his life to even have a chance at political office."

"Two things did it, I guess." Coley stared reflectively out the rain-streaked windows at the wet levee just across the road. "First of all, I got a job at Hebert's while I was in school. It's the hub of Dixie—everybody goes there—so I got to know just about everybody in that part of town."

"And the second?"

"I got a medal or two at Tarawa."

"A medal or two."

"Just about everybody there got at least one, I think—except for the ones whose parents or wives got it instead. It was *that* kind of battle."

Maria doubted that almost everyone got a medal. Enjoying the sound of Coley's voice, she saw the memories flicker in his eyes as he spoke.

"Well, to make a long, boring story short and boring, I went through a little rehabilitation, moved back to Dixie, and finished law school."

"And started practicing law and got elected to the House of Representatives," Maria finished for him.

"That's about it."

"What about your folks?"

Coley tapped his spoon on the side of his empty bowl. "You doing a biography on me?"

"I might someday."

"Daddy was a trapper and fisherman," Coley continued, the light in his eyes now going softer at the memory of those long ago mornings in the Atchafalaya Basin when he would run the crawfish traps with his father. He could almost see the misty cypress hung with long streamers of Spanish moss, could almost hear the sound of the paddle swishing softly though the dark water, and the voice of his father speaking the Cajun dialect that had been Coley's only language for the first ten years of his life.

"And. . . ."

"Mama made the best bisque and etouffee in the whole basin," Coley answered, "but then I might be a little bit prejudiced about that part."

"You know, I just *may* write a book about you one day." Maria placed her napkin on the table and sat back in her chair, giving a contented sigh. "That is, if the details are as interesting as the outline you just drew for me."

"And now for the story of Maria Genero, girl of mystery, late of the 'Crescent City.' "

"Another day."

"You're right," Coley agreed. "It's time to get back to work. I doubt Lane's taking time out for corn soup up at Angola."

"What's our next step?"

"I don't know. We've about run out of places to get any more information."

"Well?"

"We put some pressure on."

"How?"

"I was hoping *you* had that part figured out!"

TWELVE

ACADIANS

★ ★ ★

"I'll bet you didn't know that St. Martinville used to be called 'Little Paris,' did you?" André Catelon, wearing pale yellow slacks, a royal blue shirt, and a tan linen sport coat, strolled along the broad walkway leading up to St. Martin de Tours Catholic Church, dominating the town square.

Bonnie unconsciously pulled at the ruffled throat of her mulberry-colored blouse as she walked next to her father. Her black slacks, a perfect fit when she bought them six months before, hung loosely on her hips. "No, I didn't. Maybe somebody'll tell me one day."

Catelon braced himself against his daughter's mild sarcasm, determined not to spoil the day. "A whole bunch of the aristocracy left France during the Revolution and settled here," he explained. "That's how it got the name."

"Interesting."

Catelon glanced at his daughter. Her dark hair

hung like a thicket about her pale face. "You need to get to the beauty parlor and have something done about that hair. It used to be so pretty and shiny."

"Okay."

Pointing to the massive front doors of the church, Catelon tried to divert his daughter's mind from the anxiety that he had seen tormenting her. "You want to go inside? There's supposed to be a baptismal font that Louis XVI donated to the church. And a replica of the grotto at Lourdes."

Bonnie merely shook her head.

"C'mon, Bonnie," Catelon urged. "This is the mother church of the Acadians."

Shrugging, Bonnie turned to the left when she reached the steps and walked along toward the side of the church. "I'm just not interested."

"What *are* you interested in?" Catelon quickened his step to catch up.

"A drink, maybe."

"Bonnie, it's not even noon yet! Don't tell me you're becoming a lush."

"Okay, I won't tell you." Bonnie giggled like a girl, except that the sound of it bordered on hysteria. She skipped along the walk ahead of her father.

"Hold on now." Catelon caught up with her again. "Bonnie, I'm *really* worried about you."

Bonnie responded with a skeptical look.

"I mean it."

"I believe you."

"I thought when this Temple character went to prison, you'd be satisfied."

Bonnie was no longer sure when, or even *if* she had decided she wanted Lane to be sent to prison. Her thoughts often seemed as though they were not her own.

"Well, isn't that what you wanted?"

"The whole thing was *your* idea, not *mine*, Daddy," Bonnie corrected, defending herself with righteous indignation. "You just wanted revenge because he made you look silly in front of all your big-shot friends."

"That's enough!" The flush in Catelon's neck began to creep up toward his face. "You knew full well what was going on. You wanted him ruined just as much as *I* did!"

"Maybe I did," Bonnie agreed reluctantly, "but it *still* doesn't help."

"You want him *dead?*" Catelon almost shrieked. "Will that satisfy you?"

Bonnie glanced away from her father's blazing eyes.

Catelon took a deep breath, letting it out slowly. He had believed for some time that only Lane's death would rid Bonnie of her obsession.

Recalling the words of the sergeant in security at Angola made Catelon even angrier: *Don't worry, Senator. I'll sic the ol' 'Hog Man' on Temple. He'll either kill him or make him kill hisself.* At his next phone call, the sergeant had grudgingly admitted that 'Hog Man' was barely alive in the prison hospital, and that it might be hard to find another prisoner to take the job on.

"I'm sorry, Bonnie." Catelon was determined that the day wouldn't be wasted on tantrums. "But *you* can make me lose my temper like nobody else."

"Except Mama." A faraway look saddening her eyes, Bonnie stopped and gazed at the statue of Evangeline sitting in the shadow of the towering church. "I wonder if it's true."

"What?"

"The story of Evangeline."

Grateful that his daughter was finally showing some interest in something—anything, Catelon fell gleefully into a diversion he dearly loved, the sound of his own voice. "Sure, it's true. But Evangeline was really Emmeline LaBiche."

"I know that," Bonnie insisted. "And her lover Gabriel was Louis Arcenaux."

Smiling slyly, Catelon said, "I'll bet you don't know who gave that statue to the town."

Bonnie glanced up at the stone maiden and then at her father. "Huey Long."

Catelon laughed in spite of himself. "No, there are a *few* things in this state that ol' Huey isn't connected to."

With a final glance up at the statue, Bonnie walked away toward the front of the church.

Keeping up with her this time, Catelon continued his tale. "In 1929 a movie called *The Romance of Evangeline* was made right here. The cast and crew gave the statue to the town."

Bonnie made no reply.

"Delores del Rio actually posed for it." Puzzled by his daughter's actions yet angered by her rudeness, Catelon demanded, "Where're you going now?"

"To see the Evangeline Oak," she replied as though it should have been obvious.

Catelon's sober expression reflected his concern for his daughter's mental state. The sound of her giggling only a few minutes before had caused a chill to prickle the back of his neck. He remembered the same kind of inane laughter in Bonnie's mother shortly before her first commitment. *I've got to find a way to snap Bonnie out of this state before she ends up like Dorothy.*

Bonnie strolled along the sidewalk toward Bayou

Teche, reaching the site of the old port where tradition held that Evangeline's boat docked beneath the ancient oak that still bore her name. A bronze plaque told the story:

> Separated from Gabriel when the people of the village of Grand Pre, Acadia, were forced into exile by the British during the French and Indian Wars, Evangeline ended her long and perilous journey in St. Martinville. The Acadian lovers sought each other in vain and were reunited only when the aged Evangeline recognized Gabriel as a dying victim of the plague. To have all the years and all the miles apart end in such tragedy proved too much for her and she succumbed to the shock of his death.

In the little park area commemorating the story of Evangeline, Bonnie walked beneath the legendary oak, spreading its massive limbs out over the sluggish old bayou on one side and the new paved street on the other. She looked up at the afternoon sunlight shattering into a green-gold haze as it struck the leaves in the crown of the tree.

Losing herself in the dazzle of light, Bonnie sat down on a wrought-iron bench. She heard her father sit beside her, but somehow couldn't bring herself to look at him. The water in the Teche, dark and inviting, seemed to beckon to her in a language she remembered from a dream.

Frustrated with Bonnie's perplexing, sometimes incoherent responses, Catelon restrained from speaking to her. In a gesture of comfort as futile as Evangeline's search for Gabriel, he reached over and patted her hand.

Gazing across the sunlit water, Bonnie watched a

man in khakis and a wide-brimmed straw hat glide silently down the Teche in a homemade pirogue. He sat as though the tiny boat were a part of him, his paddle barely rippling the surface with his long, smooth strokes. Near the lily pads just offshore, an alligator gar broke the surface, the scales of its great belly flashing a dull yellow as it rolled over and disappeared.

Beneath the same oak immortalized in verse, Bonnie could almost smell the chalk dust and floor polish of the long-ago classroom; could almost hear the lines of the poem returning to her in the voice of a teacher barely remembered:

> Vainly he strove to rise;
> and Evangeline, kneeling beside him,
> Kissed his dying lips,
> and laid his head on her bosom. . . .
> All was ended now—
> the hope, and the fear, and the sorrow.
> All the aching of heart,
> the restless, unsatisfied longing. . . .

Bonnie found herself envying the Evangeline of Longfellow's poem, who even as she died could utter the words, "Father, I thank Thee!" Then anger and disgust with herself flared up abruptly. *How could I remember something so sickly sentimental as that stupid poem?*

Catelon began to squirm on the bench. Finally, the politician in him relenting under the intolerable burden of silence, spoke. "Are you having a good time, sweetheart?"

Bonnie merely nodded.

Catelon pressed on. "You know I postponed that committee meeting and canceled the speech at the Kiwanis just so we could have this time together."

"Remind me to submit your name for the 'Father of the Year' award," Bonnie muttered, her eyes still following the man in the pirogue.

Catelon's short fuse burned out. "I've had enough of your insolence, young woman! You're nothing but a spoiled, pampered little brat!"

Bonnie didn't flinch or show any sign that the tirade had bothered her in the least. "Sometimes you show remarkable insight, Daddy."

Realizing that the flattened affect in his daughter represented a grim portent, Catelon forced himself to be civil. "What can I do to help pull you out of this, Bonnie?"

"Out of *what*?"

Catelon refused to succumb to temper again. "Why don't we have an early lunch?"

"Fine with me."

Savoring his tiny victory, Catelon glanced back toward St. Martin de Tours. "They tell me that little café across from the church makes great oyster po-boys."

"Let's go." Bonnie stood up and walked back toward the town square.

Across the street from the church, they entered the narrow brick building with *Thibodeaux's Café* boldly hand-painted on the plate glass. Adjacent to businesses on both sides, its thick walls had once housed a bank.

In the dim recesses of the kitchen at the rear, Catelon saw a short, dark-haired man in a white apron washing dishes. He walked to the counter, gave their order, and joined Bonnie at the table she had selected. A white tablecloth and a plastic rose in a green vase decorated the table that stood next to the glass front looking out over the town square, empty on that mild midwinter day.

Bonnie contented herself staring at the slow traffic crossing the bridge over the bayou to the left of the church. A gangly boy of about fifteen wearing jeans and a *John Deere* baseball cap slouched along the sidewalk. Spotting Bonnie through the glass only a few feet away, he straightened up and gave her a hesitant and toothy smile. When she returned it, his step quickened as he pranced down the sidewalk like a young colt.

Thinking of her own youth, which now seemed as remote as the Renaissance, Bonnie made an effort to brighten her father's day. "I'm glad you brought me here, Daddy."

For a moment, Catelon thought he was losing touch with reality himself at the sound of the pleasant voice from across the table. "M—me too."

"We probably should have done this a lot more often," Bonnie mused out loud, then tried to cover up the implication of her words. "I know you *would* have if you'd had the time."

Catelon had removed guilt from his catalogue of emotions decades before, but felt a slight quickening somewhere deep inside. "I'm glad you understand, Bonnie." He felt the tiny stirring inside him die, replaced by a sense of loss and desolation. "But we've got today, haven't we? Let's make the best of it."

Bonnie nodded and smiled up at the man who placed the two white platters holding their po-boys on the table. Then the silence returned and they ate and watched the pale winter sunlight gleaming on the church.

★ ★ ★

Catherine, dressed in a severe navy suit, glanced to her right at her family sitting beside her in the high-backed oak pew: Sharon in her lace and ribbons, the boys wearing suits and ties, and Jessie looking poised and elegant in her lavender dress with its lace-trimmed bodice. She gave Cassidy a stern glance as the congregation rose. Tugging at the collar of his shirt with one finger, he reluctantly got to his feet.

Catherine looked down on the congregation, washed in the early amber light slanting down through the tall windows, as she opened her hymnal without looking at its pages. Since Lane's "trouble" as she had come to think of it, she had taken to sitting in the balcony of the church rather than on the main floor. No one had given her anything but words of encouragement to her face, but the whispers and behind-the-back glances had become unmistakable.

Holy, Holy, Holy,
Lord God Almighty!
Early in the morning
Our song shall rise to Thee.

When the singing and the announcements were over and the offering taken, the pastor stepped to the pulpit. With his gray hair, his safe and sedate dark brown suit and tie, and his smile that crinkled the corners of his eyes, he made even first-time visitors feel at home in the church. Opening his brown leather Bible, he began to read, his voice lingering over the words as he drove them home: " '. . . full of envy, murder, debate, deceit, malignity; whisperers, backbiters, haters of God. . . .'

"If I whisper something hateful about my brother or sister in Christ behind his back; if I gossip about him, surely that's not as bad as being a murderer, certainly not the same as being someone who hates God—or is it?"

The pastor gazed out upon his congregation, his smile gone, a flinty light filling his hazel eyes. "Paul made no distinction between people who do these things when he said that, 'God gave them over to a reprobate mind.'"

Never one for long sermons, the pastor gave several examples of how he had seen gossip help destroy families during his years as a pastor. He admonished his people to abhor the petty and cruel remarks that damage the reputations and well-being of their neighbors.

"Before you gossip about your neighbor, remember the words of Paul, 'Therefore thou art inexcusable, O man, whosoever thou art that judgest: for wherein thou judgest another, thou condemnest thyself; for thou that judgest doest the same things.'

"God's Word is plain about how we are to treat one another," the pastor continued, turning the pages of his Bible. " 'For all the law is fulfilled in one word, even in this; Thou shalt love thy neighbor as thyself.'

"I can't think of a better way to close this message than with the words of Jesus: 'A new commandment I give unto you, That ye love one another; as I have loved you, that ye also love one another. By this shall all men know that ye are my disciples, if ye have love one to another. . . . This is my commandment, That ye love one another, as I have loved you.' "

After the pastor had concluded his sermon and prayed, Catherine lifted her head and sang the old hymn "Softly and Tenderly," along with the rest of the congregation. She knew there was barely a soul in church who didn't understand the meaning and purpose of that morning's message, even though no names were spoken. As the building filled with song, the altar began to fill with those coming forward in response to the message.

Twenty minutes later, outside the church in the noonday glare of sunlight, Catherine and her children were greeted by friends and even mere acquaintances more warmly and openly than they had been in weeks. Many of those who had shunned them since Lane's trial offered their assistance, and others slipped cash to Catherine as they shook hands.

Pulling out of the church parking lot, Catherine gave thanks for her pastor's providential sermon. After the weeks of virtual isolation, she felt a sense of comfort, knowing that her church family was behind her.

"Mama, you think what the preacher talked about made people be nicer to us today?" Cassidy leaned over the seat, his bright face close to his mother's.

"When a preacher talks up at the podium, it's called a sermon, Cass," Sharon explained, feeling that it had fallen to her lot to educate her unpolished little brother.

"I know that, 'Four Eyes.'" Cassidy shot back. "You got enough to do trying to trick some goofy boy into liking you without worrying about me."

"Mama, you can't let this little *heathen* talk to me like that!" Sharon insisted.

"Settle down, you two," Catherine said in a level tone. "Cassidy, apologize to your sister."

"Aw, for Pete's sake!"

Dalton grabbed Cassidy by the arm. "You do what Mama said, you little heathen!"

"Git your hands off me, Dalton!" Cassidy grunted, pulling free of Dalton's grip.

"That's enough!" Catherine shouted.

The noise and fighting in the back ceased abruptly.

Catherine pulled the car over to the curb next to a gnarled old cedar standing in front of a white cottage with green shutters. She put the gearshift in reverse and killed the engine.

"You two should be ashamed of yourselves," Jessie chided her brothers.

Taking a deep breath, Catherine let it out slowly. "This has been hard on all of us, children, but you know your daddy would be simply disgusted *and* disappointed if he could see how you're acting—especially you two in the back seat."

"I'm sorry, Mama," Cassidy and Dalton mumbled almost in unison.

"We had a real blessing at church today and I just think we should be grateful for that."

"Yes, ma'am," came the mutual agreement from the boys in the backseat.

"I'm sorry too, Mama," Sharon added, her deep blue eyes shining with remorse.

"Well, I don't remember that you did anything wrong, but thanks anyway," Catherine smiled down at her most affectionate and most fragile child.

Jessie laughed and gave her little sister a quick hug. "I think we all need to be more like you, Sharon."

Sharon blushed, smoothing her skirt down over her primly crossed legs.

"Now. . . . Are we all agreed that we're going to have a happy Sunday?" Catherine asked her brood.

She was answered with two nods and two "Yes, ma'ams."

"Good," Catherine replied, starting the engine and pulling out into the street.

"What we having for dinner, Mama?" Cassidy leaned over the seat again.

"The proper word is *lunch*, Cass," Sharon corrected. "Dinner is the meal you have at night."

Cassidy jerked his head toward his sister, his mouth open to fire away at her, then he thought of the sadness he had seen in his mother's eyes at his misbehavior. "So it is," he replied almost formally, "and thank you for your help, dear sister."

★ ★ ★

Bonnie watched the twelve-year-old girl in her plaid skirt and green sweater pull the little red Western Flyer wagon down her driveway, turning west on the sidewalk that ran along Evangeline Street.

As she had done several times in the past few weeks, Bonnie had parked her red MG next to a vacant lot on the opposite side of the street and almost a block-and-a-half away from the white-columned home. Catching a few glimpses of Catherine and her family had somehow come to replace the void left in her life when she could no longer watch Lane arrive at his office through the window of Hebert's Coffee Shop.

Staring at the dark clouds building across the river, Sharon pulled Jessie's baggy sweater closer about her and ducked her head slightly into the wind. Her brown hair swirled about her face and as she held on to the wagon, she brushed it back every few seconds with her free hand.

On an impulse, Bonnie got out of her car, walked to the end of the block in the direction Sharon was heading, and waited for her. When she had almost reached the corner, Bonnie crossed the street, putting herself directly in the girl's path.

"Hi." Bonnie smiled at Sharon, thinking that the child's hair was the exact color of her father's. The blue eyes, she knew, came from Catherine. "That's a pretty wagon."

Sharon adjusted her glasses on the bridge of her nose, gazing at the dark-haired lady in the black leather jacket and gray slacks as though trying to remember if she had met her before. Bonnie's warm smile and the touch of sadness in her eyes seemed to win her over. "I don't know you, do I?"

"No," Bonnie admitted, walking along next to Sharon as she turned south on Baton Rouge Avenue. "But I know that your name's Sharon."

Sharon gave Bonnie a shy smile. "What's *your* name?"

"Emmeline," Bonnie lied, "but you can just call me Emma if you want to."

"Okay. Did you know me when I was little?"

Bonnie glanced down at Sharon's worn and scuffed saddle oxfords. "No, but I knew your daddy—a long time ago."

"Oh."

"Where are you going?"

Pointing down the street, Sharon pushed her hair back from her face and said, "To Avery's Grocery. Mama usually sends *me* because Cassidy's too hard to run down."

Bonnie smiled. "Why don't you go to the one over on Plank Road. It's bigger and closer."

Her cheeks coloring slightly, Sharon glanced at Bonnie, then stared down at the sidewalk as she changed hands on the wagon handle. "Sometimes we don't have enough money, and Mr. Avery lets us charge things."

"Oh, I see." Bonnie found herself growing attached to Sharon in a way she could have never imagined.

"Well, that's awfully nice of him. What are you buying today?"

"Two quarts of Lily milk, a pound of Community dark roast coffee, and a loaf of bread," Sharon rattled off the grocery list proudly.

"I can see that *you* don't need a list."

Sharon nodded her agreement. "Are you going to the grocery too?"

"I guess I could use a little snack; an apple or maybe a banana."

"Do you live around here?"

"No, I was just out for a drive."

Sharon shrugged. "Oh."

"I felt like taking a walk so I left my car parked back there on the street."

"You have any children?"

"No. I'm not married." Without warning, Bonnie felt a new sorrow welling up in her breast. She gazed at Sharon, her face a miniature, delicate, feminine version of Lane's.

"Are you all right?"

"What?" Bonnie found herself standing on a slab of concrete broken and tilted by the roots of a white oak that grew near the sidewalk. "Oh yes! I was just thinking of something. I find myself doing that more and more."

"Maybe a Coke will make you feel better," Sharon suggested, an expression of concern on her face. "Mr. Avery keeps them in a big box with water and blocks of ice in it. I like Orange Crush the best of all."

Bonnie could see the little neighborhood grocery in the next block. A red, white, and yellow Holsum bread sign hung from the eave and metal signs advertising such products as Pepsi, Coca-Cola, Camel cigarettes, and Brach's candy bars were tacked at random on the frame building's weathered front.

When they reached the store, Sharon left the wagon next to a bench that stood against the front wall. "Come on in. I'll show you the cold-drink box."

"All right."

When the creaking screen door slammed shut behind her, Bonnie let her eyes adjust to the gloom of the store's interior. The smell of bananas, plums, and onions in a wooden bin, and hoop cheese on an ancient carving block reminded her of the little neighborhood grocery her mother used to take her to when she was younger than Sharon.

"Can I help you, ladies?"

Bonnie looked over at the thin man in horn-rimmed glasses, wiping his hands on his once-white apron. His brown hair, thinning in front, needed a trim.

"I need some milk, coffee, and bread, Mr. Avery," Sharon replied.

"Well, I can certainly fill that order."

"Oh, I'll get it," Sharon insisted. "You can keep stocking your shelves.

"Who's this pretty lady?" Avery smiled, with a glance at Bonnie.

"This is Emma," Sharon announced proudly. She's a friend of the family."

"Nice to meet you, Emma," Avery nodded and went back to his shelves.

Bonnie helped collect the groceries and placed them on the counter next to the bulky cash register. "Oh, look how pretty!" She pointed to one of the heart-shaped necklaces hanging on a card next to the candy bars.

Sharon stared at the tiny heart, its burnished gold-colored surface gleaming faintly in the gray light filtering through the window. "I think you can open it up and put a picture inside if you want to."

"Let's get one."

Taking a crumpled dollar bill from her sweater pocket, Sharon placed it on the counter, then took a final look at the necklace. "No. It's not *real* gold anyway."

Avery left his shelf-stocking, rang up the groceries, and put them in a pasteboard box. Handing Sharon a nickel and three pennies he said, "Tell your mama if she needs anything else to just let me know."

"Yes sir, I will."

Bonnie bought a Coke and an Orange Crush, then followed Sharon out through the creaky screen door. "You want to sit and have some girl-talk for a few minutes?"

Sharon noticed the dark brown bottle of Orange Crush, then gazed west at the darker clouds beyond the river. "Mama said to hurry back before it rains."

"Oh, you've got plenty of time."

With another glance at the Crush, Sharon relented. "Okay. Just for a minute though."

Bonnie sat on the bench, handing Sharon her drink.

Sharon took a swallow. "I just love this. Better than a real orange, I think."

Speaking from her heart before her mind could stop her, Bonnie asked, "How's your daddy?"

A shadow crossed Sharon's face. Then, lifting her chin sternly, she said, "He's in prison because some bad people lied about him."

Seeing the pain in the child's eyes, Bonnie felt a cold aching begin in her breast. "Oh, I'm so sorry!"

"We know he's going to get out though," Sharon insisted, "'cause we pray for him every night and Uncle Coley is helping us too."

"I'm glad for you then." Bonnie stared out at the clouds climbing up the horizon.

"My Sunday school teacher said Paul was in prison for just being a Christian."

"Who?"

"Paul the apostle," Sharon explained. "He wrote a lot of the Bible when he was in prison in Rome."

"Oh, yes," Bonnie nodded, "*that* Paul."

Sharon got up and set the bottle down next to the bench. "I have to go now."

"Don't you want to finish your drink?"

"No ma'am. Thank you for buying it though."

When they reached the corner where Bonnie had crossed the street from her car, the first heavy drops fell from the clouds rolling slowly across the sky. She glanced at her car parked across the street and down from them. "You want me to give you a ride? We can hold the wagon on our laps."

Shivering in the rising wind, Sharon shook her head. A sudden coughing spasm almost took her breath away. "No ma'am. I'm almost home now." With a final wave, Sharon hurried down the sidewalk as the first heavy gusts of the storm hit, blowing leaves and scraps of paper along the street.

Bonnie got in her car and gripped the steering wheel tightly with both hands. In spite of her efforts to stop them, tears spilled forth as great sobs racked her body. She folded her arms across the wheel, resting her head on them as the terrible grief poured out of her in waves.

As the storm hit in earnest, rain beat down loudly on the canvas roof of the little car. Bonnie felt a dark

remorse coursing through her. *Oh, God! What's hap-*
pening to me? How did I end up such a terrible person?
I don't know what to do anymore. I don't know where
to turn!

THIRTEEN

CHAPLAIN

★ ★ ★

Roger Mitchell pastored a small church that his daddy had helped build in the piney hills of Feliciana, but made the living for his family as a chaplain at Angola. Stocky and of medium height, he had sandy hair, neatly trimmed and parted on the right. He bought his suits at J. C. Penney's and had never owned a new car in his life. People who didn't know him well wondered why he never seemed to have a bad day.

Lane sat outside Mitchell's office in a battered wooden chair with dozens of names scratched on its nearly paintless surface. Summoned from the field, he still wore his sweat-stained prison garb and heavy brogans.

The door opened and Mitchell stuck his head out. "You want to come in"—he glanced down at the manilla folder in his hand— "Mr. Temple?"

Lane felt a sense of bewilderment at the sound of *Mr.* used with his name. It had never happened during his two months at the prison. He rose and followed

Mitchell, glancing around at the files and stacks of forms and other papers that cluttered the small office like the leavings of a windstorm.

"Roger Mitchell," he said, holding out his hand. "I'm what passes for a chaplain at this place."

"Lane Temple." Lane shook hands, surprised at the strength of Mitchell's grip.

"Have a seat."

At the side of Mitchell's cluttered desk, Lane sat in a chair that looked like the twin of the one in the hall.

"I never could figure out how the men in here always get ahold of something to carve their names with," Mitchell remarked absently as he plopped down.

Lane's eyes were drawn to a wooden sign hanging on the wall just behind Mitchell. It looked identical to the one he had seen for years in Coley's office.

"You recognize the work?" Mitchell kept his pale blue eyes fixed on Lane.

"Friend of mine has one like it." Lane felt as awkward as a first-time truant in the principal's office. More used to muted conversations with Buckels and a few other convicts, he hardly remembered how to speak normally.

"Coley?"

Lane, feeling almost as though he had found a friend, gazed at Mitchell in surprise. "You know him?"

"For a long time," Mitchell smiled. "He used to come up here a lot to minister to the prisoners, but the last few times he came, it seemed like he was awfully tired. He never said anything about it though. I guess it just got to be too much for him to handle in his condition."

Lane thought of the times Coley had appeared pale, his face drawn after a particularly long day in court or a tiring legislative session. "Yeah, he does tire out easier now."

"Coley told me a lot about you, Lane." Mitchell's placid gaze held Lane's. "You don't mind if I call you Lane, do you?"

Lane shook his head.

Mitchell held up a thin file. "There's precious little in here about you."

Lane rubbed his hands together, then stared at their cuts and thick callouses.

" 'That if thou shalt confess with thy mouth the Lord Jesus, and shalt believe in thine heart that God has raised him from the dead, thou shalt be saved.' "

Lane glanced up, puzzled by Mitchell's quoting the Scripture without some kind of introduction.

"What shall I do then with Jesus? That's *still* the question."

"I'm sorry. I must be missing something."

"You are," Mitchell continued in an even voice. "Peace, joy and the best Friend you'll ever have."

Lane glanced at the sign. "Friend?"

"Does that surprise you?"

"A little, I guess." Lane found himself being pulled into Mitchell's bewildering presentation in spite of himself.

"In the fifteenth chapter of John, Jesus said, 'I have called you friends,' and that if we keep His commandments we would abide in Jesus' love as He kept His Father's commandments and abides in the Father's love."

"Friends, huh?"

"That's what He said."

Lane smiled at Mitchell and it felt strange on his face. He couldn't remember smiling since he came through the front gate on that strange and terrible night. "You're not like any preacher *I* ever heard before."

"I imagine this isn't like any *place* you've ever been before either."

Lane merely nodded, knowing the statement was purely academic.

"I have to agree with you about my being different though." Mitchell never took his eyes from Lane's. "But I've got so many men I have to look out for—scattered over this eighteen thousand acres—that I go for six months to a year without seeing some of them. Sometimes I don't know if I'm coming or going around this place."

Feeling somehow put at ease by the sound of Mitchell's voice, Lane relaxed and listened.

"I figure if I can get a man to know Jesus, then most of his other problems have a way of working themselves out." Mitchell shrugged. "It may not be the *best* way to handle things, but I haven't figured out anything better yet."

Lane gazed at the gray steel filing cabinets lining one wall. With half the drawers left open and case records left splayed open on their tops, they seemed to fit right in with the rest of the clutter in the office.

Mitchell guessed at what Lane was thinking. "I suppose an attorney like you is appalled at my record-keeping and filing methods."

"Never was my strength, either."

"I had an assistant until the warden's nephew said *he* needed help."

"So they took your helper."

"Yep." Mitchell grinned at the irony that occurred to him. "They seemed to think that the bloodhounds were a lot more important than the sheep."

"I know a little bit about state politics myself," Lane muttered dryly.

"Coley wrote me a long letter about it." Mitchell pulled an official-looking letterhead from his middle desk drawer. "He helped me get an unofficial assistant in here. People running this place wouldn't even let me have volunteer help."

Lane glanced around the office. "Maybe you can get this straightened out then."

"Maybe." Mitchell took a deep breath. "I sent for you a week ago, Lane."

Feeling that he was about to hear some more bad news, Lane braced himself inwardly.

"After finding out about you from your file and from Coley, I figured you'd be the perfect man for the job. There's always somebody wanting legal advice, help with petitioning the courts about one thing or the other, and I don't know beans about that part of the system."

"And?"

"And somebody out there with a lot more pull than Coley blocked everything I tried to get you in here." Mitchell held the letter up. "This is a letter from the head of the department telling me in no uncertain terms to lay off trying to get you the job. You're stuck in the fields."

"I didn't expect anything else."

"There's a bright side to it though."

"Maybe you could point it out to me then," Lane replied somberly. "Since I came to this place everywhere I look seems pretty dark."

"After what you did to Hogeman, the rest of the tough guys in here don't want any part of you."

An image of Hogeman flattened out on his back on the bare wood floor flashed through Lane's mind—the

221

whole scene bathed in the murky light and shadows cast by the single bulb hanging from the ceiling. He had never asked about the big man's condition.

"He's still in Charity Hospital down in New Orleans," Mitchell volunteered. "Fortunately, any change you made to his face would have to be for the better."

Lane found himself unable to smile at Mitchell's remark. He stared out the narrow window at a hawk perched on the branch of a pine just beyond the tall fence. Spreading his wings, the great bird launched into flight, soaring high above the wire and the bars and the guards.

"No matter how bleak things look, there's always tomorrow, Lane."

"You sound like Scarlett O'Hara." Lane found no humor in his own remark.

"I mean tomorrow specifically," Mitchell continued. "There's *some* rights a man has that even the powers down at the Capitol can't block forever."

Locked in darkness for what seemed like eons, Lane couldn't imagine a break coming his way.

"Catherine's coming to see you in the morning."

★ ★ ★

Lane wondered if it was more than coincidence that the same two guards who had welcomed him into Angola on that first night now escorted him down the narrow hall toward the visitor's room. Summoned again directly from his work in the fields, he was not allowed to clean up. He glanced down at the wet, muddy prison stripes and his hands, grimy and cut and scraped, that no longer seemed to belong to him.

The burly guards, their bodies as rigid as drill sergeants, the heels of their heavy boots thudding on the concrete floor, set a painstakingly slow pace that Lane knew he must hold to exactly or feel the stunning pain of a nightstick across his body. He matched them step for step.

Suddenly the dimness of the corridor gave way to the bright expanse of a mess hall set up for visiting day. A long file of tables had been arranged directly across the big room, dividing it in half. Rough-cut one-by-twelve boards, fitted with braces to hold them upright, stood in the center of the tables, marking the final edge of freedom.

Lane watched the men filing into the visiting area from one of three doors. Some already sat in folding chairs at the tables, awaiting citizens of the real world. He found an empty chair against the wall closest to him and next to an emaciated man who looked to be in his seventies. As he sat down, he nodded to the man who stared blankly back at him as though Lane's simple gesture was far too complicated for him to understand.

On a closer inspection of his neighbor, Lane realized that he was probably much younger than he appeared. The white hair and drawn face caused him to look old, but it was primarily the vacant, hollow hopeless stare that aged him far beyond his years. *I wonder if I'll end up like this poor devil?*

Lane tore his eyes away from the man and gazed out across the empty tiled floor of the dining hall, the hazy day seeming brighter than it was through the expanse of high windows.

And then he saw her! She came in the opposite door behind a fat woman in a flowered dress and drab brown coat.

Catherine! Catherine! Catherine! The name kept repeating itself over and over in Lane's mind. He wanted to jump to his feet and call out to her, to shout her name to everyone in the place, to tell them all that this was *his* wife!

But this was Angola. . . . So he sat and stared at Catherine while she went to the far end of the line of tables, gradually working her way down to the end where he sat.

Catherine had listened carefully to the instructions outlining the strict rules laid down for visitors. She sat in the chair, placed her hands on the table and gazed directly into Lane's eyes. "I love you, Lane. I love you. . . . I love you. . . . I love you."

Lane tried to speak. Nothing but a hoarse croak forced its way up from his throat. In her white blouse and simple pale blue sweater, Catherine seemed to represent all things soft and fragile and feminine.

So long in a world of darkness and brutality, of things hard and drab and cold, Lane felt as though Catherine was nothing more than an apparition, another of the dreams he would awaken from in the dark hours before dawn to the sound of coughing or men turning in their bunks, unable to sleep, or crying out as they awakened from a nightmare of their own.

Lane clasped his hands tightly together and stared at the table, feeling hot tears fill his eyes as the grief and his own hopelessness finally overcame him. As he sat there in the few moments it took for him to regain control, he tried to remember the last time he had cried.

"It's so good to see you, darling." Catherine kept her hands firmly in place as her own tears rolled down her cheeks, dropping unnoticed onto the table.

"I'm sorry, Cath." Lane glanced around self-consciously, quickly brushing his eyes. "I sure got our first visit off to a bad start."

Catherine shook her head slowly, her eyes full of light. "*Nothing* could make seeing you bad, Lane. It's almost like a dream—like I'm not really here at all."

"I think I know exactly how you feel." Lane tried to imagine how he must look to Catherine—dirty, haggard, his eyes hollow and dark-looking.

"It's going to be all right, Lane."

"What is?" Lane thought maybe he had missed part of the conversation already, that his mind had begun to fail him. "I don't understand."

"*Everything*—you, me, our family," Catherine replied, her face aglow with the meaning of her words.

Lane merely stared at her, perplexed, wondering now if maybe the strain had been too great for her.

"I can't explain it, darling." Catherine's voice held an unmistakable confidence. "I've been praying so hard for you and God finally answered me."

Opening his mouth to speak, Lane realized he had no words for what he wanted to ask.

"I can't explain it," Catherine admitted, "and I don't know what's going to happen. I just know everything's going to be all right."

"How?"

"I know it in my heart," Catherine said in that same level, undeniable tone.

She has to think that to get by? Lane nodded his head and changed the subject, not wanting to let Catherine in on his own doubts. "How're the kids getting along?"

"You'd be so proud of them, Lane. I thought they'd just go to pieces, but they've held up like little soldiers," Catherine beamed. "And they all send their love."

"Good." Lane realized that it couldn't be that easy but didn't want to press Catherine any further.

"Sharon cries a little once in a while when I put her to bed, but that's to be expected," Catherine admitted, knowing that her husband would want to hear everything about his children. "She's still making all A's and sleeps well, so there can't be any serious problems."

Lane almost didn't ask the next question. "How's Cass taking it?"

"He's down to about one fight every two weeks. That's not bad for him."

The corners of Lane's mouth turned slightly upward. "That boy never was one for turning the other cheek."

Catherine smiled at her husband, as though performing some task that he could not quite handle himself. "The church has been a big help to us."

Lane felt he just needed to listen to Catherine while she brought him up-to-date.

"And most of the people all over Dixie and the rest of the district still have your campaign signs up."

"That doesn't make much sense, does it?"

"It does to *them*," Catherine explained. "It's their way of telling the whole town that they believe you're innocent and that they're still behind you."

"Cajuns and rednecks," Lane muttered. "Once they make up their minds, they sure stick by you."

"Hinton's got signs up too."

It was a subject Lane didn't want to think about. From the day of his arrest when he had seen Hinton executing the search warrant in his office, Lane had known that he was part of the plot. Now Catelon would have the people of the whole district in his pocket if Hinton got elected.

"All six of them."

"What?"

"There may be a few more than that, but Coley said that's all he knows about."

Lane felt a deep sense of gratitude for the people of Dixie. He recalled the words of J. E. Ball, the deputy who had driven him to prison, *You got more friends than you think, Lane.* It suddenly occurred to him that even a place like Angola couldn't stop good things from happening to him, couldn't stop people from standing behind him. *I hope I can pay them back for their friendship someday.*

Catherine spoke with a slight hesitation, as though she didn't quite know what or even *if* she wanted to ask Lane the next question. "It . . . it's not very dangerous in here, is it? I mean, the guards keep things in order, don't they?"

An image flashed through Lane's mind:

Sitting astride their horses, two guards, one with a rifle cradled in his arms, the other holding a shotgun, watched a beefy red-headed man beating a boy of about eighteen with a hoe handle. The boy had accidently bumped the man, spilling his coffee. In a short time, the boy lay on the raw plowed earth next to the road, his face a mass of bloody bruises, a dark swelling the size of a golf ball over his left eye.

"You win." The man with the .30-.30 Winchester leaned over, his saddle leather creaking loudly in the silence that descended after the boy's futile struggle, and handed the other guard a fifty-cent piece. "He didn't last a minute."

The guard with the shotgun stuffed the coin into his watch pocket. "After a while you can jist tell."

"No . . . it's not dangerous." Lane remarked absently. "The guards take care of everything."

"Good," Catherine sighed with relief. "That makes me feel so much better."

"How's Coley?"

"Good as ever. He's trying so hard to find some kind of evidence to get you out of this place." Catherine glanced suspiciously at the closest guards. "But he's not getting any cooperation from the DA's office."

Lane noticed Catherine's look, thinking that it was almost the same as the one most all prisoners soon adopted. *This place is having its effect on her already.*

"The judge's law clerk is helping him though," Catherine continued. "Coley says she's a big help."

"She?"

"A pretty girl." Catherine appeared to have difficulty smiling in the presence of the guards. "Her name's Maria Genero and she's from New Orleans."

"Pretty, huh?"

"And just as nice as can be."

"But can she make good coffee and crawfish etouffee and shrimp creole?" Lane pictured his best friend with a slight paunch, married, and settled into a little Acadian cabin on some sleepy bayou across the river. *Nah! I can see it all but the paunch. He'll never put on weight.*

"I'm sure Coley's found all that out by now."

Noticing Catherine tremble slightly, Lane fought the urge to reach across the board and take her hand. "That's just what he needs—somebody to cook for him and put some meat on his bones."

Catherine gazed somberly at Lane. "He's so frustrated, Lane, knowing who did this to you and not being able to do anything about it."

"They've had a lot of practice at this kind of stuff, Cath." Lane kept to himself the thought that he would probably have to serve the entire sentence. "They'll have covered their tracks so well, it'll be tough digging out something we can use against them."

228

"We'll find it though," Catherine assured her husband. "Don't you worry about that."

"One thing I know for sure," Lane said with conviction, "Coley won't ever quit."

Catherine and Lane sat and talked to each other like they had done on their first date; never kissing, never holding hands, never one brief touch. They talked of the times in high school and college, of their first years of marriage, and of the war years. Like two star-crossed lovers, they cherished each moment together as time rushed past them.

The harsh shrieking of a guard's whistle ended the visit. With a final word of encouragement, Catherine rose and walked away, turning briefly as she went through the door on the opposite side of the big room.

Lane fixed Catherine in is mind as she turned around, that final goodbye wave, a bright corona of light surrounding her face from the sun going down behind her.

★ ★ ★

The lounge area near the prison chapel was nothing more than a concrete-block building, twenty-by-forty feet, with an old leather-and-chrome sofa donated by a local doctor, a few cast-off tables and chairs, decks of ragged playing cards, and a few worn-out musical instruments.

"That wasn't a bad sermon ol' Mitchell preached this morning." Buckels sat in a folding chair next to a wobbly card table, the ancient saxophone across his lap, putting on the final touches of his polish job as he rubbed it with an almost-clean white handkerchief. "He's got a long Sunday. Coming way out here for the eight o'clock and then two sermons at his own church."

Lane looked up from the New Testament Mitchell had given him after the service that morning. "One thing's for sure. He isn't in it for the money."

"They don't pay him?"

"Not for coming out here on Sunday," Lane replied as he returned to his reading.

"Hmmm. . . ." Buckels pondered Mitchell's motives as he adjusted the reed mouthpiece in the saxophone. "I wonder why he does it then?"

Lane continued to read.

Satisfied that he had done all he could with the saxophone, Buckels put the mouthpiece to his lips and coaxed out a slow, soulful rendition of "Heart and Soul."

Lane lowered the little Testament to his lap, marking his place with his finger as he gazed out the window toward the distant purple hills of Tunica. But what he saw was a quilt spread out in the sun-dappled shade on the bank of a creek—and Catherine, whose eyes, blue as periwinkle and full of soft light, gazed down at him, his head pillowed in her lap. He could almost feel her slim fingers trailing through his hair.

"This thing's hopeless," Buckels grumbled, pulling the mouthpiece off the saxophone and adjusting the reed for the twelfth time.

"Sounds good to me," Lane offered.

"You know as much about music as I do about lawyering." Buckels inserted the mouthpiece and raised the ancient instrument to his lips.

"Why'd you play that song?"

"I don't know." Buckels lowered the sax. "It's one of the first songs I ever learned. Simple, mainly for kids. Guess it sounds kind of silly."

"Not the way you played it."

Buckels raised the sax again. The haunting melody

230

of "Stardust" filled the little room.

Lane saw five guards enter the only door of the building, some squatting down, some leaning against the wall at the opposite end away from the men. After a few remarks, they settled down and listened to the song without another word.

When Buckels had finished and lay the sax on the table, the youngest man, who looked more like a high-school sophomore than a prison guard, applauded, then glanced around self-consciously. With scowls of disapproval on their faces that he would violate their unwritten code of conduct, the other four filed silently out the door ahead of him.

"I thought they'd come in to hassle us," Buckels said with a sigh of relief. "Guess they saw you and decided not to."

"Me?"

"Sure." Buckels pulled his handkerchief out of his back pocket and began polishing the sax. "Haven't you noticed that none of them have given you a hard time since that night you put the Hog Man down?"

"I guess I hadn't thought about it."

"You did them a big favor. Nobody felt safe, not even the guards, when that animal was around." Buckels held the sax up to the light. "It's their way of thanking you."

★ ★ ★

PART FOUR

NIGHTMIST AT SUNRISE

FOURTEEN

ELEGANCE AND SLOW GRACE

★ ★ ★

"I'll bet you didn't know that statue goes all the way back to 1885." Maria, wearing a white cotton pullover, jeans, and white sandals, pointed out the window.

In the few minutes since they had boarded, Coley had almost been lulled to sleep by the humming of the old green streetcar, swaying gently along St. Charles Avenue. He stared out the window at the statue of Robert E. Lee standing in the middle of Lee Circle. "He looks good for his age."

Maria laughed and adjusted Coley's wheelchair, folded and propped against the side of the seat. Leaning gently against his shoulder, she straightened the collar of his battered old marine fatigue jacket and said, "I'm so glad you decided to come with me today, Coley!"

Coley's mind jumped back to Lane's trial. "I just *know* there's something we're overlooking, Maria. *No-*

body pulls something like this without making mistakes."

"Remember what we agreed on." Maria sat up, staring at him in mild rebuke. "No talking about work. Today is for resting and fun."

The soft February breeze felt soothing on Coley's face as he leaned his elbow on the open window. "You're right—seventy degrees, the sky as clear as a bell. We can't afford to waste a day like this."

"Absolutely. After the all-nighters you've pulled the past few weeks, you're due a break."

In a few minutes, they had left the downtown business district behind them. Pale gold sunlight flickered down through the live oaks along the avenue as Coley gazed out the window at the Garden District. The old streetcar rocked gently down the grassy esplanade, passing Victorian and Greek Revival homes, many of them built by wealthy planters shortly after the Louisiana Purchase in 1803.

Their white-columned galleries gleaming like Aegean temples, a few of the old homes displayed second-story verandas with intricate lattice work wreathed with long tendrils of ivy. Widow's walks topped some of the roofs, built so that wives could see all the way to the Mississippi as they waited for a first glimpse of the ships of their seafaring husbands.

Against this historical backdrop, even the automobiles seemed to belong to an earlier age of elegance and slow grace as they passed by unhurriedly on both sides of the streetcar. Only occasionally would the illusion be broken by the blaring of a horn or the squealing of brakes.

Coley stared beyond a scrolled iron fence at a huge camellia bush, its blossoms deep red against the dark green foliage. "I'd forgotten how nice it is down here."

236

"The prettiest part of New Orleans," Maria observed. "Of course, I'm prejudiced."

"I'm almost afraid to ask why." Coley wondered why Maria hadn't told him before.

"Yes," Maria admitted with some reluctance. "I was raised just a few blocks down the street."

"What's the matter with that? You act like you're ashamed of it."

Maria shrugged and watched a plump, middle-aged woman wearing a yellow sun bonnet kneel and begin digging in her rose garden.

Never one for succumbing to the subtleties and nuances of polite conversation, Coley forged ahead. "Are you rich, Maria? Is that your dark secret?"

"I'm afraid so." Maria straightened up and leaned back against her seat, giving Coley an oblique glance. "It doesn't bother you, does it?"

"Should it?"

"I don't know. It's just that when people find out, they always treat me so differently, like they're afraid they might say something to offend me."

"Not me. Other than being an oppressive capitalist swine, supporting your decadent lifestyle on the backs of the proletariat, I think you're all right," Coley remarked offhandedly.

Maria turned a stunned expression on him, then noticed the rumor of a smile crinkling the corners of his gray eyes.

"Why would you think something like that?" Coley asked innocently.

"It's silly, I suppose." Suppressing her reaction to Coley's remark just in time, Maria said in a remote tone, "Most people are nice about it. Of course, there *are* some unwashed, ignorant backwater Cajuns who always overreact."

"That's to be expected." Coley had folded his arms and continued to stare at the passing homes. "They're part of the oppressed masses."

"You want to meet my family?"

Coley shrugged. "Why do you think I wore my Sunday britches?"

Glancing at his faded Levis, Maria held to the game, beginning to enjoy it now. "I thought maybe you were giving a speech somewhere. We'll still go to the zoo first, okay?"

"Fine with me."

"That's where I live." Maria pointed to a two-story stone mansion set among ancient live oaks hung with moss. In places, their spreading limbs touched the ground. Rising behind a tall wrought-iron fence, the house had a series of stone steps leading up the sloping lawn to its wide front porch. A single turret flanking the gabled roof gave it a storybook appearance. "Or maybe I should say it's where I grew up."

With a hint of a smile, Coley pictured the little shotgun house on the bayou in Grosse Tete where he was born and raised. "I thought you said you were rich."

★ ★ ★

Coasting along in his wheelchair in the dappled sunlight beneath the crepe myrtles, Coley felt completely at ease with Maria for the first time since he had met her. At the back of his mind, he had felt that she had been holding something back from him all along. As he had grown more attached to her every day, he had conjured up scenes where she ended their relationship for one reason or another.

"You're not mad because I didn't tell you about my family, are you?"

"Nope."

Maria still felt a twinge of guilt. In a matter of a weeks, she had found out through Baton Rouge's legal and political grapevine that Coley was one of the few politicians in the state who couldn't be bought at any price. The word on him was that money held little attraction for the representative from north Baton Rouge's blue-collar district.

Coley spoke through Maria's silence, feeling that she was giving the matter too much weight. "I've always harbored this desire to be a kept man anyway."

"Well, don't *un*harbor it on my account, Mr. Thibodeaux," Maria shot back.

"I think I like you, even if you are a spoiled rich kid," Coley grinned.

Maria stepped closer to the chair and placed her hand on Coley's shoulder as they moved down the tunnel of crepe myrtles toward the animals.

Stopping in front of the first cage, Maria gazed through the bars at the huge Bengal tiger, its yellow eyes gleaming with cold fire in the shadows. As it paced tirelessly back and forth on the smooth concrete floor, the muscles in its powerful shoulders and hindquarters rippled with fearsome power beneath the brownish orange and black-striped coat.

Abruptly the tiger stopped and gazed directly at Maria as a deep rumbling growl began deep in its massive chest. Then it opened a mouth white with teeth and roared.

Maria jumped back involuntarily. "My goodness! What did *I* do?"

"I think he just likes you," Coley offered.

Stepping closer to the wheelchair, Maria said, "I feel good being with you, Coley." She stroked his hand affectionately.

239

Coley wanted to respond with something poetic or at least romantic, but his mind went blank. "What does your daddy do for a living?"

Maria looked around at him with a puzzled expression on her face, then shrugged, "He raises sugarcane on land along the river. It's been in the family—my mother's family, that is—for generations. Oil leases, investments, that sort of thing too. Why do you ask?"

"Because I couldn't think of how to tell you how much I like being with you."

"You just said it."

"I guess I did, didn't I," Coley agreed, "but I wanted to say it better than that."

"Write me a sonnet."

"Would you take a legal brief instead? Or maybe a piece of legislation. I've done lots of those. One or two of them even became law."

"Write me a law, Coley Thibodeaux," Maria said in a sing-song voice. "In iambic pentameter or maybe free verse. A legal brief would be shorter, and could be no worse." She bent down so that she could meet Coley's eyes.

"That's the most romantic thing I've ever heard." Coley touched Maria's face with his fingertips, turning it toward him, his face as somber as a deacon's on a Sunday morning. "It really touched me, Maria."

Maria tried not to laugh.

"No fooling." Coley placed his clenched fist over his heart. "I felt something turning over in there!"

Maria put her arms around Coley's neck and placed her cheek against his. "Why do you think we're acting so giddy?" she murmured in his ear.

"Must be something in the water down here." Coley felt a pleasant warmth spreading in his chest. It

240

seemed as though the world had grown brighter, its troubles and heartaches suddenly far away. Again, he had no idea how to express in words what he felt for Maria.

Maria shifted slightly, her arms resting on Coley's upper chest. Leaning forward slowly, she closed her eyes and placed her lips on his.

Coley's arms went around her; his fingers slipped through her hair and touched her cheek. The fragrance of gardenia seemed to surround him.

Moments later, Maria pushed back and sighed. "That was fun. Why did we wait so long?"

"I always was a slow learner, I guess . . ." Coley felt the warmth now in his face. The flowery taste of Maria's lipstick lingered like a memory of their kiss. ". . . especially in the things that matter."

The tiger roared again.

Maria shrieked in terror, throwing her arms around Coley's neck.

"I *told* you he liked you," Coley said somberly, glancing over at the tiger. "See, he's already jealous."

Maria slipped out of Coley's embrace, glancing nervously through the bars. "Let's go see some of the other animals. Maybe I'll make a quieter friend."

Coley smiled and spun his wheelchair around, heading down the walk between the line of cages. "How about the lions? They're always fun."

Maria watched Coley stop and whirl around toward her. "I was thinking more along the lines of the giraffes. They don't make any sound at all."

★ ★ ★

Sipping a Barq's Root Beer from the bottle, Coley watched several children playing in the shade of the oaks. At the refreshment stand behind him, others noisily gave their orders for popcorn, candy, and cold drinks. "I know we're not supposed to, but I—"

Maria sat next to him on a wooden bench carved with dozens of names. "You promised, Coley," she interrupted, holding her finger to her lips.

"I know," Coley agreed reluctantly, "today is for having a good time only."

Maria took a bite of her cotton candy, letting it melt in her mouth as she mumbled at Coley. "What's on your overactive little brain, counselor?"

"I knew you'd give in," Coley grinned. "I think I finally realized what our next step's got to be."

"Wazzat?" Maria continued to savor her cotton candy with childlike contentment.

"We've got to put some pressure on Latiolais."

"Who?"

"You remember him," Coley reminded her. "Our friend with the baseball bat."

"Oh, him," Maria frowned. "How could I forget that axle-grease hairdo?"

"I just haven't figured out yet how to do it."

"Why'd you pick Latiolais?"

Coley gazed at the children busy with their games. "I think he's the one chink in their armor."

"You may be right," Maria said thoughtfully, her cotton candy dangling in one hand. "Catelon's as tough as they come and this Bruce Crain is just a mystery man."

Coley's eyes narrowed in thought. *I may just as well get it over with.* "I don't think they could have pulled it off without Hinton's help."

"That's pretty obvious," Maria remarked absently, taking a bite of cotton candy.

Stunned into silence at the casualness of her reply, Coley merely stared at her.

"You probably thought I didn't know about Hinton, huh?" Maria asked innocently.

"I've been afraid to mention it," Coley admitted. "I didn't know if you . . ."

Maria turned on Coley, too incredulous to speak for a moment. "Do you *really* think that six-foot-two walking ego is *my* type?"

"Well, I—"

"*Do* you?"

"He wears nice suits," Coley said, and as an afterthought, "and he *is* well-groomed."

"So's my friend the tiger back there," Maria pointed behind her, "and he's a lot more subtle than Hinton. One breakfast with that man was *all* I needed."

"What do *I* know?" Coley shrugged, feeling better the more he found out about Maria.

"Not much, obviously."

Coley took a swallow of his root beer. "Does everybody in your family have a temper like yours?"

"I'll let you find out for yourself," Maria offered. "Now, about our friend Latiolais."

Coley thought briefly of Lane, working in the cane fields of Angola. "I think he'll break if we can make him think we've got him dead to rights on his little swindle."

Maria tossed the remains of her cotton candy into a trash barrel. "Somebody with a badge. Preferably somebody big and mean-looking."

"I think you're on to something there," Coley nodded. "Badges and guns always have a way of getting people's attention when nothing else will."

"Let's do it then."

Coley sat his bottle on the concrete next to his chair. Rubbing his chin with the knuckle of his right forefinger, he frowned, "The problem is jurisdiction."

"In what way?"

"I know one or two people in Baton Rouge who might help us, but they won't cross parish lines and Latiolais lives in Ascension Parish."

"How about state troopers?" Maria suggested. "They've got statewide jurisdiction."

"Not in all matters—and besides, they're directly under the governor. Catelon's contacts would be on to that before we got started."

"That's right," Maria added. "The governor and Catelon are close as—"

"Thieves," Coley finished for her.

"You really have a way with words."

"I've got to figure out some way to convince Latiolais to come into my office."

"Is that all? Well, put your mind at ease then."

"You've got a plan that quick?"

Maria shook her head. "Not exactly, but I will before we get back to Baton Rouge."

★ ★ ★

By midafternoon, a cold front had moved in from the northwest. Wind stirred the long stringers of moss in the old oaks of Audubon Park and rattled the palm fronds out on the esplanade. Dusk had fallen on the Garden District along with a misty rain when Coley and Maria boarded the streetcar for their trip downtown to her car. All along St. Charles Avenue, the lights on the automobiles and the lights from the tall porches of the old houses reflected in the glistening streets.

"Well?" Maria, wearing Coley's jacket, sat next to him, her face full of expectation.

"Well—what?"

"What did you think of my parents?"

Coley stared out at the rain falling in the live oaks. A man in a business suit held a newspaper over his head as he hurried across a side street. "Your dad's not at *all* what I expected him to be. But then, people seldom are."

"I don't think I know how to take that," Maria replied defensively.

"What I expected was—royalty, I guess," Coley explained. "What I saw was a man who won a Silver Star fighting in the Ardennes."

"How did you find out about that?"

"Your mother told me when she gave me a tour of your little cottage."

"I never heard Daddy talk about it much," Maria said. "What else?"

"I expected somebody who inherited his money," Coley added, "not a man who made a fortune from his own hard work and determination in the sugarcane business."

"Mother's land gave him a pretty good start in that," Maria added, "but her family would have probably lost it all if Daddy hadn't come along when he did."

Coley nodded, seeing in Maria the same determination that had carried her father from the poverty of a ten-year-old boy just off the boat from Sicily, to the power and wealth and elegance of the Garden District. "I gather that your mother's family has lived down here for a long time."

"Since the Mississippi was just a puddle," Maria grinned, "or so family tradition has it."

The streetcar whined down to a stop. The doors whooshed open, and a stooped gray-haired woman carrying a large Maison Blanche shopping bag climbed painfully aboard. After handing her fare to the driver, she shuffled down the aisle and took a seat opposite Coley and Maria.

Coley nodded politely to the woman when she glanced in his direction.

"How ya'll doing?" she replied. "This is *some* weather we got tonight, huh?"

"Yes, ma'am."

Maria smiled at the woman, thinking that she looked vaguely like an old linotype photograph of her grandmother, one that her father had carried with him on the trip over from Sicily. "Your hair surely looks nice."

The woman's face colored slightly as she unconsciously patted the back of her head. "Thanks, darling. I gave myself one of them Toni Home Permanents. It costs too much to go to the beauty shop these days."

Coley immediately liked the woman who reminded him of his mother's friends from the bayou.

"I can tell your hair's got that natural wave, sweetheart." The woman pointed with an arthritic finger, the joints swollen and painful-looking. "This kind of weather we got makes it get them cute curls on the ends. Reminds me of little Camille, my youngest grandbaby."

"I bet you've got her spoiled," Maria said, reaching over and taking Coley's hand.

"You two make a nice couple," the woman smiled, showing a missing tooth on the bottom. "How long ya'll been married?"

"Oh, we—" Coley started to answer.

"Seems like forever," Maria interrupted. "And

we've never had even one argument."

"I can tell," the woman said, her features seeming to soften as she spoke. "Some people are just born for each other."

FIFTEEN

RUBY

★ ★ ★

René Latiolais felt awkward and out of place whenever he had to come to Baton Rouge. The coat of his ten-year-old suit would no longer button and the green-and-gold striped tie, like its owner, was slightly soiled.

Pushing the heavy blue drape aside, Latiolais gazed out the east windows at the landscaped grounds of the Capitol. Five stories below, a stocky black man in a green maintenance uniform worked on his hands and knees in the flower beds. Digging out weeds with a trowel, he tossed them into a wheelbarrow standing on the sidewalk a few feet away.

Latiolais rubbed his eyes, red and swollen from drink and lack of sleep. Since his alarm had awakened him at 6:00 A.M., he had felt as though he walked around in a fog, his thoughts grown muddled and flighty from the fear he carried inside him.

"This had *better* be important!" André Catelon swept into his office like a whirlwind, his custom-made suit in marked contrast to Latiolais'.

Startled, Latiolais jerked around and shuffled over to the closest of five smoke-gray leather chairs arranged in front of Catelon's desk.

Catelon plopped into his own plush chair, snatched his middle drawer open and grabbed a cigar. Uncapping the wooden tube, he tossed it into the trash can and jammed the cigar into his mouth. "Well . . ."

Latiolais shifted back and forth nervously, waiting for Catelon to ask him to sit down. When he realized it wasn't likely to happen, he began shakily, "I . . . I . . . uh."

"C'mon man, you sound like Mortimer Snerd!" Catelon snapped. "Out with it!"

"I'm scared, me!"

Why do I let myself get involved with imbeciles? "Any particular reason, or did you just have a bad night and need somebody to hold your hand?"

"I don't want to go to prison, no." Latiolais seemed to collapse slowly into the chair.

"That's a healthy sign, René," Catelon smirked, "If you came in here asking to be sent to Angola, then I might be a little concerned about you."

Latiolais took a red handkerchief out of his back pocket and wiped his face.

Now that Latiolais was no longer of any use to Catelon, he had become nothing more than a pest. Seeing him was merely time wasted, but there was always the possibility that Latiolais could still be a source of problems, so he found himself forced to listen to the frightened little man.

"Coley Thibodeaux come to my place a week or two ago," Latiolais mumbled.

"And . . ."

Latiolais took a deep breath, letting it out in a moan. "And he said he'd see dat I got sent to Angola."

Catelon shook his head in disgust. "You actually took him seriously?"

"He's a state representative!"

"Judges and juries send people to prison, not politicians," Catelon explained impatiently.

Latiolais forced himself to hold Catelon's gaze. "You ain't no judge and you ain't no jury, but *you* de one got Temple put in Angola."

Catelon glanced down at his diamond-studded watch. "Is there a point to all this, René?"

"I don't know," Latiolais muttered, wiping his face again and jamming the handkerchief into his back pocket. "I jes' didn't know where else to go when I left Thibodeaux's office."

Hardly able to believe what he had just heard, Catelon leaned slowly forward in his chair, his eyes narrowing in anger. "You did *what*?"

"I came here."

"I don't mean *that*, idiot!" Catelon almost screamed. "What were you doing in Thibodeaux's office?"

Latiolais seemed to shrivel up in his chair, clasping his hands together in his lap. "I *had* to go."

Taking a deep breath, Catelon tried to control his voice. "Why did you *have* to go, René?"

Latiolais spoke to an invisible object in the air three feet to the right of Catelon's nose. "I got a call from de judge's office and she said Thibodeaux was working on dat . . . appeal and needed some stuff from me."

"She?"

"De lady dat was wid Thibodeaux when he come down to my place."

251

He's dangerous now. Something has to be done. "It was just a ploy, René. You've been duped."

"Huh?"

"Never mind." Catelon knew he had to remain calm. "What did you tell him?"

"I ain't tole him nuttin'!" Latiolais assumed the defensive posture of a cornered animal.

"What did he ask you about?"

"Jes' de land and stuff like dat."

"What did you tell him?" Catelon demanded, his voice as hard as iron.

Latiolais stood up, shaking his head slowly back and forth as he began to pace in front of the desk. "He kept axing me about you and somebody named Cain or Crain dat I ain't never heard of before."

"What else?"

"About Mr. Hinton," Latiolais whined. "He axe me a lot of stuff about him."

"Take it easy, René." Catelon's voice took on a syrupy sweet quality.

Confused by the sudden change in Catelon, Latiolais gave him a blank look.

"Sit down."

Latiolais climbed back into the chair.

"Did you answer *any* of his questions?"

"I tole you I ain't said nuttin'."

I'll never get the truth out of him. He's too scared and too stupid to even remember. "Okay, René, just settle down. Everything's going to be all right."

"No it ain't."

"Why not?"

"He said he gonna talk to me some more."

"You don't have to talk to him at all, René. He doesn't have any power over you."

"But he's a state representative!" Latiolais insisted. "He makes the laws."

Realizing that he could never make Latiolais understand how the legal system worked or rid him of the idea that he *must* do everything Coley told him to, Catelon gave up. His face relaxed as he spoke in a soothing voice, but his eyes had gone as dark and barren as the backside of the moon. "You just go on home now and don't worry."

"Huh?"

"I'll take care of everything."

"You will?"

"You can trust me, René." Catelon stood up and walked Latiolais to the door.

"I 'preciate dis," Latiolais said in parting. "I just don't know what to do no more. I don't mind talking to Thibodeaux though. He don't never get ugly wid me."

"I'll take care of everything. You run on home now."

"T'anks. You a good friend, Senator."

As soon as the door clicked shut, Catelon sat down behind his desk and picked up his telephone. Dialing the number, he stuck the cigar back in his mouth and chewed on it. "Are you working on anything now? . . . I've got a job for you. . . . You'll find the envelope in the same box. It'll have everything you need."

Catelon hung up the phone, satisfied that another problem would be taken care of.

★ ★ ★

"I think we've finally found the answer we've been looking for." Coley sat behind his desk, piled high with law books, case files, and several yellow legal tablets of scribbled notes.

Shivering slightly, Maria pulled the jacket of her pearl gray suit closer around her. "I'm so glad for you—and especially for Lane and his family."

"And all of this work"—Coley waved his hand across the clutter of his desk—"was nothing but a big waste of time." He paused, giving Maria a pensive glance. "Well, maybe not *completely* wasted. I've found enough precedents to use in a dozen more trials if they happen to be the right kind, but I sure didn't find anything to help with Lane's case. They've got it wrapped up so tight, water couldn't get through it."

"You still think Latiolais is going to break?" Maria looked over at the space heater against the wall just inside the door, wishing for the little blue-white flames to sputter out of its gas jets.

"I'm sorry," Coley said, shaking his head as he noticed that Maria was cold. "I'm so used to being by myself, I just forget my manners sometimes." He wheeled over to the little heater, took a box of kitchen matches off the floor beside it, and struck one. Turning the gas on, he held the match through the grates. With a soft popping sound, the heater blazed to life.

Maria stood up and walked over to the heater, holding her hands out over it. "That feels good."

Coley dropped the burnt match back inside the box. "This is always the coldest part of a front, this wind and rain when it first comes through. It just seeps into your bones."

Maria gazed at Coley, his face in partial shadow from the amber glow of his desk lamp, his slightly hawklike features softened. She thought that he resembled the holy picture she had had as a child of the patron saint of schoolchildren, St. Dominic Savio, who died a young man. *There is something of the priest, something saintlike about him. Maybe that's*

254

why I like him so much. "All those long nights digging through law books and now it comes down to one scared little man."

"That's the way it goes sometimes," Coley said, "but at least with Latiolais we've got a good shot at turning this whole thing around."

"I hope he doesn't cause any problems for our office. I'd hate for the judge to have any trouble over this."

"Don't worry. The last thing Latiolais, or Catelon for that matter, wants is to have attention drawn to him."

"I guess you're right." Maria reached over and took Coley's hand as she listened to the muted hissing of the little heater. "You really think Latiolais will confess?"

"I'm sure of it." Coley used his other hand to gently rub Maria's, warming it as they talked. "For one thing he's scared to death and I think he actually feels guilty about what happened to Lane too. Unless I'm badly mistaken, he'll eventually have to get it off his conscience."

"At least he's got one."

"Yeah," Coley agreed, "I sometimes wonder if the good senator *ever* did."

"What about Hinton?"

"He'll just *fall*—right along with the rest of them. No sense even bothering with him."

"And this Crain fellow?"

"I doubt that Latiolais or Hinton ever met him." Coley felt a comforting warmth in the touch of Maria's hand. "Catelon's not going to say anything, no matter *what* happens."

"When do you want to talk to Latiolais again?"

"Let's give him a couple of days to think it over,"

Coley suggested, "then you can call him and tell him we need some more information. I just have an idea he'll come clean the next time I talk to him."

"I hope so. Catherine may not hold up under much more of this."

"Catherine's going to be just fine." Coley stared at the gas flames, their steady whisper driving the damp chill out of his office. "When I was a kid, we used to make toast on the space heater in our kitchen."

"Didn't you have a toaster?"

"We didn't even have electricity," Coley smiled, remembering the flickering light of the coal oil lanterns in his home. "We were lucky to have gas. A lot of people in that part of the country didn't have anything but wood-burning stoves."

"How'd you make toast?"

"We'd stand the bread up inside the metal guards and it wouldn't take very long to brown it. Then we'd turn it around and do the other side."

"That sounds like a lot more fun than sticking it in a toaster," Maria said.

Releasing Maria's hand, Coley rolled over to the window. Through the streaked glass, slightly cloudy now from the heater's warmth, he watched the traffic on Scenic Highway, tires sibilant on the wet pavement and headlights shining pathways through the blowing rain.

Coley thought of the flickering light from the heater, dancing in Maria's eyes, and of the warm glow of her skin. When did she leave his mind and spill over into his heart? Maybe on that first morning when he saw her walking across the gleaming tile floor toward him; maybe later as they worked together to get Lane's conviction overturned.

The physical and economic barriers between them

seemed almost insurmountable, and they had barely
touched on the spiritual. What chance did he have
with someone like her, anyway? Better to lay aside
ideas that had little chance of becoming the stuff of
reality.

Maria walked softly over to the window and sat
down next to Coley. "You're worried about Lane. I've
known you long enough to know that."

Nodding, Coley turned to Maria. "Sometimes it's
hard to have faith when things like this happen; when
the powers and principalities have things going their
way."

Maria found herself enjoying the sound of Coley's
voice more and more, the lengthened vowels and soft
consonants spiced with a touch of Cajun accent that
would always stay with him.

Coley glanced at her, then held out his thumb and
forefinger, not quite touching, "But all we need is as
much as a mustard seed, and they're little bitty
things."

"You sure are religious for a lawyer."

"I'm not *religious* at all," Coley said absently. "I'm
just a Christian."

Maria admitted to herself that she had never met
a man quite like Coley Thibodeaux, a man who considered himself little more than incidental, almost irrelevant even, in the favors and the work that he did
for other people in the legislature, in his law practice,
or just as a friend. She thought that Jesus must have
been something like that. It occurred to her that He
treated everyone alike and spoke of himself as meek
and lowly in heart.

Coley watched the cars spinning through the rain,
and beyond them the thousands of glittering lights of

the Standard Oil complex stretching all the way to the river.

"Coley. . ."

Gazing at Maria's face close to his, Coley felt her hand close over his.

"Do you think we'll still see each other after this business with Catelon is finally over?"

"I hadn't really thought much about it."

Maria felt her spirits sink.

"I guess it's because I don't see us being held together just because we're both trying to help Lane. I kind of hoped it was because we enjoyed being together."

Maria smiled, leaned over, and kissed him on the cheek. "That's the way I feel too."

A shadow crossed Coley's face. "Are you sure about this, Maria?"

She guessed what was on his mind. "I know that I feel better when I'm with you than when I'm with anyone else—you make me laugh and you make me very, very happy, and that's enough for me right now."

Coley smiled, feeling Maria's hand seem to grow warmer on his. Staring at the endless lights of Standard Oil, misty and softened by the rain, he wondered why he had never thought of them as pretty before.

★ ★ ★

Carrying a case of Dixie Beer, Latiolais waddled along the duckboards behind the bar. He waved to his last customers as they went out the door, sat the case down, and began stocking the cooler. The minor exertion caused beads of perspiration to break out on his forehead. His breath became slightly ragged as he finished the last of his nightly tasks.

They say, Ruby,
you're like a song. . . .

The words drifted from the jukebox, the sad melody an apt theme song for the late-night closing of
Home, Sweet Home.

"I'm glad dey finally wrote a song about you."

The woman with bleached-blond hair, wearing a
red satin dress, sat on her stool at the end of the bar
nearest the door to Latiolais' living quarters. "Isn't it
beautiful?"

"I guess so, but it don't sound so good after I hear
it t'irty—maybe forty times."

Ruby took a rhinestone-covered compact out of
her purse and checked her lipstick. "I'm sorry, I just
like it so much I guess I lose count."

Latiolais returned with the empty beer case,
leaned it against the wall, and sat down on a stool he
had built out of scrap lumber. "You play it all you want
to, cher."

Giving Latiolais a skeptical glance, Ruby closed
the compact and put it away. "You know something,
René?"

"Not much, I don't."

"You been acting different since you went to talk
to that Coley Thibodeaux up in Baton Rouge yesterday."

Picking up his empty coffee mug with both hands,
Latiolais rubbed his left thumb in a circular motion
across it smooth surface. "Maybe I *am* different, me."

"What'd he do to you?"

Latiolais gazed at the thick darkness beyond the
screen door. "He scared me at first, yeah," he muttered, "den, after I got home, I started t'inking about
what he said."

Ruby leaned forward, her elbows resting on the bar. "And what did he tell you?"

"I don't remember exactly," Latiolais admitted, "but it was kinda like talking to a priest or maybe a preacher even—no, dat ain't it either."

Resting her plump chin on her hands, Ruby listened intently to Latiolais' story.

"When I get around priests or preachers, I feel like I ain't as good as dey are, no—like they jes' want me not to get too close to dem." Latiolais set the cup back down. A trace of a smile crossed his face, lingering for a while in his eyes. "Coley didn't make me feel like dat at all, even when he tole me some bad t'ings about myself—and *he's* a state representative."

"Sounds like you had fun."

"No—not exactly *fun*." Latiolais gazed at Ruby, wishing he could remember the words Coley had spoken to him after they had finished talking about Lane Temple's trial. But, even as a young man, he had never been able to remember words well. He could not have begun to describe the feeling inside him and the way he looked at things differently now.

The song ended. Outside in the willow-lined coulee, frogs had begun their nightly symphony. A pickup with a busted muffler blared by out on the blacktop.

Ruby dug into her purse for another nickel, slid off her stool, and walked over to the jukebox.

Latiolais stared at the little path her frequent trips had made in the powdery coating of oyster shell dust tracked in from the parking lot. "I t'ink I might jes' get out of dis barroom business, me," Latiolais called out.

Leaning against the jukebox, Ruby stared at the selections as though she hadn't decided yet what to play. "You going to live off that money you got for the land?"

260

"I don't t'ink so."

"You've got to do *something* to make a living," Ruby said, dropping her nickel in.

"How about if I open a restaurant right in here?" Latiolais liked the sound of the word. "Ever'body says I'm de bes' cook north of New Orleans."

Ruby punched the buttons, standing for a moment in the jukebox's amber glow as she watched the record drop into place. "Why close the bar?"

"I jes' don't like it no more, me."

Sashaying back to the bar, Ruby climbed onto the stool and smiled sleepily at Latiolais. "Whatever makes you happy is fine with me, René."

"You know I been t'inking about somet'ing else, me," Latiolais said, returning her smile.

"I don't think I've ever known you to think so much—or make so many decisions before."

Latiolais didn't understand the change that had come about inside him after his visit with Coley, but he felt at peace for what seemed like the first time in his life. "Would you—I mean do you t'ink that we could—"

"It's okay. I'm your friend, remember?" Ruby reached over and patted Latiolais on the hand.

"Yeah," he sighed. "Ruby, will you marry me?"

Ruby's eyebrows arched in surprise as she sat up straight. "Will I *what*?"

"Marry me."

Her face softened, and Ruby took Latiolais' hand again. "You know I will, René. You're the best friend I ever had."

Latiolais climbed off his stool and put his arms around Ruby. They embraced until the song finished playing.

Ruby took a handkerchief from her purse and

dabbed at her eyes. "I must look a mess," she sniffed.

"You look like an angel."

Shivering slightly, Ruby clasped Latiolais' hand tightly. "Don't go tonight!"

"Why not?"

She hesitated, her eyes darting around the room as though she might find an answer. "I don't know, it's just—there's going to be a lot of fog on the river."

"I been taking this money over to Donaldsonville for a long time now and I ain't never had no trouble, me. That night deposit means I don't have to worry about nobody breaking in here and stealing it."

"But it's so late."

"You worry too much," Latiolais laughed, then kissed her on the cheek. "I'll be just fine."

"Okay. If you say so."

"I'm gonna be a good husband to you, Ruby." Latiolais gazed at her with eyes grown placid and gentle.

Ruby sniffed and wiped her eyes again.

"Starting tomorrow I'm gonna get my life on de right track. I'm gonna get some money out of my safe deposit box and then I'm driving in to Baton Rouge and tell the truth about something that's gotta be straightened out."

"You can take the deposit in the morning then if you're already going over to the bank."

Latiolais shook his head. "I wouldn't sleep good knowing it was here in de house. Besides, these old habits of mine are hard to break."

Ruby slid off her stool and lifted Latiolais' green work jacket off a twenty-penny nail driven into the wall. "Here you go," she said, helping him into it. "Keep it zipped up so you won't catch cold. It's so damp out on the river."

Latiolais grabbed a felt hat off another nail and

jammed it on his head. "See you in a couple of hours."

Ruby took his face in her hands and kissed him on the lips. "Be careful."

Latiolais nodded, grabbed his bank bag off the counter, and walked toward the door.

"René!" Ruby called out just as he was stepping through the door.

Latiolais turned around to see her hurrying across the concrete floor toward him.

Ruby rushed into his arms, kissing him and holding him tightly. Then she stepped back, her eyes bright with tears. "I love you, René."

"Me too," he smiled, and stepped out into the night.

SIXTEEN

NIGHT ON THE WATER

★ ★ ★

Crew-cut and muscular, he could have passed for a bull rider or a high-school football coach—until you stared into the soulless depths of his eyes.

On this moonless, misty February night, he stood in chest-deep water hidden by the ferry's shadow. Over on the bank, where the drive down the levee ended, a dented, rusty pickup and a '48 Chevrolet waited beneath the anemic light cast from a fixture mounted thirty feet up on a creosote pole. The wooden ramp lowered slowly and both vehicles lumbered up it, bouncing onto the ferry's steel deck.

The solitary deckhand pulled the winch lever and the ramp began to raise with a noisy whine.

The man in the shadows, wearing a wet suit, a heavy tire rim hanging over his back by a chain, waded over to the side of the ferry and pulled himself up, looping one leg through a tire bumper that hung from a thick hemp rope. He hung there almost effortlessly while the deckhand secured the ramp and cast off, returning immediately to the warmth of his little room beneath the wheelhouse. Once inside, he sat in a folding chair and buried his mind in a Captain Marvel comic book.

With the engine revving up, churning the ferry away from the shore, the man climbed up the rope attached to the tire and eased under the rail onto the deck, keeping the ferry cabin between him and the two vehicles. Laying the rim down carefully, he peered around the edge of the cabin. The man in the pickup looked half asleep behind the wheel. A man in a green work coat and felt hat climbed out of the Chevrolet and walked on the other side of the cabin toward the rear of the ferry.

"Hey, Captain," Latiolais waved up at the wheelhouse. "Nasty night, ain't it?"

"Not if you're Dracula."

With a hoarse laugh, Latiolais ambled on back to the stern, cast in deep shadow from the ferry's two-story cabin. Leaning both arms on the railing, he stared at the cottony mist that had already obscured the shoreline. The white wake of the ferry spread out behind the heavy props, churning with a deep throbbing sound beneath him.

The short, bulky man in the wet suit peered around the corner of the cabin, catching a glimpse of Latiolais. The palms of his hands felt hot, as though he held them before an open flame. Since that first time with the Raiders on Savo Island more than a decade earlier, the burning sensation had always started just before he made the kill.

A cold smile pulled at the corners of his mouth as he made five quick, noiseless steps over to the railing. With his knees bent slightly, his feet spread apart just enough for balance, he grabbed Latiolais' chin with his left hand, pulled him backward, and using his right hand for leverage twisted the head savagely to the left. Latiolais' neck made a dull snapping sound like a stick breaking underwater.

Easing the limp body down to the deck, the man slipped Latiolais' coat, trousers, and shoes off and quickly put them on. Then snatching the hat off, he jammed it on his head. Hurrying to the rail, he carried the tire rim over to Latiolais' body and chained it to his ankles with a padlock.

The man in Latiolais' clothes quickly checked around both corners, then eased the body beneath the rail, holding the chain at midpoint so that Latiolais and the rim reached the surface of the water at the same time. Lying flat on his belly, the man let the tire rim slip beneath the surface of the muddy water, then turned the chain loose. Latiolais' body turned over slowly in the wake, then the chain drew taut, jerking it abruptly out of sight.

Waiting until the ferry was close enough to the opposite shore so that the captain would be occupied with judging the current for his docking, but before the deckhand emerged from his cabin, the man who had murdered Latiolais ambled slowly over to the Chevrolet and got in it.

In less than a minute, the deckhand stepped out onto the deck and walked toward the winch, passing within five feet of the Chevrolet. "See you on the trip back, René."

The man slumped down behind the wheel, pulled his hat down slightly, and nodded.

When the ferry knocked against the landing, the deckhand tied off both ends and lowered the ramp.

The man in the Chevrolet let the pickup clear the ramp, then with a wave to the deckhand followed it up the shell drive, disappearing over the top of the levee. As he rode down the other side that led onto the river road, his mouth slowly opened in a twisted smile. Opening the bank bag on the seat, he pulled out the neatly stacked bills, crumpling them in his hands. "Thanks for the bonus, you little fat worm."

★ ★ ★

"You did your best, Coley," Catherine almost whispered, her voice choked with restrained grief. "Anyone else would have given up long ago."

Coley stared glumly at the headline of the open newspaper laying on the kitchen table:

LOCAL BAR OWNER VANISHES—
CAR FOUND IN FRENCH QUARTER

"I wish I could offer you more hope, Catherine, but I don't know which way to turn now."

Catherine gazed at the gray winter light, gathering like smoke at the windows looking out onto the backyard. When Jessie had left earlier to drop the children off at school and go on to her classes at LSU, Catherine had felt alone and defeated.

Hearing the sound of someone dropping Coley off in her back drive had lifted her spirits and set her thoughts on firmer ground. Even though he had brought her no good news, his mere presence gave her comfort.

"I'm *sure* that Latiolais was going to come clean with me," Coley muttered.

Catherine pulled her black sweater together in front and crossed her arms. "You really think someone would . . . *do* something like that?"

Coley nodded, his eyes still fixed on the headlines.

"It's too much of a coincidence for him to just *disap-pear* right after he came to my office."

"Maybe they'll find him somewhere in New Or-leans," Catherine offered.

Poking with his fork at the scrambled eggs on his plate, Coley shook his head slowly. "They won't find him at all. This was done by a pro."

"Eat your breakfast, Coley," Catherine admon-ished gently. "You've lost weight with all the hours you've been putting in. It won't help the situation any if you work yourself right into a sickbed."

"I guess I'd better go see Lane tomorrow, break the news to him in person." Coley took a bite of eggs and chewed them slowly before swallowing. "The prison-ers hardly ever get newspapers up there, but I still want to tell him before he finds out through the grape-vine."

"I wish I could go with you," Catherine said, sitting down at the end of the table.

Coley sipped his coffee. "One visit a month except for legal counsel. I tried to get an exception to that rule, but the corrections people wouldn't budge."

"I know," Catherine nodded, tracing the grapevine pattern of the cup with the tip of her forefinger.

Coley dropped his fork onto the plate and rested his forehead in both hands. "I'm really beaten on this one, Catherine!" He lifted his head, gazing at her with eyes grown weary and dazed from too many long nights.

Catherine reached over and lay her hand on his shoulder. "Oh, Coley, you've done so much for us! There's no way to express my gratitude."

Coley stared out the window, his face slack with defeat. "When I saw this morning's headlines, I prayed for a miracle. It's all I could think of to do." He

269

glanced at Catherine, the look in his eyes bordering on desperation. "But I didn't get an answer. I felt like the windows of heaven were closed against me."

Picking up Coley's cup, Catherine walked over to the stove and refilled it. She placed it in front of him and sat back down. "I've felt like that myself so often since all this happened. I guess my faith isn't as strong as I thought."

"I'm sorry, Catherine." Coley rubbed his eyes and sat up straight. "I should never have said that. There's *always* hope. I guess what I need is a good night's sleep."

"I'm glad you did."

Coley's face held a perplexed expression. "You're glad I said I felt defeated?"

"Yes." Catherine's eyes held a gentle light as she spoke. "You've been so strong for the rest of us during these terrible days that maybe it's good to get your doubts out in the open. We all have them; we all go through these times when everything looks bleak and hopeless. I think it makes us feel better when we have someone to tell it to."

"I believe you're right." Coley watched a sparrow flash across the span of the back windows, alighting on the crossbar of a clothesline pole. He opened his small beak, singing out against the dreary winter day. " 'The substance of things hoped for; the evidence of things not seen.' We're *not* giving up hope, Catherine. This is just a temporary setback."

Catherine sipped her tea. She still felt the cold ache of separation from Lane lying like a stone in her breast, but in spite of the despair that sometimes crept into her bedroom at night, she could somehow see a small light shining behind all the darkness.

★ ★ ★

Bonnie pulled her MG into the little parking lot used for out-of-town officials. Located between the Capitol building and the lake, it usually held several cars even if the legislature wasn't in session. She stared out at the lake, picking up the faint reflection of the massive stone structure behind her, its few lights barely casting an image on the dark surface.

For days now, Bonnie had known what she must do. Finally, at half past one on this chilly February morning as she lay awake tormented by what she had become, she decided that she could wait no longer.

Bonnie waited until the Capitol security car crept by behind her on its hourly rounds. Then, buttoning her tan trench coat, she tied a black scarf over her head, grabbed the tan briefcase, and opened the car door. From out on the river, a tugboat's whistle sounded like a lost soul moaning in the night.

Hurrying across the street, Bonnie walked underneath the tall rear portico and up the stone steps to the back entrance of the Capitol. She slipped her key into the brass lock of the center door and, with a furtive glance around her, went inside. Her high heels rang with a hollow sound on the marble floors. Taking the stairs, she climbed to the fifth floor, walked directly across the hall to the office, and let herself in with a second key.

Light filtering past the partially opened drapes cast Catelon's office into a murky pattern of shadows. Bonnie's steps were silenced by the thick carpet as she walked to the closet in the corner next to a private bath, went inside, and flicked the light on. Pushing aside her father's jackets and extra white shirts, she spun the dial of a wall safe four times and opened it.

As Bonnie sorted through the documents inside the safe, she trembled slightly, feeling fear descend on her like a cold, clammy blanket. Carefully selecting three files and several legal sheets stapled together, she put them into her briefcase, closed the safe, and spun the dial.

Bonnie retraced her steps, being especially careful not to trip on the stairs. As she stepped out into the wide hall that led to the rear of the Capitol, she saw the shadow of the night watchman sliding across the floor just ahead of him. She quickly backed into a darkened alcove until he passed by.

Once she had settled herself behind the steering wheel of her car, Bonnie gave a deep sigh of relief. She spun out of the parking lot, turning right on North Third Street. East of her, the surface of the lake winked with light.

By the time Bonnie found herself spinning along Scenic Highway with the lights of Standard Oil glittering like an industrial version of Las Vegas, she had regained control of her taut nerves. She turned off her headlights just before pulling into the parking spot that she had seen Lane use dozens of times.

Turning off the engine, Bonnie rolled down her window and listened for several moments before getting out. The great industrial complex behind her filled the night with its muffled roar. Off in the distance an ambulance wailed its way toward some neon-bright emergency room.

Bonnie's face was suffused with a fleeting serenity as she contemplated what she must do. She felt her act a form of betrayal, yet hoped it would somehow free her of the unbearably sad dreams, the intolerable awakenings that had plagued her since Lane's trial. Summoning all her will power, she grasped the briefcase firmly, got out of the car, and walked toward the office.

★ ★ ★

Catherine pulled into the lot, parking her Chrysler in Lane's space, and rushed inside to Coley's office. She had hurriedly thrown on a print house dress and her leather coat after Coley's phone call. "You said you had some good news. Did you find some new evidence?"

Coley set his coffee cup on his desk and took both of Catherine's hands in his own. "You remember that miracle I told you I prayed for?"

"Of course."

"Well it's happened."

Catherine sat down heavily, still holding on to Coley's hands. She opened her mouth to speak, then decided not to, as though the sound of her voice might awaken her from what now seemed like a dream.

"Lane's getting out of prison."

Catherine's eyes grew bright with tears. As she broke into a smile that became half-sobs and half-laughter, they began to stream down her cheeks. She remembered all the times she had prayed for Lane in those cold, hard hours before dawn, all the times her prayers had seemed nothing but dry, dead words reaching no higher than her ceiling. They now rushed back to her and the memory of them seemed as precious as family heirlooms.

Coley gazed at Catherine's dazed expression. "Catherine, are you going to be all right?"

"Oh yes!" she said, her voice full of joy and wonder. *"Everything's* going to be all right now."

"You want to know how it happened?"

"I—I must seem deranged," Catherine admitted. "Of course I do."

Coley picked up a file from a neat stack on his desk. Opening it, he took out several legal-sized documents stapled together. "I've already made a few phone calls to verify some of this—enough for our purposes right now. The rest we can do later."

Catherine felt the dreamlike state settle over her again. Coley's voice sounded faraway, but she understood every word and let herself bask in their meaning.

"This is an act of sale transferring Latiolais' property to a corporation whose principal stockholders are Harlan Hinton and Bruce Crain. The names on the documents are phony, but a typed note clipped to the documents listed those two as the legal owners. I verified it with a couple of phone calls."

"But wouldn't Latiolais be able to sell the property to them legally?"

Coley pointed to the bottom of the last page. "The act of sale is dated thirty days before Lane passed his. That proves that Hinton and this mystery man Crain knew ahead of time that Lane's transaction would be overturned. I think that's enough in itself to make a good case for conspiracy to commit fraud."

"How will you ever find Crain?"

"Right here," Coley smiled, slipping a three-by-five card from the file. Crain's address and phone number in Milwaukee. I've already checked it out."

The obvious question in all the good news suddenly hit Catherine. "Where did you *get* all this?"

Coley placed his hand on the thin stack of files lying in front of him. "They were right here on my desk when I came in this morning. I guess whoever brought them knew that I never lock my doors."

"But how—who would . . ." Unable to comprehend their good fortune, Catherine found herself too confused to ask a simple question."

"I haven't even had time to consider who could have done it," Coley admitted. "Right now it's enough to use what we have to get Lane out of prison."

"Do we have enough?"

"More than enough."

"But how can it happen so fast?"

"It's the nature of the legal beast," Coley explained. "Just when you're sure nothing will ever happen—bingo, it's all over. That's the way it works sometimes."

Catherine felt she would never stop smiling as she continued to listen to Coley.

He took a single typed page from a file and glanced at it from time to time as he spoke. "I have the names and locations of safety deposit boxes containing the forty thousand dollars Lane got from Crain."

"I didn't know it was missing."

"Neither did I, until this morning." Coley gazed thoughtfully at the window, full of morning sunshine. "The officer in charge of the evidence room is a stickler for details and I can almost guarantee that he listed *every* serial number of those forty one-thousand-dollar bills."

"Who got the money?"

"Latiolais and Hinton."

"Poor Mr. Latiolais," Catherine said somberly. "I wonder what happened to him?"

Coley thought back to the last time he had seen Latiolais—in that very room. "I can't imagine how word got out that he was planning to come clean about this whole sordid mess. He must have told the wrong person."

Catherine felt almost unable to ask the next ques-

275

tion for fear that something Coley might have forgotten to tell her would somehow prevent it. "When can Lane come home?"

"Today, if everything goes well."

"Today?" Catherine felt weak, a slight buzzing sound seeming to fill her head.

"I've already talked to Judge Robichaux," Coley said, sorting deliberately though the papers.

"Is that all it takes?"

"He usually has to see the physical evidence and take it under advisement for a day or two, but this time he made an exception to his rule for me."

"I guess sometimes it really pays to have a reputation for honesty, even in politics."

Coley gave Catherine an embarrassed smile. "He's getting the order cut to overturn the conviction based on the information I gave him over the phone."

"Can *we* go get Lane—now?"

"I'm afraid it's not quite that easy."

"Why not?" Now that Lane's prison term was ending so abruptly, Catherine wanted to jump right into her car and race up to Angola.

"Procedural reasons," Coley explained without going into detail. "As soon as the order is filed with the Clerk of Court, the sheriff's office takes it from there."

"Won't they at least let *me* go?"

Coley shook his head. "Maria's hand-carrying the order to the clerk's office, then she'll take a certified copy over to the sheriff. That could be the only delay."

"What kind of delay?"

"Finding a deputy who's available to go pick Lane up. That's the final step."

"When will we know something?"

"Maria's going to stay there until a deputy is assigned, then she'll call us."

Catherine's face clouded over slightly. "But what if they can't get somebody until tomorrow—or even later?"

"Don't worry," Coley smiled, "Maria's a very persuasive young woman. She'll get somebody to do it."

SEVENTEEN

FRIENDS

★ ★ ★

Catherine glanced at her watch for the tenth time in as many minutes. Sitting behind the steering wheel of the big Chrysler, she checked her lipstick in the rearview mirror and smoothed out the skirt of her iris-colored dress. Trimmed in white lace at the throat and cuffs, it was several years old, but still Lane's favorite. "Why is it *taking* so long?"

"They haven't had time to get back here yet, Catherine," Coley explained to her as he rested his arm on the passenger door, unable himself to keep his eyes off the dashboard clock. "Even with hard driving, it's still a four-hour round trip. And there's always the paperwork to fight."

"I wish the children were here." Catherine gazed around at the parking lot behind the courthouse. City police and sheriff's units filled most of the spaces. She watched two uniformed officers lead a handcuffed man in cowboy boots and a denim jacket down the concrete ramp that led to the basement beneath the

279

courthouse. From there an elevator would take them up to the fourth-floor jail.

Coley merely lent his ear to Catherine's comments, knowing they were born of almost three months of anxiety for her husband's safety.

"No, I guess I really don't wish they were here. I don't want them to see Lane in a place like this."

"You're right. It's best that they didn't come," Coley encouraged, his eye on the street corner where the sheriff's unit from Angola would turn.

"And what if he comes out in handcuffs?" Catherine closed her eyes and shook her head quickly. "It would be just awful if they saw him in handcuffs."

"You did the right thing, Catherine," Coley assured her. He patted her gently on the shoulder. "Now, settle down and just be glad that this nightmare is almost over."

"I know—I know," Catherine agreed. "We're through all the bad part and here I am acting like Lane's on his way *to* prison instead of on his way home."

Coley felt the soft breeze, harbinger of spring, on his face and watched it stir the leaves on the live oaks, flickering patterns of light and shadow across the sidewalk and the street. Freed from the burden of Lane's imprisonment, he looked years younger already. The pinched and drawn look his face had taken on since the trial had almost disappeared.

Catherine thought of other times she had waited for Lane to come back to her. She saw herself on the platform at the railway depot in Sweetwater when he had returned from World War II. He had sprinted across the platform just in time to rescue Cassidy from falling beneath the wheels of the departing train. Then, alone at that other depot in New Orleans, she had seen hardly more than a shell of a man, frail and gaunt, and back from the brink of death, hobble painfully toward her on a cane.

At those times, he had returned a hero—a soldier who had shed his blood for his country. What would happen this time? What had prison done to him? How would his friends and neighbors accept *this* homecoming?

The Plymouth sedan with sheriff's office decals on the doors turned the corner on North Boulevard across from the City Club and headed toward the back lot of the courthouse. Coley spotted it first and nodded to Catherine.

Catherine's face grew slightly pale, her left hand rising to her throat as she let out a half-suppressed gasp. "Oh, Coley, he's home! He's finally home!"

Staring at the Plymouth as it passed along the street in front of them, Coley was surprised at what he saw. Lane sat in the front seat, not the caged rear one, next to Corporal J. E. Ball, the deputy who had driven him to Angola and a man known for strict adherence to procedure. The two of them were carrying on an animated conversation. Coley could plainly see that Lane had no handcuffs on, although he knew that they were required until the prisoner was officially clocked in.

The Plymouth rocked slightly over the hump that led into the lot, passed along the rows of automobiles, and finally pulled into the slot next to Catherine and Coley.

Catherine, already out her door, ran around the Chrysler toward Lane.

Lane, noticing her for the first time, spoke quickly to Ball and jumped out of the Plymouth.

"Oh, Lane, Lane!" Catherine rushed into his arms,

covering his face with kisses, feeling him lift her off the ground, holding her tightly against his hard body. Pressing her lips against his, she lost herself in his kiss, the memories of all the long nights without him fading like mist at sunrise.

In a few moments, Catherine pushed back, holding tightly to Lane's hands. Nearly a month had passed since she had seen him. She expected the time to have taken its heavy toll, leaving him more lean-faced and hollow-eyed.

The man Catherine saw looked the picture of health, his face tan, his eyes confident and full of good humor. Something had changed about him. She felt somehow that she should know what it was, but even with him standing so close, it eluded her.

"Are you all right, Cath?" Lane lay his left hand softly against her face.

Catherine went up on tiptoe, kissing him again. "I'm just *perfect!*"

"Hey, don't I get a kiss too?" Coley called from the window of the car.

Lane walked over to the car with Catherine clinging to his arm and shook hands with Coley. "Nope. I'm afraid you're not pretty enough."

Coley glanced down at the muddy brogans Lane wore with his rumpled suit. "What happened to your shoes?"

"They weren't in the little wire basket with my suit," Lane explained. "Somebody took them, I guess."

"Didn't you ask about them?" Coley joked, trying to imagine Lane hanging around Angola for the sake of a pair of shoes. "Those were pretty nice shoes, if I remember right."

"I left 'em." Lane glanced down at the brogans. "I think I might have left my *feet* if it meant I could get out of that place a minute sooner."

"Good to have you back, partner," Coley grinned. "Now we can get down to some real work, like getting you elected to my House seat."

Lane gave him a dubious glance, thinking that he would be fortunate if he could just make a living for his family. Then suddenly he turned back toward the Plymouth where Ball still sat behind the wheel filling out his paper work. "I forgot all about thanking J. E."

"Maria said he came in on his day off just to go pick you up," Coley said.

"Maria?"

"Coley's been courting since you left, Lane," Catherine answered for him. "Remember, he met this nice girl from New Orleans."

Lane's eyes registered the memory. "Hold that thought. I'll be right back." He walked over to the Plymouth.

Ball looked up from his clipboard. "Well, you made it home, boy. Maybe there *is* some justice left in this ol' world."

"I just wanted to thank you again for what you did for me—and for Catherine. I owe you one."

"I told you that night I brought you up there you still had some friends on the outside." Ball held out his beefy hand to Lane. "There's more than just me too."

Lane gripped Ball's hand firmly. "Well, let's go get me clocked in."

"Don't worry. I'll take care of it myself," Ball assured him. "You get on home to them kids."

Lane's face showed his appreciation as he nodded and went back to Catherine and Coley. "Now, tell me about this Maria and why in the world she would be interested in a skinny little Cajun like you?"

Catherine found herself still amazed by Lane's attitude. She had expected him to be depressed or at the least subdued after almost three months in one of the worst prisons in the country. Instead, he acted confident and at ease, as if he had just returned from an extended vacation.

"What's not to like about me?" Coley answered Lane. "Wit, charm, good looks—"

"Poverty," Lane finished for him.

"There's that too," Coley agreed, "which, I might add, is why I'm so humble. I bet you didn't know I won the Louisiana Trial Lawyer's Humility Award three years in a row."

"You two want to finish this later?" Catherine suggested, tugging at Lane's arm. "We have children at home who haven't seen their daddy in a while."

"Yes, ma'am." Lane gave Catherine a quick, firm kiss on the mouth, then led her around the car, letting her slip over next to Coley while he took the wheel.

★ ★ ★

Bright red and white azalea blossoms flanking the front walk caught Lane's eye with his first glimpse of home.

WELCOME HOME, DADDY

As he turned into his driveway, Lane stared at the sign, an old bed sheet hanging between two of the columns on the front gallery and hand-lettered in what looked to be shoe polish and crayon. He felt his heart fill up. "What a sight!"

"Well, the thought is what counts, I guess," Catherine smiled, "even if the artwork could be better."

Lane braked the car to a stop, beaming at the sheet billowing softly in the March wind. "I think it's as pretty as the Mona Lisa—no, prettier!"

Lane drove to the back beneath an archway of brightly colored balloons. When he got out of the car, all four children ran pell-mell down the walkway toward him.

"Daddy's home!" Cassidy, always the quickest to react in any situation, reached Lane first, leaping onto his chest and wrapping his arms around Lane's neck.

After a quick romp with Cassidy and a grown-up handshake and sheepish grin from Dalton, whose voice barely quavered when he spoke, Lane motioned for Sharon. "Come here, precious. I need a big hug from my sweet girl."

Sharon ran into his arms. "Oh, Daddy, I missed you so much! I'm *so* glad you're back!"

"I missed you too, baby." Lane held her close, feeling her trembling slightly, then eased her back, brushing a tear from her soft cheek. "There, there, it's all right, sweetheart. I'm home for good now."

Catherine followed Coley along the brick walkway, joining Lane and the children.

Jessie hung back until Lane had given Sharon the attention that she needed.

Lane held his arms out to Jessie. "Anybody else around here feeling like giving their ol' daddy a hug?"

"Do you have one left for me?" Jessie embraced her father quickly, kissing him on the cheek.

"Look who else came to welcome you home, Lane," Catherine said.

In the deep shade of a live oak, Homer McCurley, wearing his usual brown slacks and white shirt, sat on a bench next to the three-tiered fountain. Next to him sat Maria. Having come straight from work, she wore a tailored gray suit and white silk blouse. They seemed to be listening to the music of the flowing water.

Next to the brick patio where Homer sat, a picnic table covered in a white cloth held a big bowl of salad, another three of boiled shrimp on ice, and platters of hors d'oeuvres. On the lawn, at the edge of the shade, a huge pot sat on a butane burner awaiting the hundred pounds of crawfish that would soon be boiled in it.

Bunting had been strung through the spreading limbs of the live oak and baskets of impatiens hung from the ceiling along the edge the rear gallery.

"How did ya'll get all this done so quickly?" Lane asked, walking with Catherine and Coley over to where Homer and Maria sat. "You only had a few hours' notice."

"Word got out and people just started showing up with things to welcome you home." Catherine held Lane around the waist as though something might spirit him away from her.

Maria smiled up at Lane as Coley introduced them. "I can't tell you how good it is to see you at home with your family, Lane. I already feel like I've known you for a long time."

"Coley's been telling me about you on the trip over here," Lane replied, glancing at his friend. "I might still be up there digging up stumps if it hadn't been for your help."

"Coley did most of the work."

"Pretty, smart, and modest." Lane smiled, and turned to Coley. "You'd better not let her get away from you."

Coley cleared his throat, started to reply, then gave Maria a slightly embarrassed smile.

"Homer—it's sure good to see you again." Lane

shook hands with him as Catherine sat down on the bench.

"Looks good, doesn't he, Homer?" Coley kidded. "For a jailbird, that is."

"Don't let him get you down, Lane," Homer grinned. "Paul and Silas had a song service in a jailhouse one time, if I recall."

"You see, Coley, I'm in pretty good company." Lane gazed at the little white-haired missionary who seemed to have an almost visible aura of serenity about him. When he'd visited him with Catherine at Carville, Lane had seen only an old man with a disease that had slightly disfigured him. Now he stood in awe of Homer's courage and fortitude at having taken the gospel to turn-of-the-century Africa, with its swift and terrible dangers.

"I sure appreciate you folks asking me here today." Homer gazed about the backyard.

"We're happy you could come." Lane reached down and took Sharon by the hand. She seemed unwilling to get more than a few feet from him. "Your face sure looks a lot better, Homer. Those bumps are about all gone."

"Sulfides," Homer responded absently, as though his face was hardly a concern. He watched Jessie bring more food from the kitchen out to the folding table that Dalton and Cassidy were setting up next to the already full one. "They take good care of me down at Carville."

Lane squatted down next to the bench with Sharon leaning against him. "You remember the question you posed to me the time I visited you with Catherine?"

"Yep."

"Well, a man named Mitchell brought up the same

287

question when I was at Angola."

"I know what your answer was and is, Lane." Homer spoke with a soft confidence. "And I'm glad to see you finally came around, son. I was gettin' kinda tired of praying for you so often."

Catherine stared at Lane in wonder. An unrelenting joy began to rise in her breast as she wondered how she could have missed that unmistakable change in his spirit. *I've hoped and prayed for this so long! And to think it happened in a place like Angola!*

"Well, you can ease up, Homer." Lane smiled warmly at Catherine. "Your prayers were answered."

Homer nodded, his eyes filled with a joyful light. "Good. Now I can get back to some easier work."

"Easier?"

"Yep." Homer winked at Coley. "Like praying for the redemption of China."

Still feeling disoriented by the sudden change from prison back to his own home and friends, Lane's mind flashed on the stark and brutal images of Angola. "I know that I made it through that place alive only by His grace."

"His grace—and a mop wringer," Coley said, a Cheshire-cat smile spreading across his face.

Lane frowned at Coley, not wanting Catherine to find out about his encounter with Hogeman.

Noticing Lane's expression, Catherine said, "It's all right, sweetheart. Coley told me while we were waiting for you. He figured it would be all right, now that you were getting out. Besides, if David could use a slingshot, I think it was all right for you to use a mop wringer."

"Not as miraculous, maybe," Coley added, "but it sure got the job done."

Catherine glanced at the back drive where a gray-haired man of about sixty rounded the corner of the house and headed toward them down the brick walk. He wore black oxfords and neatly pressed khakis with a metal Standard Oil ID badge pinned to the left pocket of his shirt.

"Hello, folks!" Abner called out. "Ya'll keep your seats. I can't stay long."

Lane stood up from force of habit to greet Abner. "You'll have to excuse the way I look, Abner," Lane apologized, glancing down at his wrinkled suit and the scuffed brogans. "They've really relaxed the dress code up at Angola."

Abner smiled. "I just wanted to stop by and welcome you home, Lane."

"I really appreciate that, Abner. You'll never know how much it means to have friends who stick by you no matter what." Lane introduced Abner to Homer. "Abner Hollis, here, was my first client when I opened my law practice."

"Yep," Abner agreed. "I saw Lane back ol' Thurman down that day in Hebert's Coffee Shop, and figured he'd do just as good in a courtroom."

"Tell your wife I really appreciate the coconut cake, Abner. She dropped it off while we were waiting for Lane."

"I'll do that, Catherine."

After a brief visit, Abner said his goodbyes and turned to leave, motioning for Lane to follow him.

When they reached the driveway, Abner handed Lane a twenty-dollar bill.

"What's this for?"

"For your campaign, naturally," Abner replied, as though Lane should have known. "We've got to have somebody down at the legislature who'll stand up against men like Catelon—somebody who's on the side of the workingman."

From prisoner to a free man with family and friends backing him for political office, all in a matter of hours—Lane struggled with a feeling of unreality. "I'll do my best, Abner. You can count on that."

"I know you will, Lane," Abner said, shaking Lane's hand. "That's why there's a lot more folks out here in Dixie that're standing behind you."

When Lane returned to the backyard, he saw Dalton and Cassidy struggling down the steps of the gallery with a hundred-pound burlap bag full of live crawfish.

"Let me have that, boys." Lane hefted the bag easily over his shoulder, carrying it out to the big stainless-steel pot.

Dalton tagged along behind Lane. "How'd you get so strong, Daddy? I want to train like you did."

Lane thought of the long days clearing new ground and of the dozens of stumps he and Buckels had dug up and hauled off. "No, you don't."

"Come on over here," Lane called out to Coley, who sat at the bottom of the back steps talking to Maria at the open door of the kitchen. "Get this burner going and let's cook some of these mud bugs."

Jessie, who stood next to Maria, reached behind her and tossed Coley a box of kitchen matches. He wheeled his chair down the walk past the fountain and tables and across the brown winter grass.

Sitting on the bench next to Homer, Catherine watched Lane with Coley and her boys as they made preparations for the crawfish boil. "This is the third time he's come back to me, Homer, when I didn't know if he'd make it or not."

"But he always *did* come back." Homer eased his

right foot in its molded, protective sandal into a more comfortable position. He had learned over the years to accept gifts without question and to store up the good memories against those days that would surely come when things would not turn out so well.

"Yes," Catherine replied, her voice little more than a whisper. She smiled at Homer. "He always did."

★ ★ ★

"What a great day." Lane sat in a wrought-iron chair on the second-story gallery outside the French doors leading into his and Catherine's bedroom. He wore faded Levis and had thrown on his old fatigue jacket against the night chill.

Catherine sat next to him in a heavy terry cloth robe and slippers. "Friends."

"What?"

"I think it's a beautiful word." Catherine slipped her hand in Lane's.

"I didn't know we had so many until today," Lane admitted, putting his free arm around Catherine's shoulders.

"I counted 153 people that came by to say hello and welcome you home."

Lane thought back twenty-four hours when he had lain in his bunk staring at the rough ceiling of his dormitory at Angola. He wondered if Buckels, ravaged by hard drugs, would last out his sentence.

Catherine sensed that Lane's mind had turned to those dark memories that he would have to learn to live with. "It's going to be all right, sweetheart."

"I know that," Lane replied confidently.

Pushing herself out of the chair, Catherine curled up in Lane's lap, laying her head on his shoulder while he encircled her with his arms.

"I'm ashamed of myself, Cath," Lane said abruptly.

Catherine sat up, gazing into her husband's eyes. "Whatever are you talking about?"

Lane gazed thoughtfully at his wife. "I had to hit rock bottom to become a Christian. I've heard preaching all my life—but it was only words. I found out the truth sitting in a muddy field up at Angola."

The night wind rustled the leaves of the great oak next to the gallery. Catherine shivered slightly.

"You're cold. Let's go inside." Lane stood up, carrying Catherine in his arms into their bedroom.

Sitting next to Lane on the edge of their bed, Catherine held his hand in both of hers, feeling its rough calluses. She felt joy spilling out of her heart as she listened to the sound of his voice, listened to his story as old as time—as new as a baby's first breath.

"I had just finished my cornbread and collard greens, and we had a few minutes left before we went back to work. I remember the wind blowing off the Mississippi was freezing me half to death. I thought I'd never get out of that place alive."

Catherine raised Lane's hand and pressed her lips against it.

"Right then, Cath, I just *knew* that Jesus is who He said He was. I said right out loud, 'Jesus, I'm sorry for the way I've lived. There ain't much left to me now, but I give my life to You.'"

Lane lay back on the bed and took a deep breath, letting it out in a soft laugh. "Well, Buckels and a few others around me thought I'd finally cracked up— some of them started easing back away from me. But I didn't care. I knew then that I'd make it."

Catherine took a pillow and placed it beneath Lane's head, then lay next to him, her left arm resting across his stomach as she held his hand.

"You know something, Cath?" When I look back now I realize that He was taking care of me when I never even had a thought for Him."

Catherine raised up on one elbow, placing her left hand against the side of Lane's face. There was a soft light in his eyes that she had never remembered seeing before. "Jesus said, 'Come unto me, all ye that labour and are heavy laden, and I will give you rest.'"

A weary smile touched Lane's face as he closed his eyes. "I've done pretty good in the labor department, all right."

Catherine watched Lane's face relax, the lines of care disappearing as he drifted into sleep. In the dim light filtering through the diaphanous curtains, he almost looked like the boy he had been on that long-ago day when she first met him, and he had rescued her from the town bully. A hint of a smile lit her eyes as she remembered her girlish dream of a shining knight on a white charger. Lane had rushed to her in high-topped tennis shoes and a football letter jacket, but the thrill of it had been far better than her dream.

Lying down next to Lane, Catherine slipped her hand in his and listened to the sound of his breathing. Then she fell into a deep, dreamless sleep. Outside, the night wind moaned around the eaves of their house.

EPILOGUE

★ ★ ★

"Well, what did you think?" Lane unbuttoned the coat of his one good suit, a navy pinstripe he saved for special occasions, and loosened the ruby-colored tie.

Cassidy, his hair bright and blowing about his face in the sunshine, picked up a rock from the levee and sailed it out into the river. It splashed next to a dark log rolling slowly in the current. "It was okay, I guess."

Lane rumpled his son's hair. "I can see you're all excited about your daddy getting sworn in as State Representative."

"That swearing-in stuff was boring." Cassidy took his tie off and crammed it in his coat pocket. "The punch and cake afterward wasn't bad though."

"I think you've gotten to the heart of it, Cass."

"Daddy . . ." Cassidy squinted up at Lane.

"Yep."

"Who was that man that kept staring at you? You know, the short one in the fancy suit."

Lane remembered André Catelon standing at the

back of the House Chambers, glaring at him as he took the oath of office. "You don't miss much, do you?"

"I didn't miss *him*." Cassidy kicked an RC bottle, spinning it around in the dust. "He's got mean eyes."

"His name's André Catelon. He's a senator."

"How come he's not in jail?"

Lane laughed, continually fascinated at the way his youngest child could see beneath the surface of things. "You don't get sent to jail for having mean eyes, Cass."

"I know that, Daddy. You think I'm a kid?" Cassidy protested. "I heard Coley say he was the main one that got you sent up to Angola."

Lane stopped and squatted down on the levee. He watched the glare of sunlight on the river's muddy surface. "The world's not always like a Roy Rogers movie, Cass. Sometimes the bad guys get away."

"But why didn't the cops arrest him?"

"It's kind of complicated," Lane explained, "but what it amounts to is, his name wasn't on any of the legal papers that got the others convicted."

"Why didn't Hinton or that guy Crain tell about what he did then? *They* had to go to prison."

Lane glanced up at his son in surprise. "You *have* been listening, haven't you?"

"Yes, sir, I do all right—for a kid."

"I think they were too scared to testify," Lane smiled. Then his face clouded slightly as he remembered the scowling face of Hogeman at Angola and the lethal contract Catelon had given him. "Catelon probably threatened to have them—taken care of."

"You mean bumped off?"

"Yeah," Lane agreed, "I mean bumped off."

Cassidy sat down next to Lane. "You think you're gonna like politics?"

Standing up, Lane continued walking along the levee. "Some of it, I guess."

Getting back up, Cassidy brushed off the seat of his trousers and caught up to Lane. "Even with people like Catelon?"

Lane gazed eastward at the capitol building, its towering limestone walls gleaming in the sunlight. "Everybody's not like André Catelon. A lot of them are just like—"

"Hey! Look at that!" Cassidy interrupted.

Lane stared down at the water's edge where his son was pointing.

"Look at the size of that thing! What is it?"

Images flashed through Lane's mind: That chilly afternoon in New Orleans when he had first seen one; staring two feet down in the murky water as he sat with Coley in his pirogue; and the time with Cass on a fishing trip.

"I remember now!" Cassidy shouted. "It's like that thing I stuck with the frog gig down at Coley's camp!" He ran down the grassy levee toward the river.

"Hold on, Cass," Lane warned, trotting along behind him. "You'll fall in."

Cassidy stopped halfway down the levee, seemingly reluctant to get any closer.

Lane stopped next to him. Down below them, the giant alligator gar lay half out of the water on the muddy bank, his ponderous torpedo-shaped body with its rounded head and tapering tail barely rocking from the wake of a passing tug far out on the river.

"Look at those teeth! How big is he?"

"Twelve, maybe fourteen feet."

"I wonder what killed him?"

Lane put his arm around Cassidy, turning him away. They walked together back up the levee.

"How'd you like to get some ice cream?"

"Yes, sir!" Cassidy yelled, running on ahead of Lane.

Below them, the first bluebottle fly, its iridescent wings glinting in the hard light, buzzed loudly above the slimy and mottled green body of the gar.

GENEVA PUBLIC LIBRARY